StyleNoir

THE

FIRST

HOW-TO GUIDE

TO

FASHION

WRITTEN

WITH

BLACK

WOMEN

IN

MIND

Style Noir

CONSTANCE C.R. WHITE

ORIGINAL ILLUSTRATIONS BY ALVIN BELL

A PERIGEE BOOK

A Perigee Book
Published by The Berkley Publishing Group
A member of Penguin Putnam Inc.
200 Madison Avenue
New York, NY 10016

Book design by Debbie Glasserman
Cover design by Joe Lanni
Cover photograph by Anthony Barboza
Interior illustrations by Alvin Bell
See page 227 for credits for interior photography.

First edition: February 1998

Published simultaneously in Canada.

The Putnam Berkley World Wide Web site address is
http://www.berkley.com

Library of Congress Cataloging-in-Publication Data
White, Constance C.R.
StyleNoir: the first how-to guide to fashion written with Black
women in mind / Constance C.R. White.
p. cm.
"A Perigee book."
Includes bibliographical references.
ISBN 0-399-52379-0
1. Afro-American women—Costume. 2. Afro-American women—Social life and customs. 3. Costume—United States. 4. Fashion—United States.
E185.86.W4387 1998
646.7'089'96073—dc21 97-27140
CIP

Printed in the United States of America

10 9 8 7 6 5 4 3 2 1

The heights by great men reached and kept
were not attained by sudden flight
But they, while their companions slept,
Were toiling upwards through the night.
–Longfellow

—to my family.

Is There Such a Thing as African-American Style?

When I was asked to do this book, the first question that arose was: Is there a definable area of style that can be called African-American? What makes us think black women want their own style book, and do they have particular style interests or needs that are different from those of, say, white women or Native American women?

The answer is a resounding yes. There is indeed such a thing as African-American style. There is an African-American style just as there is a Latina style, a Wasp style, an Asian style, or a gay style. African-American style is partly an expression of African culture and partly a collection of preferences born out of black style inventions and assimilation in America. African-American style is exactly what it says, both African and American. Resistance to the idea of a black style comes not from black women or even white designers but from some black male designers. Perhaps their fear of being hemmed in makes them agonize over the notion. After all, if there is such a thing as black style, then isn't that what black designers must create?

Like any highly evolved genre, you can discern within African-American style several subcategories. The up-in-your-face sixties revolutionary look—big Afros, beads, and dashikis—was epitomized by the seductive Black Panther men and sublime women like Angela Davis. Today there's the ghetto fabulous sexpot look, embodied by women who look like their sweat smells—Lil' Kim and Foxy Brown. Their decorous opposite is the church-going diva in her robustly colored matched suit. The hip-hop boy and flygirl wear jeans slipping down their butt and have appropriated brand-name dressing. And impossible to overlook is the mack daddy of the seventies and his properly paid alter ego the urban buppies, once fingered by writer Thulani Davis in the *Village Voice* as identifiable by their expensive coats and long jackets in the finest black leather.

Whether it adorns the ghetto fabulous queen, the black American princess, or the pious church mother, African-American style has at its core a love display. Black women and men are interested in dressing up, a characteristic also found in Latin cultures; it is the direct opposite of Wasp style, which is understated and puritanical. Black people wear clothes in an expressive way. Has anyone figured out the style DNA of Queen Aretha, Rick James, or Little Richard? Which of course brings me to Prince. Artistic, yes, but there is something undeniably materialistic about black style, from hip hop to African to Sunday best. There's not one genus of African-American style that can be said to be understated. In other communities, dressing simply or in a self-effacing way can qualify as great fashion. Looking disheveled, no matter how creatively done, is never thought stylish in our black culture—be it American, Caribbean, or African. And black church style epitomizes the constant struggle in American life between this country's conservatism on the one hand and the roots of liberalism and freedom on the other.

The many guises of black style spring from black people, but they are not limited in their application to people of African descent. African style, like other schools of art and applied art, is cultural rather than racial. People are not born with a predisposition to bright colors, kente cloth, or wearing their pants falling off their hips. Some blacks' rejection of the concept of African-American style may understandably come from their presumption that it means that all African Americans should wear, understand, and reflect black style. This is definitely not true. What is evident is that a large number of African Americans embrace black style because it is a reminder of a part of their heritage that is often negated by white America. And it thrives because style is often tribal, fostering identification and acceptance in a group. It can exist within the bounds of contemporary fashion but blossom in a hothouse prescribed by a company, a school, an industry, or a race, particularly a socially segregated one. Consider the IBM uniform, the look of the music industry, the college campus style—and its subtribes, professors and students. In 1995 IBM reached a famous watershed when it declared that its employees would no longer be expected to wear navy suits; Big Blue would allow workers to dress in more casual garb. The casual revolution has given rise to close examinations of the connection between dress and worker productivity. But what effect will the dramatic cultural shift at IBM have on workers' morale, sense of belonging, cohesiveness, and self-image?

Studies reveal that black women have certain fashion characteristics that define them as a category. In sales, targeting any definable group, focusing on what they want, and sending a message directly to them is good business. White women have been targeted for years. When American designers expand to the lucrative Japanese market, there are real cultural differences that are addressed. For instance, Japanese women respond well to brand names, and they are more petite than American women, so many clothes must be resized.

Sears and *E-Style* found that their African-American customers, compared to the statistical average, responded better to brand names, were more fashion forward, wanted more color, and in many cases required clothes with different fit specifications, like more room in the hips. In an ongoing study by Cotton Inc., the survey respondent group labeled trendsetters—those women to whom fashion was most important and who were likely to welcome fashion innovation first—included a disproportionate number (24 percent) of black women.

Separating racial or cultural groups by physical characteristics for style reasons is flirting dangerously close to Jimmy the Greek and bell curve theories that purport that blacks have certain immutable characteristics. If black women's hips are bigger, couldn't their brains be smaller? Our civilized culture, however, accepts physical differences but does not entertain mental ones, particularly when they are tabled as a means of oppression and prejudice. In fact, the black consumers' predisposition to certain styles is influenced more by history, folkways, and particular environments than racial genetics. The Texas market bears many similarities to a black woman's market, says Veronica Jones, owner of a retail store in Nyack, New York, and one of a handful of blacks who own sales agencies in the fashion business. "Traveling the country you see the differences. We like color. We like softer fabrics. Sometimes we're a subcategory within a category," she says.

Marketing to black women is a growth area because African Americans, like other women of color in America, have been ignored or patronized as consumers. "It's important because we've never been targeted," says Jones. "Our dollars came, but they've never been sought. No one celebrated us to get our dollars."

In the late 1990s, there is a flowering of interest in black style. It comes from two different directions, one market-driven, the other creativity-driven.

The push to do business in this area is fed by the growth of colored populations in the United States—African Americans,

Asians, and Hispanic peoples. The influence of these groups as a new target for makers and sellers of fashion and beauty products has manifested itself in a proliferation of stores and catalogs determined to court the black consumer, female and male. The most prominent among these are retailers that dress America, like Macy's, Sears, J.C. Penny, and Target, and catalogs like *Essence*, produced by *Essence* magazine, and *E-Style*, a joint venture of Spiegel and *Ebony* magazine.

The creative aspect has been expressed by the unprecedented number of designers creating collections inspired by black culture. For at least the first six years of the decade, designers had regurgitated old styles from the forties, sixties, seventies, and even eighties rather than trying to invent something truly fresh; there was a general paucity of new ideas. It is likely that the interest in spirituality and introspection, and curiosity about Eastern themes, that has accompanied the approach of the millennium have also provoked a desire to explore African culture. People have sought to renew their connection with the earth and their inner being. Art forms and style values developed by blacks in America and in the Diaspora have attracted attention in exhibits like "The Art of Africa," which opened in London and then New York in 1996. The love affair with Africa is part of a larger movement in fashion toward Eastern concepts—although designers like Valentino and Giorgio Armani have periodically used African motifs in their work for years. "I am fascinated by everything that is rooted in the traditions of peoples of the world because of the inherent qualities of authenticity, of cultural structures, of historical memory of the spirit," says Giorgio Armani, who often uses the African djellaba or buba as a basis of design. "This is particularly true of peoples and countries like those of Africa where those connotations are stronger."

The fulcrum on which this new creative and commercial drive toward black style in the 1990s has turned, I believe, is hip hop. In the past ten years, hip hop, invented by black city kids in America, has evolved from a marginal music form into a lifestyle and pop culture influence, which has shown irrevocably the muscle of the African-American market and the power of black style. Hip hop has become a world uniform for youths as far away as Japan and Angola. But even before fashion and beauty marketers, prodded by hip hop, began courting African Americans and nonblack designers began flirting with black style, African Americans like a seamstress at work on a singular dress were snipping away, defining their unique fashion.

Marginalization breeds creativity, which is not to suggest that one has to be marginalized or oppressed to be creative, but in fashion and the fine arts, ostracism or the feeling that you somehow don't fit in has its rewards. It's more than coincidence that the time when white women devoted lots of energy and money to the way they looked and dressed—the 1920s through the 1950s—mirrored their lack of opportunity for expression in areas like business and government. In the absence of real power, decorating oneself can be both empowering and liberating. Clothing played an emancipatory and central role in the lives of African Americans as far back as slavery. "There is a lot of talk about clothes as an expression of love," says Michele Black-Smith, a costume and textile historian. "Mothers and grandmothers would make things for their children and for their husbands—sometimes from scraps they sewed together because that's all they had." In ancient Africa, clothes and jewelry were treated not as mere covering but as art and a means of communication.

Among designers, particularly younger ones, there is general acknowledgment that African Americans have produced some exceptional and inspirational styles. Isaac Mizrahi cites the candy-colored suits and amazing hats of black churchgoing women, and he is inspired by Flip Wilson, though he doesn't say if that's Flip as Flip or Flip as Geraldine. Tommy Hilfiger refers to hip hop and to the Muddy Waters era and its impact on British style. Tom Ford, creative director for Gucci, is mesmerized by the black style of the seventies.

When slavery was abolished in the nineteenth century, one of the shackles that remained was being judged by one's appearance and found wanting. Blacks would, tragically, always strive to be neater and "cleaner" (looking) than the master, so that we might be accepted. Hence the emphasis on looking our "Sunday best." "Coming from being have-nots in this country to being haves has had an impact," says designer Tracy Reese. "As a black woman I've become aware that outward things—clothes, cars, makeup—have always been important to us. The whole Harlem Renaissance era was the first time we had money."

When it periodically becomes apparent that clothes will never make an African-American pass, outrage, discontent, and the thorough repudiation of prevailing standards give rise to another more rebellious expression of black dress, like the warrior style of the Black Panthers or the harsh gaudiness of the seventies mack daddy with his gold chains, expensive watch, and white-walled Cadillac parked in front of his apartment in the projects.

"As a Wasp and someone who grew up in Wasp culture, one of the reasons I had to leave America was to develop as a designer," says Tom Ford. "In some parts of America, too much style is bad taste. Blacks are much more fashionable. Go to a black Baptist church meeting in Texas and you'll see the most amazing clothes. Every designer I know has books on Africa. I have about twenty."

Creating fashion, he notes, requires a spirit of adventure and reconstruction, a willingness to move on to something new every three months. The story of how Jewish immigrants, the ultimate outsiders in the first half of the century, built Hollywood by finding a niche for themselves as the celluloid purveyors of the American dream is well known. Ford believes a similar hypothesis explains why Jewish immigrants flocked to the American fashion business and why African Americans, most of whose ancestors were slaves, are such a font of style ideas. "For anyone who's been uprooted, the willingness to change radically and dramatically every few months helps you not to be afraid of fashion," he says.

Tracy Reese, though black, female, and from up north, sees the same pattern in the tapestry. "The free expression is for me what's at the heart of fashions, and we've never been afraid to fully express ourselves. We're so the opposite of Wasp, we're not afraid to go all the way. I think black people enjoy being divas—men and women. In the seventies when all those black models became popular it was because they gave it that extra style, that extra personality."

The latest renaissance in African-American home décor and fashions—the last one took place in the 1970s—is happening against the backdrop of a larger interest in African culture. Black literature, discourse, film, and art have found a broad audience, black and white. America's top entertainers and sports figures are black. At a party in Paris, I was shooting the breeze with a British fashion journalist when he launched into a breathless story describing a hot, up-and-coming talk show host in England. He said, "She's the white Oprah Winfrey." Now that's a turn of the tables!

The crossover of African-American style is a positive development as long as it benefits blacks as well as whites. Hip hop has spawned black millionaires, multimillionaires, power brokers, and, thank God, just plain old jobs for black folks who work not only in the music business but in fashion, publishing, film, and advertising. Hip hop created its own film genre, its own slang; in doing so, it's gone mainstream.

And yet the assimilation of black style has sometimes proven a double-edged sword for African Americans. Black fashion expressions on black people are often seen as a political act—and they sometimes are. But because there is this Janusian quality to white society's approach to black style—both embracing it and policing it at the same time—the mainstreaming of blacks' style is not always to their benefit. Most hip-hop fashion dollars go into white-owned companies.

In 1981 the federal courts upheld American Airlines' right to forbid a black ticket agent to wear braids on the job. In explaining his ruling, the judge said the employee did not have the right to wear her braids because it was not a cultural expression, as she asserted, but was a fashion trend started by Bo Derek, the white actress who brought braids to widespread attention in the movie *10.* Here justice was not only blind, it was deaf and dumb.

I've included a brief history of black fashion in this book to help avoid such painful misreferences. To borrow the title of Paula Gidding's book, my overview is a *When and Where I Enter* of blacks and their place in fashion. However, it merely scratches the surface.

As I pored over library shelves doing the research for this book, I had a chilling thought: What if I were a child of ten—black or white—in search of information on African Americans' role in fashion? Lois Alexander, founder of the Black Fashion Museum, did invaluable work with her book *Blacks in the History of Fashion,* now out of print. But there is further study to be done and more fashion history to be noted, particularly since the generation of pioneers and affirmative-action babies—those who broke down walls in fashion during the important civil rights era—are now in middle age or are senior citizens. Their history, our history, the fashion industry's history needs to be recorded.

African-American fashion cries out for historians or scholars to dig deeper, but the subject labors under a double discrimination. Both African-American culture and fashion continually struggle for recognition as being worthy of respect and the highest academic study. I'm happy for the opportunity to tell part of the story.

Romeo Gigli inspired by Bogolan fabric, 1995.

From Kente to Kelly: An Overview of Blacks' Contributions to Fashion

March 1997, Paris, and Jean Paul Gaultier, the hip, acclaimed French designer, had survived a few rocky seasons in which his normally brilliant fashions had been less than sparkling. As hundreds of fashion journalists and retailers from around the world watched, models began to emerge slowly through a cloud of thick smoke onto the runway, which was designed to look like a boxing ring.

Most of the models were black: Naomi Campbell, Georgianna Robertson, Brandi, Chrystele, Lois Samuels, Stacey McKenzie, and Alek Wek. Kristen McNemany, a white model known for her strong, quirky personality, was included in the mix. The sound system oozed Isaac Hayes's bass rolling over "Shaft" and Miriam Makeba singing "Pit-A-Pat."

This show, Gaultier's homage to black style, was a broad, stylish sweep of fashion history, and was one of the best shows of the season. Gaultier took the glamour of 1920s African Americans, mixed it with the baaad soul of the 1970s, weaved in hip-hop flavor, and sprinkled it all with the stardust of the motherland.

There were ombre-colored pants suits and coats trimmed with fur reminiscent of the jazz age and Harlem's glory days. Elegant, sexy long wool dresses were worn under sweeping mack daddy coats; hooded cropped sweatshirts over baggy leather pants represented hip hop; and darling velvet flapper dresses in red, green, and yellow plaids deftly married two inspirations: 1920s black America and the aso oke textiles of Africa.

The striking models wore Chinese bumps, Makebas, finger waves, or huge Afro puffs that sat on the backs of their heads like regal crowns. Their lush lips

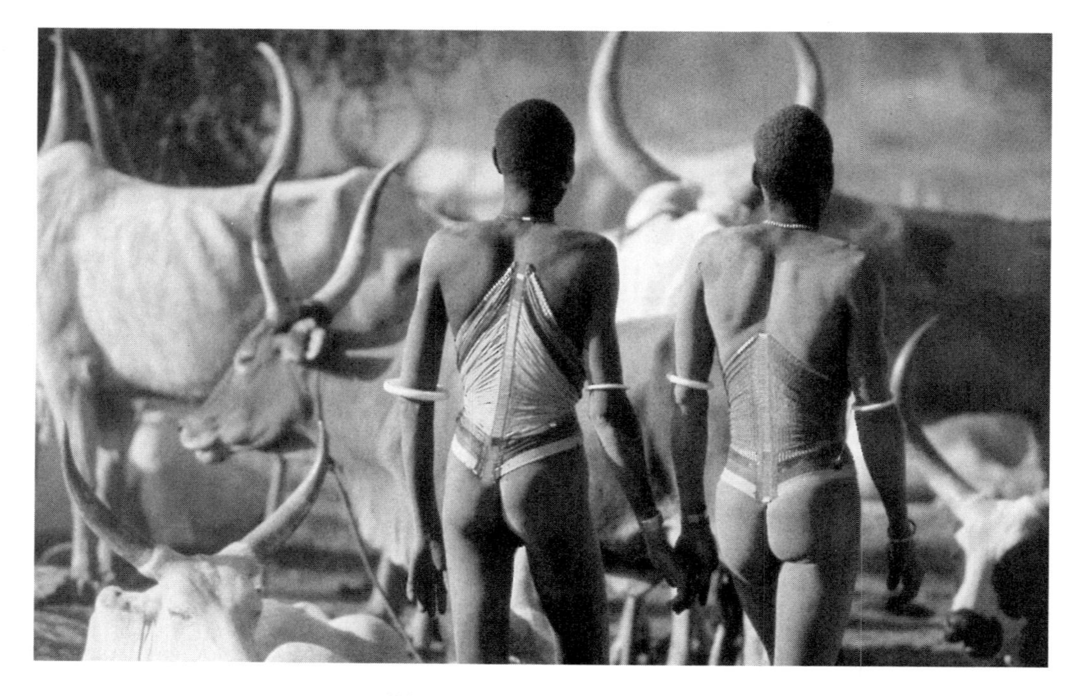

Dinka women in magnificent beaded corsets.

glistened with tones that complemented their complexions—berry browns, deep cinnamon, and mahogany.

Gaultier had often drawn on African culture for inspiration, but this was the first time he developed a collection based entirely on black style. And he was not alone. In 1997, the world's most prominent designers—from Gaultier to Ralph Lauren—designed African-influenced fashion collections.

More African Americans are becoming interested once again in expressing their African heritage in what they wear. White Americans, Japanese, and blacks in the Caribbean and in England are adopting black style.

Despite their integral role as shapers of fashion, blacks have so far not been able to put down deep roots in the business. Like shooting stars, talented black designers have come to world attention only to fizzle and disappear after a few years. Lack of financing, the silent executioner AIDS, and racism within and without the business have stalled careers. There are no top black designers, though there are several with outstanding accomplishments. In the top echelons of retailing and fashion journalism, where decisions are made about who will be promoted and who will not, their numbers are few. However, there are many African Americans working behind the scenes in

John Galliano's African-style beaded corset gown for Christian Dior, 1997.

Jean Paul Gaultier's homage to black style, 1997.

influential positions—at the right hand of Donna Karan, at a handful of top newspapers, and as buyers controlling millions of dollars for Saks and Sears.

Never before have as many high-fashion designers simultaneously shown so many clothes that rely on African culture. Two days before Gaultier's show, another important designer, the eccentric Englishman John Galliano, presented an ode to Egypt as one theme in his collection. Six months earlier, Ralph Lauren, Donna Karan, Mary McFadden, Alexander McQueen, and Hermes had been praised for their outstanding collections. All were inspired by African style. Galliano went back to the well for spring 1997, this time drawing on the Ndebele culture.

This attention from the fashion world is part of a broader revival of interest in black culture, which some observers have compared to the Harlem Renaissance in the early part of the century. Then, as now, a blossoming of talent and Afrocentrism in the fine arts flowed into music, literature, and film, finally touching home and fashion design. Just as

From Byron Lars's fierce African collection, 1994: leather mask handbag and Mongolian lamb legwarmers over Scott Rankin boots.

Tracy Reese's ode to a trip to the Ivory Coast in 1993.

museum exhibits at the turn of the century in the United States and Europe galvanized interest in black culture, the Art of Africa exhibition had a profound impact on designers; it included art and artifacts at least a hundred years old, and the cultural mores and artisanal methods that produced them were older still, some dating back to the fourteenth century.

African Chiefs: Fashion Icons

Long before the Europeans colonized Africa, people of the fourteenth- and fifteenth-century empires of Ghana, Mali, Egypt, Kush, and Songhai developed fabrics and jewelry from indigenous resources. (The scurrilous idea that Africans were uncivilized was a myth advanced by Europeans to justify slavery.) Skins of leather from leopard and goats were used for clothing. The people of Songhai were already fashioning leather jackets and amulets. In places like the redoubtable Kongo to the south, cotton and bark from trees was woven into apron-like coverings, and nobles swept about in clothes made from cotton. Reports of a

Karl Lagerfeld, always on fashion's pulse, went hip hop with Chanel in the early nineties.

historic pilgrimage of the great Malian empire-builder Mansa Musa, or King Musa, in A.D. 1324, state that many of the twelve thousand servants, slaves, and companions with him decked themselves out in silk and brocade.

Since the fifteenth century, aso oke cloth weavers on the east and west coasts of Africa were trading with Indians who sold them silk in exchange for ivory, gold, and iron. Nimble African weavers would unravel the silk and weave it into their native cotton, thus developing the earliest versions of world-renowned kente cloth. Many older kentes—which now cost hundreds or thousands of dollars—are made of silk. (Contemporary kente is likely to be of cotton or rayon.)

Leopard skins, that spotted cliché and dotted classic of Western fashion, were worn as a sign of bravery and often signified nobility or high standing in society. At the time this book was being written, Zaire, now renamed Congo, was in a state of unrest. But embattled president Mobutu Sese Seko was still making public appearances in a leopard-print cap as he had done for decades to indicate his power and position. He may have been on the verge of political annihilation but he never forgot his fashion statement. Shaka Zulu, the exalted Zulu warrior of the nineteenth century, is often depicted in a leopard-skin apron, a sign of his authority and courage.

Jewelry making and cloth weaving fell under the banner of art in many African societies in the ancient empires and still do in contemporary tribal life. In the great kingdoms of Mali, Egypt, Songhai, and Kush, these artists were arranged in prestigious guilds—collectives of skilled specialists who would pass on their knowledge to succeeding generations. Most artisans served at the pleasure of the king, developing special weaves or precious metal imprints for the royal household.

In more humble circles, people wove their own cloth but often were forbidden to copy patterns reserved for kings or chiefs.

Kenyan elders wore fur pieces called gethis, and men and women would sometimes dress in leather skirts or mothurus.

When pious European missionaries overran Africa in the sixteenth–eighteenth centuries, they urged Africans, accustomed to wearing as little as they pleased, to cover up. Naturally, resistance to this practice was widespread, even among Christian converts still mindful of African traditions that were hundreds of years old. Wearing clothes that revealed the body was not only a way to keep cool in punishingly hot climates but, in Kikuyu societies, allowed suitors to check out the health of a prospective spouse. European-style clothing was considered ugly and a deceitful attempt to cover up a physical abnormality. Former president

Jomo Kenyatta of Kenya wrote in 1965 in his seminal book *Facing Mount Kenya* that a would-be son-in-law foolish enough to insist on wearing European dress would be forced to strip before witnesses to prove he was not trying to hide a deformity under his clothes!

Gold Rush

After peacefully trading with Africans for years, the Portuguese, Dutch, English, and French decided to invade Africa in the sixteenth–eighteenth centuries, not to save people's souls but to gain control of the amazing displays of gold they had seen when they traded with Africans from Mali and other empire states in western Africa. Africans had highly developed goldworks where they produced jewelry, artifacts, and sculpture. One visitor to the city of Timbuktu, the storied learning center in the heart of the Mali empire, described "plates and scepters weighing up to 1300 pounds."

The people of the Mali empire and the Kush, who ruled Egypt for several generations, were reported to bedeck themselves in dazzling amounts of gold worked into breathtaking collars, rings, necklaces, earrings, crowns, and even gold-dipped fabrics. Gold beading, which is growing in popularity among African Americans today, dates back to this time. The treasures found in the grave of the boy-king Tutankhamen of Egypt were just one indication of the central role gold adornment played in ancient African life. European museums and African families possess remarkable pieces of gold jewelry and sculpture estimated to be hundreds of years old.

Throughout Africa, in southern states like Zululand and western chiefdoms like Mali, kings controlled the gold, iron, and copper mines and regulated trade with African states as well as European and Arabian merchants. Zulus loved Venetian beads. Zulus, like other tribespeople, purchased vast quantities of glass beads from the traders who brought them from India and Venice. Beads of different colors would fall in and out of fashion, and in many societies they were so highly prized that they were sometimes used as money.

Today, Venetian-style beads—now often made from plastic—are a characteristic part of the dress of some native African people, including the Ndebele and the Masai, who work them into spectacular jewelry and clothing. It is this legacy that emerges in Ralph Lauren's spring 1997 collection and Galliano's fall 1997 couture line for Christian Dior. Todd Oldham, the New York designer and creative consultant for Escada, who is a favorite of Queen Latifah, created an Ndebele collection a few years ago inspired by this South African people's stunning beadwork.

Rich kente, gold—lots of it—and touches of leopard skin: a Ghanaian chief displays a fashion feast.

A Legacy of Fabulous Fabrics

The European invasion of Africa fueled Europe's industrial revolution, providing cheap labor in the form of slaves. Slaves' unpaid work enriched European and American textile factories. The Africans who remained in their native land under the rule of white imperialists increasingly bought European goods and absorbed European values, including fashion tastes and textiles. The large fabric houses in Manchester, England; Lowell, Massachusetts and Lyon, France, grew rich in the eighteenth century, helped along by free slave labor and demand from Africa for fabric.

Many of the fabrics destined for Africa that these factories produced were in the European mode, but most were made to suit African taste and, in fact, were copies of indigenous African patterns. The availability of European textiles, however, crushed the local African textile industry, which was outdone by the Europeans' lower prices and large supply, made possible by industrialization.

A curious legacy of this development is that today many African fabrics, like waxed prints and brocade, don't come from Africa at all. The African print you buy may well be a product of Holland.

Hair and Makeup Styles

The head is revered in African culture as the seat of spirituality, and covering the head with a hat, wrap, or creative coiffure is given great importance. Africans early on displayed a love and affinity for creating remarkable hairstyles. Wigs were worn by Egyptians, Kushites, and Zulus. There are early records of ornately carved combs, similar to what we now call picks or Afro picks, that were used to comb and style the hair.

Beauty treatments included ochre or rancid butter to protect and style the hair. Milk baths kept the skin moist. Color was applied to the hair, using henna, and around the eyes, using kohl.

Though Africans brought to America were violently separated from much of their culture, some customs, like the Afro pick, remained or were reclaimed.

Africans' Role in American Fashion at the Turn of the Nineteenth Century

Blacks in America in the eighteenth and nineteenth centuries—most of them enslaved—were often making the clothes worn by whites and blacks.

Slaves were circumscribed in what they could wear: one of the sinister tools of subjugation and a nickel-and-dime way to increase the slaveowner's profits, since he was responsible for clothing the slaves he owned. They were condemned to wear a rough cloth of beige, brown, or blue-and-beige linen or cotton, which often came from factories up north, explains Michelle Black Smith, a costume and textile historian. This plantation-issue fabric came to be known as Linsey-woolsey, or Negro cloth, and carried with it the unpleasant association of slavery even after emancipation. "It had the same effect as branding," adds Smith. "It was such an expression of slavery. There were codes on the books about what blacks were forbidden to wear to separate them from whites."

The lack of opportunity for adornment must have had a chilling effect on Africans and African Americans. Lois Alexander, the founder of the Black Fashion Museum (formerly located in Harlem and now being moved to Washington, D.C.), says it is difficult to document blacks' dressmaking work during that period since, as slaves, they were not given any credit for what they did. Nevertheless, she identifies the extraordinary Elizabeth Keckley, modiste—as designer dressmakers were called then—

Mary Todd Lincoln

as one of the first prominent black designers.

Keckley was the confidante and seamstress of Mary Todd Lincoln, and she created most of Mrs. Lincoln's clothes. It was a day of jubilation when Lincoln gave to Keckley what was not his to give: her freedom. She was the first known black to design for a first lady. Amazingly, almost sixty years later, another black designer, Anne Lowe, shared a similar distinction, creating the wedding dress of Jacqueline Bouvier Kennedy.

Meanwhile, the emancipation Declaration of 1863 abolished slavery in the United States. Free blacks moved north, their optimism and relative prosperity fueling their ambition and sowing the seeds for the harvest of music style and literature that would enrich Northern cities.

Furs and Flappers in Harlem

The end of World War I brought euphoria among all classes and races, culminating in a blossoming of interest in black culture and a receptivity on the part of many whites to the black sensibility. It was the first time a large number of blacks in America were able to share in the national prosperity that they had helped produce, and they took pains with their clothes and hair care, with dramatic results. At the turn of the century, blacks had invented a new music form that now swept the country. Someone dubbed it jazz. Whites and blacks alike were relieved that the war was over. Women were given the right to vote, and Caribbean immigrants, their eyes glazed with the promise of American working-class riches, joined the blacks up north.

From the Jazz Age on, the influence of black style was inextricably linked with the hold of black music on popular culture in America and abroad.

As non-blacks became smitten with a world that seemed exotic and unfamiliar, the Harlem Renaissance was born. "Black people were just doing what they were doing," says Thelma Goldin, a curator at the Whitney Museum. "The great fallacy of the Renaissance is that they were calling it a Renaissance. This was a time when black artists really were not welcome in white communities."

Blacks of the jazz era cultivated a glamorous look. Coats trimmed with chinchilla fur collars, loose beaded dresses that skimmed the body but revealed some leg, cloche hats, and long strings of beads were all the rage. These were the Roaring Twenties, the era when the flapper emerged with her flat chest, bobbed hair, and waistless dresses.

These liberating fashions for women were spurred by the permissiveness of the Jazz Age, the women's suffragist movement, and the prosperous, fun-loving spirit of peacetime.

Blacks and whites flocked to clubs to

be entertained by swing bands led by players like Duke Ellington, whose slicked-back hair and pale debonair suits set a standard for men's dress. Black men wore dapper, loose-fitting suits with wide shoulders and baggy pants pleated at the waist. They topped the look with fedoras. Dances like the Charleston, which required freedom of movement, emerged from the black community and took the country by storm, no doubt spurring the creation of flapper dresses.

Blacks also looked to the touring blues and jazz singers of the day for fashion direction. The style of Bessie Smith, considered the country's foremost blues singer, was decidedly drop-dead glamorous. Smith, often photographed in divalike splendor, favored furs, long beaded gowns and glittering jewelry, and well-coiffed hair.

African Americans' strong and influential dress style and music were but two expressions of black culture. Similar interest and activity flourished in black art, literature, and business, and one area fed creativity in another. Egyptian jewelry was all the rage, particularly in New York. In 1923 the Brooklyn Museum organized "Primitive Negro Art," an exhibit of more than a thousand objects from central Africa. The exhibition led the museum to commission the creation of a special fabric it called Congo Cloth, which was inspired by the work of the Kuba and Kongo people of Zaire. Embroidered dresses, characteristic of many west and central African clothes, were made from the fabric and sold not only in the museum but in stores in New York.

It was around this time of interest in black culture that artists like Pablo Picasso and Constantin Brancusi began copying African art and developing the styles that would bring them worldwide renown.

The flowering of black style was also an outgrowth of Pan-Africanism—the idea that blacks in the Diaspora should unite behind their common African ancestry—which shone a spotlight on Africa and its culture. People like W.E.B. Du Bois and Marcus Garvey, who brought his United Negro Improvement Association from Jamaica to Harlem during the Renaissance, encouraged black pride and self-reliance. Their message received global attention; among the countries that were deeply inspired by black activists and entertainers was France.

Josephine Baker, a member of a traveling troupe named La Revue Negre, reveled in the high-gloss look of renowned singers like Bessie Smith. As her fame and wealth grew, she found a home in Paris, where French women clamored to hear her sing and their men grew an extra pair of eyes to better view the nubile splendor of Baker's gorgeous body. Though she is most often portrayed as a half-naked, full-eyed performer wearing bananas around her waist, she was more often a

Glamorous blues singer Bessie Smith

Josephine Baker

vision of elegance. She helped popularize the finger-wave hairstyles popular with American blacks of the day—a style that is newly en vogue today. French women looked to her for style cues, from wearing belts made of bananas to the clothes she wore designed by Pierre Balmain and other top French couturiers of the day.

Back in America, the romance with black culture slowly withered. After the Depression hit in the 1930s, a renewed, vigorous racism forced increased migration of southern blacks to northern industrial cities like Chicago, Detroit, and New York. As this fresh blood fed the development of jazz in the 1940s and 1950s, influence of jazz on fashion remained strong with jazzmen like Duke Ellington and Miles Davis marking the sartorial compass point for men over several decades. The music became hotter and more brazen, and so did the clothes.

Zoot Suit Fever

Bebop jazz, performed by stars like Thelonius Monk, Charlie Parker, and Dizzy Gillespie, replaced swing and classic jazz in the 1940s. The beboppers bopped, and long after the music faded, the word “bop” would be associated with the distinctive rhythmic way some black men slide and dip when they walk. Dress styles became more eclectic. These jazzmen mixed jackets with pants of a different color and added whimsical touches like berets and scarves worn around the neck.

Performers began favoring a more exaggerated silhouette, which was to be copied by men and women, whites and blacks around the world. The look became known as the zoot suit.

The zoot suit was characterized by a jacket, which extended to the knee or midthigh, with broad square shoulders, wide lapels, and a nipped waist. Exceedingly baggy pants were tapered and cuffed at the hem. Women paired the jackets with knee-length pegged skirts and heavy high-heeled shoes.

Often worn with a brimmed hat, the zoot suit was a remarkably flamboyant fashion statement and one that came to signify defiance. It expressed the rage of black men who had fought and seen their comrades die for their country and returned home from World War II to find that they still faced discrimination in America. And the look caught on with Hispanic youth in California who found they shared with blacks a history of discrimination. On the West Coast, police beat zooters, primarily Latinos, whom they viewed much the way they now view today's gang bangers.

Zoot was also a seducer of the French women and men who were the forerunners of the rebellious beats of America and of Paris's left bank, who consorted with jazz musicians and other black entertainers. In France, zoot wearers were known as zazous. Across the Channel, the zoot was picked up by black Caribbean men who had begun immigrating to England in record numbers in the forties and fifties to help fill England's labor shortage. Like their American counterparts, young West Indians often had local tailors make their suits. They kept the exaggerated shoulders but adopted a shorter jacket length, which would become popular in the late 1950s. Women brought their love of bright, feminine colors in curvy suits and fit-and-flare dresses and open-toed shoes, opening English women to more adventurous style beyond the dull sobriety of traditional English dress.

Film stars in the forties and fifties wielded a huge influence on fashion, though less so in the black community. The spate of black films Hollywood released during the period with stars like Lena Horne, Diahann Carroll, Fredi Washington, and Dorothy Dandridge tended to project prevailing white style. "When I began my career I had a hard time finding role models," Carroll recalled in 1997, when she introduced the Diahann Carroll fashion collection. "There was no one who looked like me."

The central role the zoot played in black life is documented in films like *Stormy Weather*, starring Lena Horne and Cab Calloway. Calloway—no dishrag when it came to style—was widely photographed in his eye-popping white zoot

West Indian men in England in the forties and fifties adapted the zoot look and in turn influenced the English Teddy Boys.

suits with pocket chain. Even Malcolm X poured himself into a zoot suit; Spike Lee's film *Malcolm X* contains a vivid scene (from Malcolm's autobiography) in which a young Malcolm, played by Denzel Washington, takes great glee in obtaining his first zoot suit—in powder blue, no less. In his pre-activist days, Malcolm also adopted the style of many black men in the 1940s and 1950s and straightened his hair, a fashion later considered to be a pathetic attempt to imitate white people. "No kink, no curl, Conkoline will straighten your world," said one catchy advertisement.

Black women had by now left behind their twenties crimps and switched to bangs, falls, and pompadours. Men conched or pressed their hair, using dangerous lye-based chemicals, and the black community supported many hairdressers and chemists who specialized in the care and conching of black hair and the lightening of black skin. But Marcus Garvey, ever the radical, refused to accept advertisements in his organization's newspaper for products designed to straighten black hair or wash the brown out of brown skin. His oratory and newspapers helped set the tone for the black pride style of the 1960s.

The music of Garvey's generation and the young Malcolm X was jazz, but as the 1950s unfolded, young blacks—and then white kids—discovered a form of blues music that had them rockin'. They called it rock-and-roll, and black singer Chubby Checker was one of its first crossover stars. Once record companies realized that both whites and blacks were listening to this music, they created a constellation of white entertainers who copied not only black entertainers' music but their style. The most famous and influential of these was Elvis Presley.

From the hair on his head to the shoes on his feet, Presley took his cues from

Cab Calloway in *Stormy Weather,* in his flamboyant zoot suit: wide lapels, extra-long jacket, and baggy pants were copied by all races in America and abroad.

blacks. He slicked and stiffened his jet-black hair in imitation of the Memphis slicksters who sported pressed and pomaded pompadours. He adopted black singers' scandalously tight suits and pointed two-tone shoes, and he appropriated their dramatic, feline stage moves.

Similar influences were taking root among the white Teddy Boys of England, whose rockabilly look melded black Southern clothes with Elvis's caramelized fashions. Black Americans' style would be repackaged and Anglicized and sold back to America years later in the early sixties with the so-called British Invasion of groups like the Beatles and the Rolling Stones and singers like Dusty Springfield.

"I'm Mrs. It": The Fashion World Discovers a Black Model and Black Designers

Despite the strong influence of black street style from the 1920s through the 1950s, black designers and models were still scarcer than hen's teeth. If black women were to find anyone to emulate and reflect their beauty, they would have to look on the sleeves of record albums. Magazines of the era tell the story. There are virtually no dark faces gracing the pages of publications like *Vogue* and *Harper's Bazaar.*

In the 1950s, the American fashion community had an inferiority complex and looked to France for direction. It was common for American dressmakers and retailers to copy French fashion line for line, sometimes going so far as to replace an American label with a real or invented French one. The era of the celebrity designer was dawning, with people like Christian Dior rating a cover of *Time.*

Against this backdrop emerged Anne Lowe, a black designer from Alabama whose work was coveted by America's social-register set. As a result of this connection, in 1953 she was asked to create the wedding dress and the outfits for the bridal party for the marriage of a young debutante to a senator, the son of one of America's wealthiest families: Jacqueline Bouvier and John F. Kennedy.

The dress Lowe designed for Jackie Kennedy incorporated her trademark work of handmade appliqué and tier upon tier of delicate fabric on a ballgown skirt. Lowe's dresses followed the shape of the day: a cinched waist and voluminous full skirt of crinoline, tulle, or satin, with detailed seaming reminiscent of French couture dressmaking techniques.

Lowe owned her own business—an amazing feat, but one not so unusual for blacks, who prior to desegregation operated bustling business communities. But a black person becoming part of the fashion establishment was still unheard-of. The business is centered around a grimy, congested area of New York City bounded by Sixth Avenue and Eighth Avenue on the east and west and Fortieth and Thirty-fourth Streets to the north and south. What Broadway is to theatre, Seventh Avenue is to fashion. The modern fashion industry in America owes much of its existence to Jewish immigrants. There is now also a strong Asian presence from Japan, Hong Kong, China, and Korea. As in other areas of American life, blacks were not welcome and the incestual nature of the business worked to keep most of them out. Around the time Anne Lowe was scoring her Kennedy triumph, Wesley Tan was becoming one of the first blacks to break onto Seventh Avenue, with his timeless daytime dresses; he arrived in New York City from North Carolina in the early fifties. After working for a company called Casino Classics, he opened his own business. "I realized I had to get out of that working for someone else mode," he says. Henri Bendel, the exclusive store, was one of the first retailers to buy his collection. Bendel's, in fact, was instrumental in supporting the African-American designers—most of them men—who were the black pioneers on Seventh Avenue. But

Jackie Kennedy in her wedding dress designed by Anne Lowe.

that store was an exception. Prejudice was still a formidable obstacle, and the fashion business doled out its fair share of racism to designers as well as models.

"In the late fifties I was dressing models and sending them out on the runway at a fashion show, and someone complained that it wasn't right for me to be in the back dressing and touching white models," recalls James Daugherty, who came to New York in 1957 and went on to establish a foothold as a designer on Seventh Avenue in the sixties, with his festive, multipurpose day dresses.

Sepia-toned models, battling cultural standards that had little regard for African beauty, found few opportunities to establish careers on Seventh Avenue. The success of actresses like Lena Horne and Dorothy Dandridge opened doors for beautiful black women with café au lait complexions, but developing a career in modeling was even more difficult. So after landing a few bit parts in films in Los Angeles, Dorothea Towles, a tall, light-skinned teenager from Texarkana, Texas, packed her bags in 1949 and headed for Paris, where she became the first black to establish a thriving modeling career. (At the time, Towles's older sister had been touring Europe with the concert choir of Fisk University, the renowned black college, and Towles made her way to Paris by wangling a ticket through the university.)

Dorothea Towles thought she was "it" in the 1950s.

On arriving in Paris, Towles immediately started looking for work in France's top design houses. "You couldn't tell me I wasn't Mrs. It," she says. She was hired by Christian Dior, Pierre Balmain, and Elsa Schiaparelli, among others. And she, like any attractive black woman who came through France at the time, was often compared to Josephine Baker, an observation that worked her last nerve.

"To the French your skin color was an attraction, not a detraction," she explains. "Skin didn't knock them dead the way it did in America, where you couldn't get in the door."

Though the French were more racially tolerant, the situation in France was far from sublime. Towels was to be the only black in her circle for some time, even though other black American girls and many African ones were seeking work as models. And she recounts the day she first tried to borrow clothes from Pierre Balmain for an *Ebony* magazine photo shoot. (*Ebony's* food and fashion editor, Freda de Knight, started coming to Paris in the fifties, followed by the magazine's owners, John and Eunice Johnson.) "Mr. Balmain said, 'You know, Dorotay (he used to call me Dorotay), I don't mind, but I've got white American customers, those rich women, and if they ever saw my clothes in a black magazine it would be a problem.'"

From then on, Towles recalls, she would borrow clothes from the couturiers on the pretext that she needed them for a night on the town—a practice all designers encourage even today, since they want their designs to be seen on young, beautiful women. Instead of just partying in the clothes, she would secretly have them photographed and the pictures sent to *Ebony* in Chicago. The French were none the wiser. They never read the black magazines anyway.

When Towles returned to America in 1954, she began traveling around the country staging fashion shows in black communities using clothes she purchased from French houses. *Ebony* later started a similar traveling fashion show that became the pinnacle of the social season in many towns with large African-American populations.

The Power of Black: Black Leather, Black Pride, and the Youth Revolution in the Sixties

As the civil rights era dawned, black style became more austere and militant. Confrontations over segregation and a general lack of equality exploded into scattered race riots nationwide as blacks and some whites sought change. The rudeness of rock-and-roll music mirrored the rebelliousness that youths around the world were feeling, but while rock-and-roll was laying the foundation for anti-establishment, youth-oriented style, a black entrepreneur named Berry Gordy created a record company that operated like the Hollywood studio system in which as much attention was paid to how stars looked as to how they sounded.

A disciple of peaceful integration, his approach was not to ignore the injustice and frustration in the black community but to combat it with sugar-coated sounds and images. Motown Records in Detroit became a style factory, and the perky manufactured glamour of both male and female entertainers like Martha and the Vandellas, the Supremes, and Smokey Robinson and The Miracles was emulated around the world.

Style decision making for Motown's

recording stars was put in the hands of Maxine Powell, a successful local model and charm school operator in Chicago and later Detroit. Powell made sure the Motown singers were polished, and she also filled the role that now would be called stylist, suggesting clothes and outfits for the groups.

Singers in all-girl groups were decked out in custom-made outfits and clothes that were store-bought and then altered. They delivered a stylish message to young women across the nation who copied their mohair suits, bouffant coiffures, glamorous shiny gowns, and frosty lipstick. "When they wore their sweaters backward, we wore our sweaters backward," says Sandra Graham, vice-president for public relations at Halston International; she owned a boutique near Detroit in the 1960s.

"It was the first time you saw large numbers of young white Americans attempting to mimic young black Americans," says Michelle Black Smith, the costume historian, who has helped organize the exhibits at Motown Historical Museum in Detroit. "The impact of Motown fashion was tremendous. It did exactly what Berry Gordy hoped it would do, which was to make black America mainstream."

From blacks' perspective, the Motown look may have seemed a safe approach to style, but the view was different—as it often is—from the white seats. Groups like Diana Ross & the Supremes still represented, in the eyes of many whites, something exotic, a little racy, and perhaps even rebellious, and in this vision likely lay the real secret of the Motown groups' fashion influence.

"Everybody in the mid-sixties was influenced by Diana Ross," says Tom Ford, creative director of Gucci, who was a boy in his native Texas at the time. "I remember particularly the frosted lipstick. We had never seen anything like that before, and on a black woman."

Nonetheless, the world according to Motown was relatively antiseptic. While the Supremes made a string of number one hits in their decorous dresses, the streets were seething with race riots and discontent that found expression in the militant style of the Black Panthers, a quasi-military and community group that advocated black equality, to be won by violence if necessary.

The black leather jackets and berets of the Black Panthers found their way into street fashion. Hispanics—again on the West Coast—created their own version of the Black Panther style with brown berets.

A look emerged among black militants that fused the sharp, urban gear of the Black Panthers with African-inspired fashion expressions like Masai-style beads, Nigerian amulets with dashikis, and other African-print garments. Fiery black orators like Malcolm X and

The Supremes and other girl groups of Motown were style role models for a host of young black women, and white ones too.

Martin Luther King, Jr., encouraged black pride, which was expressed in Afrocentric dress.

African-influenced style in some ways fit neatly into the hippie movement, which was a catalyst behind the sudden interest in Eastern culture, be it Asian or African. Both the African-American and hippie mode were creations of the street, grass-roots fashion that was shaped by the way ordinary people lived and the way they put clothes together. It was exciting and distinctive, and high-fashion designers always on the trail for something new began looking to black culture and the street for inspiration. Yves Saint Laurent's first collection for Christian Dior in 1960 was inspired by the look of the jazz-inspired subculture of the beats, which emerged in the 1950s and early 1960s. In 1967 and 1968, he created clothes imbued with African esprit.

Despite the strong pull of black culture, the sixties brought only a smattering of black designers to Seventh Avenue. Wesley Tann continued to build a successful career, selling his clothes to tony

Can you spell D-I-V-A? The fabulous Miss Ross influenced generations.

stores like Neiman Marcus. Other designers like Arthur McGee and James Daugherty began to emerge in the first half of the decade.

"It was bad and it's still bad," says McGee, who with his then partner Diane Harris opened a popular store called Contagious in Gramercy Park, New York. "I remember a man walked in one day and couldn't believe I owned the store. He said, 'I could walk from here to 125th Street and ain't no niggers owning no stores.' And he was right."

Even so, the civil rights movement did help push more blacks into jobs in the fashion industry and give aspirants of color more hope that they would be able to contribute and have fulfilling careers. Black designers worked for fashion companies or relied on big stores to carry their creations. In the sixties, Bloomingdale's established a shop within its store for McGee, an accomplishment equal to an actor getting his own TV show. McGee's studio in New York's Chelsea district became a way station for young black designers like Stephen Burrows and Constance Saunders. And Burrows, one of America's most important modern designers, began to attract attention.

Black designers who gained a toehold in the late sixties created opportunities for black models on Seventh Avenue, and one or two white designers, motivated by their civil rights values or by fashion's natural craving for the new and exotic, began to use black models occasionally. Pauline Trigére, who had emigrated from France and set up shop in New York, used several dark-skinned models. But it was still rare to see a black face in a showroom, on a runway, or in the pages of a magazine unless it was a situation controlled by blacks and aimed at blacks, like *Ebony* magazine.

Into this white blizzard strode Naomi Sims, a mahogany-skinned beauty with high cheekbones, wide, pointed nose, and full lips. In 1969, Sims made her first big breakthrough; she was featured on the cover of *Life* magazine after being unable to get any top modeling agency in New York to represent her. Even after landing one of the most coveted modeling assignments in the business, several agencies turned her down again; they did not think they could get enough work for a black model. Wilhemina Cooper, the famous model who had opened her own agency, agreed after some pleading to allow Sims to use her agency's name.

Sims went on to be one of the most celebrated models of her era. Since retiring she has introduced a line of cosmetics and wigs for women of color and published an autobiography that documents her struggles and ascent in the fashion world. The doors she opened as one of the first well-known blacks in the business will be her lasting legacy.

The incomparable Naomi Sims. "When we first saw her [in 1969] we just about died," says Stephen Burrows.

While Sims was breaking down barriers in the modeling profession, on the music scene a flamboyant guitarist from Seattle named Johnny "Jimi" Hendrix was making an indelible impression on the world of fashion. Hendrix's talent and influence in pop music is well documented; his dress innovations were also copied

Jimi Hendrix pushed the boundaries of androgynous style.

by both blacks and whites alike, and he set the stage for the funk style that was to define the next decade.

Fitted see-through shirts, sinewy velvet pants, ruffles, and rich, bright colors were his hallmarks. He borrowed some of his psychedelic look from the acidheads and his rich colors and beads from the hippie movement. When he moved to England in the late sixties, his flamboyance and experimentation with clothes progressed. Tall, thin, and attractive, he would wear skinny pants with ruffled shirts, tie a chiffon scarf around his neck, and top the look with brocaded and festooned old-world military-style jackets. The small Afro of his American days was blown out and apparently texturized into a wild exotic crown of curly and kinky hair. English rockers like Mick Jagger, Keith Richard, and David Bowie got to study his style close up, and they incorporated it into their own wardrobes. Before there was "Ellen," black entertainers like Hendrix, and more recently Grace Jones and the former Prince, pushed the public toward an acceptance of androgynous style.

"The way he blended male and female imagery in his look was incredibly influential," says Valerie Steele, fashion curator for the Fashion Institute of Technology in New York and author of several books on fashion. "He was wearing velvet shirts and scarves but was the rock star who was ultra masculine."

In 1970, Hendrix died suddenly in London of a drug overdose. But the impact of his groundbreaking attitude endured well into the seventies, where it helped set the stage for the funky chicken style. And almost three decades later, Tom Ford at Gucci based his 1996 spring collection on Hendrix, one of his favorite fashion icons.

Mack Daddies and Clothes That Were the Mack: The Funky Seventies

In the early 1970s, blacks' outrage over racism and injustice had not been quelled, and for good reason. Still segregated in many areas of the United States, blacks were denied access to basics such as education, health care, and jobs. The 1970s dawned with the National Guard's shooting of Kent State students protesting the Vietnam War and the FBI's national manhunt, or more correctly womanhunt, for Angela Davis, a professor and activist accused of being a coconspirator in an attempt to free several black prisoners. The bloody result was the death of a judge and several defendants. Her notoriety and the empathy both blacks and whites felt for her made her a romantic figure. And since the only person stylishness ever hurt was Imelda Marcos, Davis earned points for being attractive too. Here was an eloquent, well-educated, take-no-prisoners black

Jazzmen began influencing fashion in the 1920s, when jazz was born. Here Miles Davis poses in front of his wardrobe, dressed in tight seventies "skins."

woman who wore miniskirts, dashikis, and fabulous African-inspired earrings. The big Afro that framed her intelligent face inspired more women to adopt that hairstyle. Jewish women, inspired by their civil rights politics or a highly developed fashion sense, combed their hair into Afros whenever it was curly enough to defy gravity.

The rioting of the early 1970s gave way to the promise of integration, affirmative action, and "overcoming," but a great deal of inequality and resentment persisted, mixed with blacks' need to express their growing pride in their African roots.

Dashikis mingled with acid-washed, studded jeans, African beads and amulets, acidhead psychedelia, and African tie-dye. Fashion was going over the top, and funk music—perfect for dancing the funky chicken with your bellbottoms flapping—was just the vehicle to help speed it along. With funk emerged a glamorous, mad mix of glittery and flamboyant self-expression in fashion. It was a time when Diana Ross established herself as the diva to end all divas with her stunning, decorous gowns designed by Bob Mackie. Singing groups like the Delfonics, the Chi-lites, and the Stylistics adopted flashy suits to match their flashy, soulful moves, and soul groups like the Jackson Five commercialized the eclecticism of the period.

Black women had joined the wave of whites wearing miniskirts, but they were also early champions of the maxiskirt, which white women resoundingly rejected. Part of the message of black dress was strongly carried by a spate of black films—not all of them good—that Hollywood pumped out in the seventies.

While many blacks objected to films like *Cleopatra Jones, Superfly*, and *Coffy* for their glorification of swaggering, sex-charged black antiheroes, the style of those films had an immediate impact on many people, including those in the fashion world both then and now. Blaxploitation films picked up on the street style of the black community, exaggerated it, and reserved it to young people of all races. Many of the stars of these films became style icons, including Pam Grier in *Coffy* and *Foxy Brown*, Tamara Dobson in *Cleopatra Jones*, Ron O'Neal in *Superfly*, Richard Roundtree in *Shaft*, and Billy Dee Williams and Diana Ross in *Mahogany*.

The look included dramatic Afros, long jackets with wide lapels, maxicoats, turtlenecks, hot pants, knee-high boots, and furs. Jewelry was big and bold, with huge hoop earrings for women and heavy gold chains for men. The blaxploitation films romanticized this pimp profile down to the furs—one reason some African Americans objected to the genre—but young blacks and many whites reveled in it. Here was a provocative look that was glamorous, sexy, and powerful, and it reverberated around the world.

Dashikis, African-style collars, and head scarves gave definition to black pride in the sixties and early seventies for people like the champion tennis player and activist, the late Arthur Ashe.

Ironically, but not surprisingly, many of the professionals working behind the scenes on these films were white, and that included the costume designers. Giorgio di Sant Angelo, one of the most exciting talents of the seventies, who had been taken under the wing of Diana Vreeland, editor of *Vogue*, was given the job of creating the clothes for *Cleopatra Jones.*

Valentino was asked to design the costumes for *Mahogany*, but Joan Juliet Buck, the editor of French *Vogue*, then a young reporter for *Women's Wear Daily*, recalls that Diana Ross set off a scandal in Italy (where

Soul sisters and brothers in the style immortalized in blaxploitation films: outsize Afros, hot pants, body-conscious clothes, wide lapels, bell-bottoms, fedoras.

filming was taking place) when she decided to take charge of her own wardrobe. "She ripped everything apart and decided to redesign it herself," recalled Buck.

One black designer who did benefit from the movies was James McQuay, a furrier who took Ron O'Neal's film wardrobe to baroque lengths with his floor-length furs. Another, Bernard Jacobs, who was also a dancer, made the leap from ready-to-wear designer to costume designer. He designed costumes for films like *Claudine*, starring Diahann Carroll and James Earl Jones.

Soul Goes to Seventh Avenue

By the mid-1970s, the civil rights movement had pried open windows of opportunity on Seventh Avenue for black designers, models, and—to a lesser extent—journalists. There was an effort to redress discrimination and a new awareness of blacks as professionals or, quite simply, people with good ideas that could perhaps enhance a business.

Bergdorf Goodman had staged a fashion showcase of the work of black designers in 1968. "I'm sure they didn't think we could pull it off," recalls designer Arthur McGee. "I remember how successful it turned out." The event marked a watershed of sorts, as stores became a bit more magnanimous—or afraid to appear discriminatory toward black designers.

One of the most important African-American designers to surface in the 1970s was Stephen Burrows. Slight and attractive, Burrows came to New York from his native New Jersey and in 1966 graduated from the Fashion Institute of Technology, which, with Parsons School of Design, is one of the premier design schools in the United States. Both his grandmothers had been sample makers for Hattie Carnegie, the prestigious Manhattan designer and retailer. He worked for Webber Originals, a Seventh Avenue house, and then operated O Boutique—"O" representing the symbol of infinity—with artist Jim Valkus for a year before gaining the attention of a *Vogue* fashion editor, Carrie Donavan, who later became the style editor of the *New York Times*. She put Burrows's clothes

Arthur McGee

on the young up-and-coming model Naomi Sims. "When Sims arrived for the shoot," says Burrows, recalling his excitement, "she was wearing purple eyelashes, and we thought we would just die."

Burrows would spend his weekdays toiling over his sketch book and sewing machine at O, and weekends on Long Island's Fire Island, a trendy gathering place for creative gay men and other beautiful people seeking respite from the grit of the city. There he befriended Joel Schumacher, who worked for Paraphernalia, an influential store of the time. When Schumacher moved on to become display director for Henri Bendel, he urged Burrows to show his work to Geraldine Stutz, president of the store. Burrows recalls that when he went to Stutz's office she tried on a coat and some other things and immediately said, "I'll give you a boutique on the third floor." Thus began a legendary partnership in fashion.

Joel Schumacher went on to produce blockbuster movies like *Batman Forever, A Time to Kill,* and *The Client.* And Burrows went on to fashion stardom.

In 1970, Henri Bendel opened the boutique called Stephen Burrows World; it showcased Burrows's distinctive slinky jersey dresses, skirts, and halter tops that wrapped and draped around the body sensuously. Jersey was becoming a popular medium among the leading-edge designers, and Burrows and his friend Halston excelled in it. The 1990s revival of seventies fashion is often noted for its references to Halston, but much of the flavor is also distilled from Mr. Burrows's early creations.

Burrows liked to work in bright colors—lipstick red, clear orange, daffodil yellow, and green—finishing his dresses with a distinctive rippled hem or lettuce edging around sashes, armholes, and hems. His clothes were worn by the glittering set—Cher, Diana Ross, and the models and actresses who hung out at Studio 54. The designs were perfect for people living a life of glamour and excitement, recalls Veronica Jones, a friend of Burrows and a retail executive at the time. Burrows was one of five American designers (the others were Halston, Bill Blass, Oscar de la Renta, and Anne Klein) chosen to represent American design in Paris in 1974, and he was twice awarded America's highest fashion honor, the Coty Award, in 1973 and 1977.

Retailers and fashion journalists were interested in black designers—they were innovative and had a fresh approach to style. Fashion insiders noted their courage and ability to use and mix bright colors. Scott Barrie, Lester Hayatt, Jon Weston, Jon Haggins, Jack Fuller, Alvin Bell, Bonnie Bonfield, and Constance Saunders were other black designers who gained recognition and success in the 1970s.

Some designers, for example Burrows, Barrie, and Haggins, helped define a recognizable black-influenced aesthetic of bright colors like red, green, and black jersey—the shades of Afrocentrism—or dresses that draped and wrapped rather than zipped and pinned. Others refined their expertise in what Saunders calls Judaeo-Christian clothes—the kind of middle-of-the-road, accessible dresses and suits that the Liz Claiborne company or any respectable design house might produce for the masses of American women.

Often it was in search of more "soul," or distinctive style, that owners of garment companies began pursuing black designers in the seventies. The legendary Ben Shaw, who invested in the businesses of Oscar de la Renta, Halston, and Giorgio Sant Angelo, was looking for African-American talent when Halston introduced him to Burrows. Shaw and Burrows became partners. But the situation was unusual. Most white investors were looking for black talent but hoping to keep them in the back design rooms.

Stephen Burrows was as big a star as the women he dressed in his innovative jersey dresses, shown here on models in the seventies—and he was one of the first designers to have his own fragrance.

"I have never felt racism in the business except trying to get money," says Burrows. "I always felt I had to hide being black in order to get things circulated or known," adds Jack Fuller.

The ebullient Felicia Farrar—a black designer who now owns her own business and has dressed Patti Labelle and, more recently, stars like Elizabeth Shue, Diana Ross, Lynn Whitfield, and Danielle Steele—moved from her home in North Carolina to start her career in New York's back rooms in 1974. After the 1960s youth quake, fashion began to take its cues from young people in the street rather than high-society matrons and the designers who dressed them. Farrar describes an almost comical situation involving black women and apparel company owners, probably spurred by the blaxploitation films of the era—and a twisted prejudice. "They used to take prostitutes—especially in the seventies—take them to Bloomingdale's or Bergdorf Goodman and let them go shopping," she says. "Whatever they bought, that was the line for the season, especially in the mass market."

Garment manufacturers were reluctant to hire blacks as full-fledged designers. "I was disillusioned when I first came to New York," says Farrar. "There was never any stability for black designers. They would hire you and fire you the next sea-

Jon Haggins

Scott Barrie left the jersey designs of the seventies behind when he made a comeback in the 1980s. He still wanted the top models for his clothes—Anya Bayle, Dalma, and the fabulous Roshumba.

son after taking your ideas. And there were never any promotions. Their attitude was, why should they put someone on the payroll when they could hire by the hour?"

Like many African-American designers who came of age then, Farrar ended up starting her own business. So did Willi Smith, who helped define American sportswear.

Smith, who had transferred from Philadelphia College of the Arts (Burrows, Smith's idol, had attended the school briefly in the sixties) by all accounts a precocious student, dropped out of Parsons School of Design, designed for several apparel firms, including Digits, where his contribution to the company earned him his name on the label. At Digits he met Laurie Mallet, a French immigrant, and in 1976 they started WilliWear; his clever take on cheap chic urban wear for women and men caught on instantly and became a standard designers would refer to again and again. "I don't design clothes for the queen, but for people who wave at her as she goes by," he would say. He designed loose, oversized clothes inspired by African and modern art. His wrap fatigue pants and vegetable-dyed striped cotton jackets and pants were characteristic of his work.

Willi Smith. "He was a genius," says his friend Alvin Bell.

Constance Saunders, one of the few pioneering black women with her name on the label. "Perhaps because my features are not so ethnic, I've been more accepted."

Several of Smith's friends note that his charm and urbane ways helped make him a darling of the press as well as a successful businessman. "He was intensely academic and ahead of his time," says his

She looks the same as she did way back when! Even as a *Mademoiselle* cover girl, Peggy Dillard refused to perm her hair.

friend Alvin Bell. "He was one of the first designers to do fabulous classical fashion for mass America. Yet he also dressed the richest women in the world." In 1986, when Caroline Kennedy (the daughter of President Kennedy and Jacqueline Kennedy Onassis) wed Edward Schlossberg, the groom's navy tails and silver tie, designed by Smith, caused a sensation. Coincidentally, a decade later, Caroline's brother, John F. Kennedy, Jr., asked Gordon Henderson, a black California designer living in New York, to make the suit in which he got married.

All the black designers who rose to prominence in the disco decade were male. Some designers admit it was easier for men to succeed during that period. It may be that fashion, which has always been more accepting of homosexuality than many industries, was more comfortable with gay black men than straight black women. Even in fashion journalism—an area of fashion that has been more open to women—black women found the doors locked tight. It appeared that females, white and black, faced discrimination within the business. Corporations were just beginning to open up to large numbers of women in influential positions.

African-American women were more visible as models. Willi Smith staged flamboyant, spirited fashion shows featuring his sassy sister, Toukie, who went on to star in the TV series *227* and the film *Mi Vida Loca.*

Black models' dramatic presentation, their haughty walk or their joie de vivre, became the preferred runway style until the early 1990s, when sashaying and hip swiveling became démodé. Grace was replaced by awkward movement and glassy-eyed stares, a new form of modeling

Renauld White, now an actor and model, set the pace for today's Tyson Beckfords.

Beverly Johnson, the first black model to appear on the cover of *Vogue*.

that developed alongside a new cutting-edge design that championed androgyny and casual style.

Among the most prominent brown divas of 1974 were Pat Cleveland, Alva Chen, Billie Blair, Bethann Hardison, Mounia, Katoucha, Barbara Smith, and Peggy Dillard. Dillard and Smith were among the first black women on the cover of *Mademoiselle*. Dillard developed a cult following for refusing to perm her hair. Male models Renauld White and Rashid Silvera, who was once married to Alva Chen, emerged during this period, breaking color barriers as they began to be regularly featured not only in black publications but in advertisements and magazines like *GQ*. The still-stunning Beverly Johnson became a star with her magazine work; in 1974 she was the first black model to grace the cover of *Vogue*.

When Givenchy began using some of these black models in the early seventies, he not only created a furor by hiring them for his show, but he took to partying with them all over Paris and at Studio 54 in New York.

He explained recently how he ended up with mostly black models out of necessity when on a trip to Los Angeles to present his line, the only good models he was offered happened to be African American. He invited many of them to come to Paris, and they did—Diane Washington, Caroline Miles, Sandi Bass, Billie Blair, and the African model Katoucha among them. His most famous recruit, the pouty-lipped Mounia from Martinique, was to arrive later, but after three seasons with Givenchy she was snapped up by Yves Saint Laurent, where she became one of his muses.

"There were a lot of critiques, principally by *Women's Wear* and customers," Givenchy recalls. "They said, 'Why does Givenchy only use black models?' Other critics said, 'Givenchy is crazy to dance with black models.' It was difficult for some people to accept at that time. But I didn't care. It was certainly one of my best collections. I got a lot of inspiration from the models."

As more designers demanded black models, these runway princesses had to attune themselves to the ways of the fashion trade and rein in their flamboyant style, which would later be immortalized in gay voguing parties and by Madonna in her 1990 video *Vogue*. Several of the black models had honed their style—grand entrances and triple pirouettes—on the chitlin' circuit, where the Ebony Fashion Fair was the pinnacle.

"We all followed Givenchy," says Bob Mackie, whose favorite model is African-American Lu Celania Sierra. "We all wanted black models, but some of those girls had to learn to tone it down from what they did at *Ebony* or so on."

Pat Cleveland and Richard Roundtree, later to become famous as "Shaft," were among those models who early in their careers worked for *Ebony*.

The Ebony Fashion Fair runway shows not only provided black models with scare work opportunities, but brought European high style to the American hinterlands. And it was done against great odds. *Ebony* had been building its Fashion Fair since the 1950s under the eagle eye of Eunice Johnson, the wife of John Johnson, owner of *Ebony* and *Jet* magazines and one of the country's first contemporary black millionaires. She would personally travel to Europe to select clothes for the show and join the tour on some of its many stops throughout the United States. A typical annual Fashion Fair tour can include two dozen cities spread over six months.

When Eunice Johnson traveled to Rome and Paris twice a year to buy clothes, she was not always met with open arms. Audrey Smaltz, who was the Ebony Fashion Fair commentator and accompanied Johnson to Paris in the seventies, recalls that Valentino would not let the two colleagues into a show in the early seventies, although they had been customers for years. "We told them if they didn't let us in, we weren't going to buy any more," says Smaltz. "Now we're friends." (Eunice Johnson was at the Valentino show in 1997.)

Pat Cleveland was a favorite of top designers like French couturier Thierry Mugler (left).

"Designers wouldn't sell to her because she wasn't prestigious enough," says Bill Cunningham, the *New York Times* fashion photographer who was traveling to Europe at the time. "She wasn't Bergdorf Goodman. She had to go through the door at the back or the side."

In articles in the white press on couture customers, *Ebony* is rarely mentioned, even though Eunice Johnson is one of couture's oldest clients. In the 1970s and 1980s at the height of French fashion, *Ebony* was spending about one hundred thousand per season on clothes in Paris, reckons Smaltz.

Eunice Johnson wanted only the top names for her show; sometimes she would buy designs a season old, which cost less than the latest styles. She chose designs with an eye on showmanship. Black communities historically have had to create their own entertainment. Fashion shows, organized around community church groups, sororities, and social clubs, became a popular leisure activity for the black bougeoisie. The shows were meant to be as theatrical as any play and demanded clothes that could make a connection with the woman sitting in the bleachers. Eunice Johnson understood this and featured fashions that were brightly colored and highly decorated—and a reflection of her own style. Mrs. Johnson ain't afraid to pair her tropical-colored Yves Saint Laurent suit with thigh-high boots; clearly, she has a love of fashion. But it was not only passion that drove her pioneering spirit. Each *Ebony* fashion show provided the magazine with an invaluable mailing list: A ticket to a show includes the price of a subscription to *Ebony*.

Designers and models also got valuable exposure in *Essence* magazine; its first anniversary in 1971 featured a cover shot of an Afroed beauty named Barbara Cheesborough wearing a red, green, and black draped jersey dress designed by Scott Barrie. *Essence* was the first successful fashion and lifestyle magazine for black women.

Its fashion mission was to show beautiful black people, dressed and undressed, with tattoos, pierced noses, Afros and cornrows in high-fashion and more humble fare. The magazine, a much-needed forum for black photographers and editors, also went after some of the top lenspeople of the day, featuring work by top white photographer Helmut Newton and brothers Gordon Parks and Anthony Barboza.

The age of the supermodel was yet to come. A wall existed between highly compensated photography models and the runway models who were paid much less but were coveted for their lithe walk and ability to carry clothes. When photography models crossed over to the runway, these graceful movements were no longer valuable currency; being widely known and gorgeous was more important. These new dual-purpose models monopolized more work and paved the way for supermodels. Black models, who had established a toehold on the catwalk, were the big losers, since racism made it difficult for them to get editorial jobs or advertising work. "Exotic," the category in which black models often found themselves, was fine for a limited audience of professionals at a runway show, but to appear in a magazine or advertisement aimed at Jane Lane in Peoria was another story altogether. Today, although there have been some breakthroughs in advertising, in the hallowed halls of magazines this view persists.

Probably the first black model to straddle runway and photography successfully was a cool Somalian beauty named Iman. She strode into American consciousness in 1977 with exotic East African looks and a story concocted by her handlers that she was found running around in the African bush by well-known photographer Peter Beard. In fact, Iman came from a middle-class Ethiopian family. She was one of the first black models signed to a cosmetics contract when Revlon hired her to be the spokeswoman for its Polished Ambers line (which has since been discontinued).

Iman, the first black supermodel—runways, magazines, cosmetics contracts.

Since retiring from modeling, Iman has acted in several small roles in film and television. She has been busy as the wife of David Bowie and as spokeswoman and creative director for Iman, the cosmetics company she sold to Ivax Corporation in 1996. In 1997, after eight years of modeling retirement, Donna Karan lured Iman back in front of the camera to star in her spring 1997 collection advertising campaign and is said to be working on developing a fashion collection. The heart-tugging photographs by Peter Lindbergh show a new side of Iman and of modeling imagery—an earthy, sexy, complicated woman—who happens to be black.

Bob Marley, Fashion Muse

On the street, the colors of Pan-Africanism were slowly seeping into American and global fashion. In Jamaica, Rastafarianism had blossomed into a full-scale way of life that was to have a resounding impact on fashion that is still evident today.

As reggae grew from an island interpretation of rhythm and blues to anthems of racial pride and liberation from oppression, musicians like Bob Marley and the Wailers gave up their sharkskin suits for rebel dress. Rastafarians espoused African pride, natural living, and a belief in Emperor Haile Selassie divine.

Black men and women wore their hair naturally and let it grow into long uncombed dreads as their ancestors had done. Much like the hippies, women rejected makeup and were urged to express their roles as African queens, which meant long skirts, sometimes of African prints, head wraps or knitted tam-o'-shanters, and general expressions of femininity. Identification with America's black power movement, the South Africa antiapartheid movement, the civil war in Angola, and socialist revolutionaries like Fidel Castro and Che Guevara all conspired to introduce a militaristic strain into Rastafarian dress. A Rastafarian king-man might wear tight plaid pants with a shiny patterned shirt, a knit vest, and a khaki military jacket.

Men buttoned shirts high on the neck in what was called spanglers style, an updated version of the sixties rude boys of England and Jamaica. Interestingly, like the rebels who came before them, their preferred mode of transportation was motorbikes—Triumphs or S-90s. Pants were worn tight or slim, and although Bob Marley regularly wore jeans, most Rastafarians shunned them, perhaps associating them too strongly with American capitalism and cultural corruption. West Indians prided themselves on taking fabrics—or pants lengths as they were called—to their local tailors and having trousers made. Often Rastafarians' custom-made trousers were cuffed and worn with argyle socks, Clark's shoes, a knitted tam incorporating red, green, and yellow, or a fedora or peaked cap. Rastafarians expressed their Afrocentrism in accessories in red, green, and yellow—or ites, green, and gold, as rastas called these hues taken from the colors in the flags of several African countries.

This style of dress spread throughout the world as reggae singers, many of them Rastafarians, became international stars in the 1970s. It was not unusual to see white Rastafarians in Jamaica and the United States. In Jamaica, many young people joined the Rastafarian movement, and thousands more donned the Rastafarian look as a fashion affectation or an expression of rebellion. In America, England, and African countries like Angola, where Marley was invited to perform for Zimbabwe's independence ceremonies, people of all races adopted the style with varying degrees of intensity.

The Rastafarian look was a vivid presence on the streets of London, melding not only into street fashion but into the

Jamaican Rastafarians like the late Bob Marley and the I-Threes, including his wife, Rita (center), spawned worldwide fashion trends on the street (wrapped heads, long skirts, dreadlocks) and in high fashion (Rifat Ozbek, Byblos).

collections of white high-fashion English designers like Keith Varty and Allen Cleaver, who designed for the Italian company Byblos until 1996, and Rifat Ozbek.

The African pride movement in Jamaica was fueled by the black pride movement among African Americans and had in common with American hippies a general suspicion of institutionalized authority. Hippies and others were urged to really experience life by taking LSD, and Rastafarians thought it wise to make a daily sacrament of herb or marijuana. The hippie movement espoused long flowing skirts and love beads and a withdrawal from a corrupt society into communes. Rastafarians advocated going back to Africa or retreating to the hills of Jamaica far from "Babylon." With such bases of commonality, it is no wonder that a fashion movement from a small country found such wide acceptance. Perhaps because of these similar attitudes, white Americans initially embraced Rastafarian style more wholeheartedly than black Americans. It was not until hip hop became the music of choice for a new generation that the Rasta look was dissected and incorporated into black American fashion.

Glory, Death, and Disappointment on Seventh Avenue

The 1980s dawned with expectation and excitement about the number of black designers moving to Seventh Avenue, but there were already signs that problems lay ahead. After their spectacular start, talents like Stephen Burrows did not seem able to attract the money they needed to expand their businesses.

The initial flood of press interest was beginning to look like a mirage to some black designers. "Black designer was like another trend," says Jon Haggins. "The onslaught of the press was basically a fad because of this 'black is beautiful'. It was something to fill their pages, another look, another angle. The most ridiculous question we were asked was, 'How does it feel to be a black designer?'"

In the eighties, money flowed into the coffers of rich individuals and wealthy corporations. People were weary of the pall of the seventies recession, and flashy displays of wealth in parties, cars, or clothes were as ubiquitous as Don King in a boxing ring. As women moved up the corporate ladder into middle management, a nouveau riche brand of corporate style emerged: the broad-shouldered, flashy power suit for day and the simple-minded pouf for night. The look was ostentatious and glittery.

The prices of designer apparel rose more than 50 percent between the seventies and the eighties, and designers created large empires based on the sale of expensive clothes and cheaper fragrances. Many black designers who had seemed to have such bright futures a decade earlier were unable to find the financing to compete on the scale at which fashion was now being conducted. Fashion titans like Calvin Klein, Chanel, Giorgio Armani, and Donna Karan operated businesses of global proportions. "It seems like a lot of the time the black guys had it a bit harder," said Scott Barrie in 1989. "We couldn't always get the financing we needed."

Barrie and Burrows were among those black designers forced to close their businesses. Barrie moved to Milan, where he worked for a succession of Italian and Japanese companies, including Krizia and Milan D'Or. Burrows began concentrating on small design projects and custom clothes for private clients.

Tragedy struck at an early age. In 1987, Willi Smith died at thirty-nine. Although it had been generally known he had been ill for months, he kept the nature of his illness private, perhaps afraid of the stigma that then was still associated with AIDS.

Laurie Mallet, his partner, struggled to keep the company alive. She opened a

Willi Smith store on Fifth Avenue in the Flatiron district and installed a series of designers, most notably Andre Walker, a black man who was a product of the Greenwich Village avant-garde and was known for his quirky, downtown designs. He welcomed the chance to continue the Willi Smith legacy, but he felt acutely the burden that entailed. Two days before the show that would unveil his first WilliWear line, he said, "Here I get a chance to do something and it has to be with a company on its last leg." The highly anticipated show, held in April during the ready-to-wear showings in New York, was an unmitigated flop, poorly received by the press. A few weeks later, Mallet announced that she was closing the company. Today the WilliWear trademark lives on in clothes in discount stores.

While Burrows's and Barrie's fortunes were waning in the early 1980s, Patrick Kelly from Vicksburg, Mississippi, who was the first American ever admitted to the Chambre Syndicale, the prestigious body of French designers, arrived on the fashion scene. But it was not until he moved to Paris at the urging of model Pat Cleveland that the fashion world took notice. In 1985, he staged his first collection presentation with money from his collaboration with Italian designer Roberta di Camerino.

Kelly's designs bore the imprimatur of the eighties—exuberant, showy, body-conscious clothes with whimsical prints like red lips or windmills, or strong shades of red, black, or white. He developed a button print and adorned his sexy tailored clothes with attention-getting buttons, an idea he said was inspired by his grandmother's replacing the buttons on his clothes when he was a little boy.

Kelly surrounded himself with a coterie of energetic black divas, male and female. His right-hand design assistant was Elizabeth Goodrum. His fairy godmother and constant supporter was model Pat Cleveland. Audrey Smaltz flew into Paris each season to help coordinate his shows. And his shows, advertisements, and other promotions for his clothes featured the biggest bevy of black models assembled since Hubert Givenchy had caused the fashion industry such discomfort. They included Iman, Mounia, Rebecca Ayoko, Anna Getaneh, Magic, Roshumba, Coco, and Lu Sierra. Kelly charmed the press and public dressed in navy overalls reminiscent of his Southern upbringing. Brooches in the form of full red lips and black baby doll pins became his witty trademarks. "The black bougeosie, the Black Caucus wives, they hated that pin," says Audrey Smaltz, who had recommended Kelly to Roberta di Camerino. "They thought it was a disgrace." But Kelly's fans eclipsed his detractors. "Traveling with Patrick was like traveling with Mick Jagger," says Mary Ann Wheaton, who was president of Kelly's company. "On one trip I remember it took us two hours to move from the baggage area to the sidewalk. He had just been on the cover of *Vanity Fair*."

Kelly's big break came when he met Gloria Steinem, the activist and author, who introduced him to Linda Wachner, the owner of Warnaco, a large apparel company that makes Calvin Klein underwear. Known as a shrewd, ball-breaking executive, Wachner had gained notoriety—and a pile of money—as the first woman to stage a huge leveraged buyout. She decided Kelly was a talent worth investing in, and he became a licensed division of the Warnaco stable in 1987.

In 1989, Kelly seemed on the verge of accomplishing what no black designer had done—a global, multiproduct business. But it was not to be.

That same year, Fairchild Publications, at the instigation of Monique Greenwood, produced "Soul of Seventh Avenue," a historic program honoring black models and designers at the National Association of Black Journalists convention in New York. Greenwood, now style editor for *Essence,* was editor of Fairchild's *Children's Business* at the time.

The unprecedented event was to bring together models like Beverly Johnson, Iman, Naomi Campbell, Sheila Johnson, Wanakee, and Bethann Hardison and the top black designers, including Patrick Kelly, Alvin Bell, Jeffrey Banks, Stephen Burrows, Gordon Henderson, Karl Logan, Felicia Farrar, and Isaia Rankin, a designer whose sexy stretch fashions were a favorite of the new MTV crowd.

In the midst of the arrangements for the event, in June 1989, came word that Isaia Rankin had died, struck down by AIDS. He was thirty-three. For days before the news leaked out, his shocked and confused young assistants would not confirm his death, telling inquirers that Isaia was "not here." It was several weeks before his landlord at Seventh Avenue knew his tenant had died, as the workers tried to carry on the business as usual.

As the date of "Soul of Seventh Avenue" drew near, communication with Patrick Kelly's representatives in New York and Paris became erratic. One day they said the designer would be coming; the next day he wasn't. This went on up to the day of the event, when Mary Ann Wheaton reported that he was unable to make it. "When Patrick had friends who got sick or had a problem he believed that they should face it and fight it," says Wheaton. "When he got sick himself he went into total denial." Meanwhile, rumors had begun circulating that Kelly was extremely ill. On January 1, 1990, almost six months after he had failed to make his scheduled trip to New York, word came that he had died in France. The news was carried in newspapers, on television, and on the radio throughout the United States and in France. The official cause of death was given as cancer; in fact, Kelly had died of AIDS. Kelly's

Patrick Kelly and his sexy, exuberant fashions caused gridlock at airports.

Alvin Bell

death changed the way financial backers approached designers. "After that people started taking out multi-million-dollar insurance policies on designers," says Wheaton.

By the mid-1990s three of the thirteen designers honored in "Soul of Seventh Avenue" were dead—heart-stopping odds. The third was Karl Logan, who had once won the California Designer of the

Jeffrey Banks, a Ralph Lauren alumnus; he won a Coty Award for his preppie menswear.

Year award. Altogether the fashion community had lost dozens of designers, black and white, to the AIDS plague, including luminous names like Perry Ellis, Franco Moschino, and Clovis Ruffin. For the black community the losses were more vivid because our numbers were so few. Other African-American designers who had died by the mid-1990s were Kevin Smith, Scott Barrie, Bernard Jacobs, Toyce Anderson, and Robert Miller.

Buppies and Hoodies: The Eighties and the Dawn of Hip Hop

While African Americans like Patrick Kelly were helping define eighties high fashion, the street was bubbling with a flavor that was to prove stronger than any 1980s designer-driven trend.

A decade earlier, Jamaican immigrants had begun bringing their brand of sound system parties to the Bronx, where entertainers like Whodini and Grand Master Flash "talked" over a heavy back beat, producing records that became some of the earliest rap hits.

In 1996, Gordon Henderson designed John F. Kennedy, Jr.'s wedding suit, but the nineties have brought crushing financial difficulties for young fashion stars like Henderson.

In those days hip hop looked very different from what it is now. Early rap fashion owed more to the popular soul and funk bands of the 1970s like Earth, Wind, and Fire and the Commodores than to street style. By the time Run D.M.C. and LL Cool J became rap's first megastars in the mid 1980s, a look had evolved that was discernibly hip hop.

African-American entertainers and black youth in the Bronx began wearing nylon jogging suits, gold chains big enough to chain a cow, and triple-striped Adidas sneakers, making an important break from the prevailing style of entertainers like Lionel Richie, who wore glitzy costumes when performing. Rappers in essence began performing in their street clothes, and rap lyrics by performers like Run D.M.C. glorified fashion, referring to Polo and Vuitton and extolling Versace, Adidas, and Karl Kani.

The definitive b-boy of the 1980s, LL Cool J, in Kangol cap, hoodie, heavy gold chain, sneakers, and ultimate accessory—the boombox. "I Just Can't Live without My Radio," rapped LL.

The boombox, immortalized by LL Cool J in his hit "I Just Can't Live without My Radio," became the accessory of choice for urban hip-hop kids, right behind the must-have gold chains, which might sport a Mercedes emblem as a pendant or the wearer's name in big letters. Some following the lead of LL Cool J added a Kangol—a hat brand that had been an important part of the reggae and dub scene in Jamaica.

Women wore huge "doorknocker" earrings, pierced their noses, and wore sexy, blasé outfits like tight pants, over-the-knee boots, and leather or shearling jackets. The natural hairstyles of the seventies were gradually replaced with ever more complicated permed styles made possible by hairweaving. Flygirls adorned their fingers with gold rings—nameplates that spread over three knuckles or signet rings, the better to call attention to long, nail-wrapped, brightly painted fingernails.

Even as the b-boys adopted casual dress, the girls remained more informally glamorous. By the late eighties, both sexes were making prestige logos an integral part of the hip-hop look. Gucci, Chanel, Mercedes Benz, Louis Vuitton were emblazoned on clothes, handbags, and jewelry, much of it knocked off by merchants serving the hip-hop market.

Many of the youngsters who were adapting these high-priced brands to their own needs had become teenagers or young adults as the country moved into a backlash against blacks and affirmative action under President Reagan. Social programs such as CETA and Head Start—on which many blacks relied to get a foot up into a living wage—were cut back, and courts moved away from legal redress for discrimination. A general intolerance of blacks, immigrants, and lower-income families was accompanied by gauche displays of wealth and the idolizing of material well-being. It was the age of Donald Trump, the pouf, the $1,000-designer-suit-and-everyone-better-know-it.

"A lot of these kids came of age seeing people glorified for wearing expensive designer clothes," said Lois Taylor, a social worker, who works with inner city clients. "They couldn't wear it. They rebelled. They said, 'Fuck it. I'm gonna make what I wear cool.' They went to the other extreme.'"

Hip-hop dress has always been emphatically casual, and the jewelry became almost a parody of showing off immense wealth.

As rap took hold among black urban youth, attracting thousands to concerts and selling millions of records, the dress moved beyond rap music fans to black urban kids in general. By the late eighties, baggy jeans worn low on the hips and oversize sweatshirts had replaced jogging suits. Kids took to displaying the waistband of their underpants above their low-slung jeans, a look none too popular with many older African Americans.

Some trace the emergence of low, baggy jeans to prisoners who, according to prison regulations, cannot wear belts, and so their pants fall down. (In the United States a disproportionate number of young black men are arrested and imprisoned, a higher proportion than any other racial group.)

Around the same time that the baggy look was emerging, MTV began airing rap videos. The black community had complained for years about the dearth of black performers on MTV, and in 1986 the network finally took steps to do something about it. Videos had a huge impact on fashion in general and hip-hop style in particular, making television into one long electronic fashion show. After one's peers, rappers are the most influential style-setters in hip hop.

One strain of hip hop style had an African motif superimposed on it. Rap groups like Salt-N-Pepa, whose look epitomized the flygirls of the period, added African-print kuffis to their leather-and-boots style. Queen Latifah later arrived on the scene with her baroque turbanlike headdresses evocative of an African queen, or at least a homegirl diva.

Not a little of the hip-hop style was derived from drug pushers, who were ruling inner-city streets and could afford loads of gold jewelry even though they did not have legitimate jobs. Blacks were more aware of this aspect of hip hop's early roots than were other racial groups, a fact brought home when Bloomingdale's faced an outraged black community protesting its depiction of a little boy in hip-hop gear—cow chain and all—in huge newspaper advertisements.

Hip-hop music came under increasing pressure, both inside and outside the black community, and the clothes were among the earliest targets. Even before the Bloomingdale's incident, people were protesting pants worn below the waist with underpants or butt showing as a lack of social decorum. A series of armed robberies over sneakers and leather baseball jackets—some decorated with eight-ball patchworks of color especially popular in the late eighties and early nineties—did not help quell the outrage. What did was the overwhelming influence of hip hop on fashion at every level.

As hip hop created young black moguls in music and film, many of them sought to extend their reach by getting into the fashion business. More African Americans have thus found a place in fashion because of the need to reach the urban market or infuse a collection with some hip-hop "flava." Designer Tony Shellman cofounded Mecca and was then tapped by Fila to introduce that company's new Enyce (inichay) collection. Several designers at Tommy Hilfiger are black, and Morehouse graduate Lloyd Boston is an art director there. Jeffrey Tweedy has moved from key positions at Spike Lee's clothing company to Karl Kani to Twism by Shaquille O'Neal.

Vibe and *The Source*, the leading urban music magazines, have had several white editors-in-chief, but the two main rap publications employ several young black journalists, photographers, and stylists.

Suburbia, Here We Come: Black Self-employment and Purple Jeans

Two of the biggest-ever black designing successes came out of hip hop: Cross Colours and Karl Kani.

In 1990, African-American designers Carl Jones from California and T. J. (Thomas) Walker from Mississippi decided to codify the black urban look and introduce the first hip-hop clothing line. They called their new young men's collection Cross Colours and cleverly based their marketing strategy on getting prominent rappers to wear the Cross Colours clothes in videos.

The name Cross Colours was a reference to Los Angeles gang culture, which had grown increasingly violent and influential. But Cross Colours promoted a message of peace and high self-esteem. Advertisements and slogans for Cross Colours included exhortations to keep the peace; "Stop D Violence" and "Judge 4 Yo Self" were two of the common phrases used. "We wanted to make clothes that send positive messages to kids, and at the same time make a clothing line for African Americans," Jones told *Forbes* magazine in 1992.

Cross Colours became an instant phenomenon, within two years racking up sales of $40 million as young blacks—men and women—donned Cross Colours gear. Stores like Merry Go Round, Macy's, Fred Segal, and Up Against the Wall snapped up Cross Colours's baggy jeans in purple, orange, green, and yellow, matching shirts, and sweaters emblazoned with the company logo and whipsmart sayings. The signature colors of the company were red, green, and black, a combination that exalted Afrocentrism. But Cross Colours's lightning-fast expansion was its undoing. Although Walker and Jones were experienced fashion operators (Jones had owned a company called Surf Fetish before starting Cross Colours, and Mr. Walker had been an employee), they had no way of anticipating the overwhelming response to their idea.

As early as 1992, store executives began to grumble about late deliveries as the partners scrambled to keep abreast of the demand. Trouble is always double, and in addition to the shortages, the fickle hip-hop crowd began to tire of bright denims. Kids were turning to a nautical preppie look. And Cross Colours was not moving quickly enough to respond to the change.

As Cross Colours collapsed, Karl Kani (Carl Williams), Tommy Hilfiger, Polo/Ralph Lauren, Nautica, Perry Ellis, Timberland, and Guess became popular labels. Cross Colours's ashes contained the proof that not only could blacks in fashion build large businesses, but the black market could be a gold mine. "Before Cross Colours, the big retailers and manufacturers didn't know what was going on," says designer Maurice Malone. "Cross Colours made a big impact. Cross Colours was the first to see that if they gave out clothes and got them into videos, they wouldn't have to pay that much for advertising and trade shows and they could reach black audiences." Walker and Jones also opened a portal through which several talented black fashion professionals passed. Karl Kani, Tony Shellman, Jeffrey Tweedy, and designer April Walker were all associated with Cross Colours.

Karl Kani, in late-nineties hip-hop style, is an important force in fashion.

White fashion designers had a range of reactions to their newfound popularity through hip hop. One or two enthusiastically embraced this newly visible black urban audience. Others tried to keep their distance while reaping the benefits of being targeted as a desirable label among young blacks.

By the early 1990s, hip-hop fashion was clearly a multibillion-dollar business, producing clothes that were worn by youth of every race in the city and the suburbs. Its influence spread to Africa, the West Indies, Europe, and Japan, where black street fashion captured the imagination of Japanese youth, who began to wear baggy jeans and took a liking to anything emblazoned with "Malcolm X." "As a result of black kids taking this style and taking something normal and making it very hip, it's turned into a billion-dollar business and designers into successful entrepreneurs," says Tommy Hilfiger.

Calvin Klein found a homeboy in Marky Mark and signed the white rapper to an exclusive contract to promote CK Calvin Klein jeans, a move that upset many African Americans. Was Calvin having trouble finding a black homeboy? It wasn't long before billboards and magazines around the country were emblazoned with Marky Mark's muscular form wearing baggy CK jeans with the band of his Calvin Klein underpants riding above the waistline, a look characteristic of hip-hop style.

Fashion magazines like *Vogue, Elle, Harper's Bazaar,* and *Mirabella* missed the huge impact hip hop was having on fashion or chose to ignore it—it was, after all, an African-American creation—until high-fashion designers became interested. Anna Sui mixed hip hop into her first fashion show with big, chunky chains. Chanel paid homage to hip hop as hip hop had done to Chanel years earlier. Isaac Mizrahi, inspired by the street and his elevator operator, borrowed ideas from the way urban black and Hispanic youth were dressing. "Rap was a moment that was happening at the time and was hard to ignore," he says.

Hip hop has shaped babyboomer style. Many a boomer with two kids and a mortgage is likely to wear high-tech sneakers or Timberland boots with jeans while driving a four-by-four—a picture far away from his or her parents and much closer to the style of black, urban twentysomethings.

Ralph Lauren and Tommy Hilfiger have benefited greatly from being chosen as purveyors of the hip-hop uniform. "I see a lot of rappers wearing my clothes and I think it's great," says Lauren. "It's interesting how people pick up things and wear it in their own way. But when I design it, I don't design it for anyone in particular."

When Hilfiger realized he was becoming popular with the hip-hop set, he moved to cement the relationship by looking to the street for trends and trying to start some of his own. His brother, Andy, who works for him, was in charge of making sure rappers—like Treach of Naughty by Nature and Snoop Doggy Dogg—and stylists for music videos had access to whatever clothes they needed. He hired Kidada Jones, Quincy Jones and Peggy Lipton's daughter, and put rappers like Coolio in his fashion shows.

While internationally recognized designers like Hilfiger were making hip hop a part of their business, several black entrepreneurs gained entree to fashion and began producing their own collections. Russell Simmons, the entertainment impresario responsible for shaping the hip-hop industry with acts like LL Cool J, Warren G, and RUN D.M.C. (his brother Joseph is a member), started Phat Farm. Film director Spike Lee opened Forty Acres and A Mule fashions for men and women with shops in Macy's. Lee's venture grew out of the success of his film *Do the Right Thing*, which showed popular urban fashions like Negro League–style baseball shirts on some characters.

Play of Kid N' Play, Chuck D of Public Enemy, and Doctor Dre of New York radio station 97.1 and formerly of Yo! MTV Raps, Wu Tang Clan, Naughty by Nature, Twism from Shaquille O'Neal, Salt-N-Pepa, all went into the fashion business. Some of these have since closed their doors, but their numbers are still strong. Black designers and sales executives are part of the behind-the-scenes talent at labels like Mecca, Enyce by Fila, Playaz, Fubu, Maurice Malone, Shabazz Brothers, and Karl Kani. The last three are black owned. April Walker, a Brooklyn designer behind the WalkerWear label, teamed up in 1996 with boxer Mike Tyson to form a fashion cooperative.

Unlike the large, white-owned companies they compete with, these designers face a challenge as black designers of a product that sprang from black hip-hop culture. When hip hop is over, will they be over, too? "The biggest players, Tommy Hilfiger, Ralph Lauren, Donna Karan, are not called hip hop," complains Ertis Pratt, an executive at Maurice Malone. "Right now if you're a black designer and you're selling jeans, you're a hip-hop designer."

Being branded as a designer who does one thing can be the death of a company in the fast-moving fashion business. But it's a risk many black designers will have to live with for the time being if they wish to stay in touch with their African-American urban customer base. "Saying you're hip-hop clothing helps on an inner-city level, but it hurts you with department stores who think you're not going to ship, you're not going to be around long," says Karl Kani. "The young hip-hop generation that started in 1988, 1989 is growing up now, so every-

Spike Lee's women's hip-hop collection, 1992—baseball shirts, denim, prominent logos, and Afrocentric jewelry.

one's going through stages as to what to wear. Hip-hop fashion is changing, but the name should never change, the name is too powerful."

Fast Fashion

The renaissance in black street fashion brought attention to African-American beauty rituals, from adventurous hairstyles to ornately done nails. As the ideal of integration spread, African Americans had abandoned many kinds of businesses, but black hairdressing was not one of them. White-run establishments had never learned how to handle African Americans' curly hair.

Decorated nails became a fetish in the 1990s as African-American women's interest in nail wrapping spread to other groups. Nails an inch or two long were painted in strong colors like red, blue, or orange and then decorated with patterns, tiny decals, or rhinestones. The first public figure to bring this look to wide attention was Florence Griffith Joyner, who became as well known for her flamboyant style as for her Olympic gold medal performances.

Joyner, her sister-in-law Jackie Joyner Kersee, and a clutch of other 1988 African-American Olympic athletes made an impact on style that went beyond their fingertips. For the first time on worldwide television, viewers were exposed to a group of sexy, fashionable athletes, women who showed a deep interest in looking feminine and stylish while sweating and breaking world records.

While runners from other countries made do with shorts and tank tops, Joyner sheathed herself in shiny, bright leggings, one-legged tights, running shorts that rode provocatively up her derriere, and tops that showed off curves or a well-toned midriff. While the eastern European women wore little or no make-up, Joyner and Kersee started every race with lips of bright red or deep burgundy. East German and Russian hair was strictly wash and wear: Joyner, even when speeding toward the finish line, looked like she had just spent hours at the salon.

These women's appearance not only promoted the idea of athletic clothes as feminine fashion for women but also ushered in the paradigm of a more muscular beauty ideal, setting the stage for the surge in interest in athletic bodies as a fashion alternative in the late 1990s. The women of the 1988 Olympics laid the groundwork for the women's basketball league. Athletes like basketball players Lisa Leslie and Sheryl Swoope, soccer player Mia Hamm and model-volleyball champion Gabrielle Reece are now considered mediagenic poster girls. Prior to Flo Jo, as Joyner was called, women athletes were not considered style innovators. There were two prevalent athletic role models to choose from: the preternatural, childlike delicacy of gymnasts and ice skaters or the masculine, androgynous style of tennis players like Martina Navratilova and the eastern European athletes who dominated track and field athletics. Women soundly rejected both.

Everyone wants to identify with a winner. When these trendsetting black women broke through with their performance, they also broke through to an audience of women ready to equate achievement, physical strength, and sports with traditional feminine allure.

Athletics and hip hop have since melded, creating a nexus of fashion, music, and sports referenced again and again. "African Americans are the ones that decided comfort should be king in the late eighties, and they've affected the world with it, from white American suburbia to Chelsea in London," says Tommy Hilfiger. "They're the ones that made it chic to wear athletic gear off the courts, and they're the ones that made it fashionable to wear very high-tech, expensive, athletic footwear."

In the Ateliers

Back on Seventh Avenue, designers of every race suffered in the nineties under the inhospitable business climate for small fashion houses. Sales of clothing contracted between 1990 and 1995 as women shifted some of their discretionary dollars to the pursuit of travel, home decoration, investments, and beauty. Casual clothes, which generally cost less than tailored suits, were becoming more popular.

For African-American designers—most of whom were owners or creative heads of small businesses—this shift meant fewer orders from stores and less investment money available from the financial community. It is also far more expensive to launch a fashion business today. A designer needs about $5 million to do what $50,000 would have done twenty years ago, reckons Stephen Burrows. Many of the most successful African-American designers with their own labels were forced to close their businesses or were shown the door. Gordon Henderson's company was shut down by his backer, World Hong Kong; he went on to design an exclusive collection for Saks, but that too went belly up. Tracy Reese left Magaschoni and is now operating her small company on her own. Byron Lars's partnership with C. Itoh ended abruptly. He then became embroiled in a lawsuit when he attempted to continue his collection with a new investor, San Siro, and he was compelled to scale back his company. Alvin Bell left HERO, and Stephen Burrows—with the help of Veronica Jones and backing by the New York theatre producer and radio personality Vy Higgenson—reopened his business, only to close it a year later when stores did not respond. The talented Nigerian designer Lola Faturoti and Haitian designer Fabrice also fell victim to the punishing retail environment.

Black models too were becoming less visible in the 1990s, culminating in 1996 in what Katie Ford, chief executive of Ford Models, described to the *New York Times* as "the blond collections." She was commenting on the almost complete absence of black models on the runways in 1995 and 1996. Fashion shows have a tremendous impact beyond the runway, as the images of the models find their way into print media, videos, and television around the world and are seen by millions of people. While in the previous years models had begun to represent ethnic diversity, designers in the nineties seemed to favor pale Caucasians as suitable mannequins for their clothes.

Designers blame agents for the status quo, saying the agents don't recruit and send them great black models. The agents point the finger at the designers and advertising directors who do not hire black models, thus making it bad business to retain African Americans on their roster. In the mid-nineties, Naomi Campbell was often the only black model who made it onto the runways. Black models are still living with the reality that when the call goes out for "a great model" or an "American-looking model," most fashion power brokers take that to mean a model who is white. We will need an extremely sharp knife to cut through such deeply ingrained values. Magazine editors justify their limited use of black models by pointing to their audience of largely white readers, yet the French-owned *Elle* magazine, which also has a French editor-in-chief and a French creative director, has proven that multiracial images can enhance a magazine's prestige and bottom line. "The frustration is being told you can't be on covers because you won't sell," says Naomi Campbell, one of the most successful models in the world. For years editors have defended themselves from accusations of racism by saying they would like to use a more diverse range of models, particularly on their covers, but that black models do not sell magazines. This argument leaves unexplained why top model Amber Valleta, for example, who—according to a report in *Women's Wear Daily*—was on the cover of two of the worst-selling issues of fashion magazines, continues to get prestigious bookings, including covers.

Vogue found itself with its slip showing when fashion insiders began gossiping about how unhappy Naomi Campbell was when her promised cover became an inside cover, while the real cover had blond Niki Taylor smiling out. "They shouldn't have promised me if they weren't going to do it," said Campbell, whose call to Anna Wintour to complain rated a call-back from Wintour's assistant. *Vogue* has put her on a cover four times, said Campbell. Yet one could count on two hands the number of times a top magazine has had a black woman on its cover in the last twenty years.

"The only editor who doesn't see color is Bensimon at *Elle*," said John Gnerre, who represents top talents like Campbell, Chandra North, and Kate Moss. "They say black models don't sell. Naomi's black but she's Naomi. She's a star."

For designers the decision to use—or more often not use—black models is, on the surface at least, one of aesthetics. (Of course, aesthetics are shaped by prejudices, too). And in 1995, a pervasive fashion mood emanating from Europe, particularly England, was the washed-out look of a drug addict—bringing new meaning to the term "high" fashion. In America, this trend was transmuted into not only a druggie look but the seedy, blue-collar style known in impolite circles as white trash. The black trash look had yet to inspire designers, so black models found themselves left on the bench because they didn't look the part.

However, there is a racism, conscious or unconscious, in using skin color to convey a fashion message. Thus, the fact that black models have started showing up on runways again to coincide with the African inspiration sweeping through fashion in the last few years of the 1990s is not necessarily reason to break out the champagne. If black models are only to be considered when the inspiration is black culture—though certainly an improvement over being ignored—then the ugly underbelly of that reasoning is surely that only whites should be considered when the leitmotif is Anglo culture.

"We were excluded from that mod thing," said Tracy Reese. Designers in the United States and Europe began reviving mod dressing of the sixties, in the mid-1990s. "That's when the whole 'no-black-models' thing started happening that we're just now getting out of. It was like we never happened. If either Byron [Lars] or I were having shows at the time we would have addressed it, but we weren't."

It will come as a surprise to some that, among major designers, the most consistent employer of black models in America has been Ralph Lauren. Even when African Americans were nonexistent in his advertising, he had from two to several of the best black models in his show. Billie Blair, Renauld White, Aria, Karen Alexander, and Naomi Campbell are among those who have walked his runway and occasionally been featured in his advertisements. "I used Billie Blair and Beverly Johnson in my first show in 1977," says Lauren. "I thought they were beautiful girls. The world is a little narrow in the people designers use. It's something I want to change, but I don't want to get on a soapbox about it."

Driven by money, integrity, or esprit, Lauren, who has built his empire on an ideal of white Anglo Protestant style, in 1997 had the strongest black imagery in fashion. He continued to use Tyson Beckford (under contract exclusively to Lauren's company for the past three years) to represent his menswear division and he signed on Naomi Campbell to be the face for his top women's collection for one season and for Polo Sport, his casual, less expensive line, for a year.

He may have been lifting a leaf out of Tommy Hilfiger's book. In a few short years, Hilfiger had become a powerhouse in the fashion business, his conservative, middle-class suburban clothes made cutting-edge by b-boys and flygirls.

Hilfiger's rapid rise was attributable to his decision to court black youth once he realized they liked his clothes. It was a bold move, one that ultimately paid off in profits that outstripped those of designers like Donna Karan. Hilfiger recalls the reaction in the fashion community to his success among young black men. "When I first designed big logos for spring 1989, people reacted immediately, and the press and other people would ask me, 'What do you feel about all these African Americans wearing your clothes? Do you think it's going to hurt?' And I said, 'Oh no.'"

African-American designers have not disappeared from Seventh Avenue in the 1990s, though after the spurt of talent

The top male model in the world, Tyson Beckford, with his agent, Bethann Hardison, a rebel and pioneer, at a Fashion Outreach fundraiser.

in the decade's early years, it certainly seemed that way. Their presence has taken on a form that has become increasingly familiar among designers heading small businesses: They consult for big companies who do not want the expense of investing in another designer's business but are willing to hire talent as roving creators. Stephen Burrows was a consultant for Mary McFadden. Tracy Reese and Byron Lars both consulted for *E-Style,* the catalog that was produced by *Ebony* and *Spiegel,* while continuing their own businesses in a more limited way.

Small companies—headed by Patrick Robinson, CD Green, Eric Gaskins, Montgomery Harris, Shaka King, Lawrence Steele in Italy, and Lamine Kouyaté of Xuly Bet in Paris—are holding their own and growing slowly. New on

Seventh Avenue is menswear designer Maurice Malone, who still produces hip-hop gear but is expanding into tailored clothing. Several more gifted black designers are content to work behind the scenes helping to shape some of the most influential fashion labels in the world. Edward Wilkerson and Ximora Gosset have each been designers with Donna Karan for more than a decade. Max Wilson is a senior designer at Ralph Lauren, Kevan Hall designs for Halston, Eric Wright is a creative director for Karl Lagerfeld and Fendi, Karen Pugh is a design consultant at The Limited, and until 1997 Michael Roberts helped create the look of Company Ellen Tracy.

When high-end designers in Europe and America presented African-motif collections in 1997, many of them were inspired by the massive "Art of Africa" exhibit that was held in London and then came to New York in the summer of 1996. For at least four years, however, midtier retailers and black grass-roots designers had noticed the growth in the black and Hispanic populations and their interest in clothes that reflected the non-Anglo part of their American heritage, J.C. Penney had contracted with African-American designers like Anthony Mark Hankins to create collections with black women in mind. *Essence* developed its own mail-order catalog.

In 1997, Sears introduced Mosaic by Alvin Bell, a fashionable collection for

Designer Patrick Robinson

women of color that drew on Bell's experience designing for high-end customers. Sears created this collection exclusively for its stores as part of a program aimed at market segments such as large-size women, Hispanics, Asians, and white suburbanites. The store was adopting a strategy that more marketers are likely to use in the next few years as minority populations grow and cultural identification becomes stronger.

And what of black and white designers serving the high-fashion market—Gaultier, Lauren, Reese, and Lars? The influence of Africa on couture design will continue with the ebb and flow of fashion. Designers like Reese, Gaultier, Dries van Noten, and Rifat Ozbek have continuously dipped into the African Diaspora to find inspiration for exciting, modern clothes.

Further evolution in marrying African and Western style may not necessarily come from black designers, many of whom create European-style clothes. Designers of any background should feel free to embrace or reject inspirations from around the world. African art and style are both modern and ancient at the same time—the clean seemingly contemporary lines of Benin sculpture of Ivoarian jewelry are juxtaposed with the continuing respect for artisanal traditions.

The next chapter of African-American influence on fashion is likely to be written in the streets rather than the catwalks. Increasingly, lifestyle is directing fashion. The tenets of hip-hop dress are more than fashion—they are a way of life, both a catalyst and a product of the demand for relaxed clothing and technically advanced fabrics. Now that we know all this, let's get dressed.

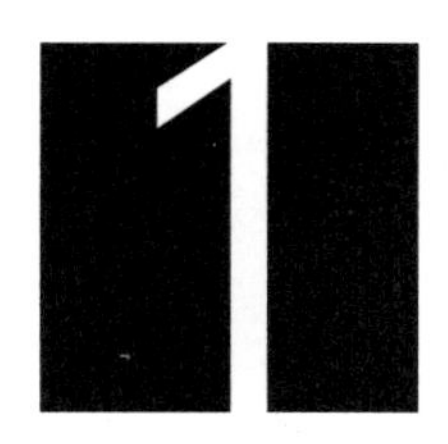

The Basics of Style: Laying the Foundation for Your Own Great Look

Everyone, including you, has style. The problem is that not all women have great style. Great style enhances the wearer and her surroundings and adds some drama or point of interest beyond the end result. A wonderful sense of style communicates a positive message about a woman. Clothes and the way we wear them help shape our concept of ourselves and the perceptions of those we interact with. This book is intended to help you reach your full style potential, to help you look your best and feel your most powerful.

Think for a moment of a woman you have met who impressed you. Do you remember the particular way she carried herself? The clothes she was wearing? If her clothes were not memorable but she was, this too can be indicative of good taste. Her clothes were not upstaging her.

Great style is the ability to identify your strongest features—both physical and emotional—and choose your wardrobe, hair, and makeup for maximum enhancement. So great style relies first on self-knowledge. Then you need a full-length mirror.

What's Your Style?

What looks good on you, and what are you comfortable wearing? If you are conservative, then no amount of prodding by your best friend or saleswoman should convince you to buy the bright kente-print pants suit with the gold trim. You won't be able to pull it off. You'll feel all wrong on the inside, and this will communicate itself in your posture and lack of confidence. On the other hand, if you're basically a bring-on-the-red kind of women, then you are not going to feel good in navy unless it's a PMS day. "Lena Horne can get away with wearing three kimonos at once," says designer Isaac Mizrahi. "But not everyone can. The real key to great style is simply feeling good about yourself. The worst thing to do is present yourself as something you are not. Whenever a woman is uncomfortable, either physically or psychically, I can tell."

What is your essential nature? Are you reserved or flamboyant? We are complex beings, and most of us have some of both tendencies. Nor should we dress one way all the time. But there is one facet of your personality that is more dominant. You should emphasize that attitude in your style, because it is where you will feel most comfortable and confident. So first, let's identify where you fit in.

Answer the following questions: Which color do you wear that gets you the most compliments? Consider your favorite dress or outfit. What does it look like? Note its color, fit—close to the body or loose—length, shoulder construction, fabric, and neckline. Now ask yourself which of your outfits draws the most compliments (and we don't mean from your mother, she'll say you look good in anything). Describe it. Why do you think it looks good on you? The two items, your favorite outfit and the one that draws the most compliments, may not be the same, but they should have some characteristics in common.

I have learned over the years that I look my best in sleek, tailored clothes. Although I am told I look great in bright colors, since I was a teenager I've preferred dark ones. The minimalist style goes with my nature. I'm sociable, but I tend to be reserved. The core of your wardrobe should draw on features of your favorite outfit, while incorporating elements of the clothes that objectively look best on you and project the image you are most at ease with.

Let's discover one more insight into your style attitude: With whom do you identify most—over-the-top Aretha, safe and pretty Whitney Houston, flamboyant yet conservative Patti Labelle, sleek and feminine Faye Wattleton, hip and streetwise Alliyah, or perhaps grand diva Jessye Norman?

You will need to pull a wardrobe together that is full of clothes that look great on you and reflect how you feel about yourself. To build your wardrobe it is necessary to start fresh. Your goal should be the ability to show up for work or any occasion nine times out of ten looking and feeling your best—with a minimum of headache and drama. Shopping for new clothes, as the need arises, will then be a pleasure rather than a migraine waiting to happen.

Starting fresh means assessing what you have and getting rid of what you are not using efficiently—that includes the red sweater with the pompoms your brother gave you for Christmas and the bell-bottom pants that have been waiting for you to lose weight since 1977.

Don't be meek. You must take a hatchet to your wardrobe. Follow these guidelines if you're having difficulty.

- If you haven't worn it in three years—THROW IT OUT.
- If you've tried stain-out and your dry cleaner, and it's still stained—THROW IT OUT.
- Mend all torn clothes, or see if they can be repaired at a reasonable cost. If not—THROW IT OUT.
- If it's too tight, THROW IT OUT.

Now, I don't mean dump it in the garbage. Separate clothes into items for friends and relatives, a bag for your local charity, and a bag for the clothing consignment shop. Many boutiques that sell used designer clothes have sprung up around the country, and you may be able to make a few hundred dollars on new or slightly worn clothes of good quality with prestige labels. If you give clothes away to charity, you can deduct up to five hundred dollars on your itemized tax return each year. Any more, and you have to fill out special forms and perhaps contend with the IRS.

Sort out the items you have left in your closet. As you go through this book, you will probably find that you already have many of the clothes mentioned. As you read, you'll pick up ideas on how to utilize them differently and creatively. You will also come across suggestions that will encourage you to purchase a few new pieces. But you don't have to go out and spend a lot of money at once. Creating a great style takes time. Furthermore, something that doesn't feel right now may feel more appropriate later, even a year from now. Stay on top of current fashion trends, but before you jump on them, make sure they make you look or feel better.

The Essential Wardrobe

For your core wardrobe, you want pieces that are timeless and of top quality. Your basic essentials are your no-brainer clothes for work. The goal is to build a core wardrobe that you can turn to again and again. Try this exercise: Pretend you are going on a seven-day business trip. You'll work for five days and have two days off to relax. You can only bring one standard-size suitcase. What would you take? Often in fashion, knowing what looks good is knowing when to stop. This suitcase exercise forces you to pare down your look to essential pieces. Then, like any good builder who creates a beautifully designed house, you can add to this solid foundation.

The core pieces of any modern wardrobe include:

One trouser suit
A jacket and skirt that work together
A blouse
A knit top
A basic cotton man's T-shirt
A pair of jeans
A short black evening dress
A glossy raincoat of water-repellent microfiber
A pair of black pumps—with medium or low heels
Three pairs of stockings, one pair of trouser socks
A large silk scarf
A black leather or nylon handbag—medium size
A small evening bag.

On the first day of your hypothetical business trip, you would wear your trouser suit. The second day, you would pair your skirt with the knit top. The next day, you would mix the trouser suit jacket with the skirt and wear the shirt underneath and so on. You have everything you need for five days of work and some recreation without wearing the same outfit twice.

Lift the look with a few accessories: a short triple band of pearls or a twist of Tutsi pound-bead necklaces (more about this accessory later); gold hoops or a pair of pearls or diamond (fake is okay) studs. A good understated watch is sometimes the only accessory you need. It may be delicate and jeweled or a gutsy sports watch or a man's model.

Sunglasses are great for throwing shade of all kinds and giving a quick touch of glamour. And the scarf comes in handy for tucking into the neck of a jacket to frame the face and for warding off cold on the plane. It can then serve as a shawl for the evening cocktail party you may have to attend and work as a styling belt looped through the waist of your jeans on the weekend.

When I'm packing for vacation or for my twice-yearly trips to Europe to view the runway shows in Paris, the first thing I think about is a color scheme. Limiting my wardrobe to one or two basic colors helps me pack less and well.

There are four important things you should bear in mind if you want to look your best and get the most out of your clothes:

- Color
- Quality
- Fabric
- Fit

Color

Before you build your wardrobe, decide on a color scheme. Choose a core color based on practicality and convenience.

Colors that you love—ones that give you an emotional charge but are impractical—can be used when you're filling out your closet. A sensible core offers more options because it allows for more combinations and there's less chance of making a mistake with mixes that don't work.

Choose one shade and then two more as second colors for your primary wardrobe pieces. Black goes with everything, but it looks better against some colors than others. Here are some ideas.

BLACK works well with white, cream, and red.

BROWN with beige, ecru, orange, and lime green.

NAVY with red, fuchsia, white, and robin's-egg blue.

CAMEL with brown, ivory, red, and tan.

CHARCOAL with silver gray, pink, white, navy, and red.

OLIVE GREEN with parchment, cream, brown, and metallic gold.

Many women feel that they cannot wear certain colors; this, however, is rarely true. Black women's deep coloring allows for a wide range of color choices. The trick is to find the tone and intensity of a particular color that suits your complexion. Model Veronica Webb, a former Revlon cover girl, has light brown skin, yet she wears orange or green, which are thought to be difficult colors.

If your skin tone tends toward sallowness or a yellowish tan, olive-based greens like army green will look good on you; a brassy emerald green would be wrong. But both shades can be fantastic against skin that's chocolate brown or darker.

A clear red is more flattering to dark skin than a red with a blue or orange cast to it. Whether you're light or dark, you should wear colors that play against the warm brown tones in your skin and draw them out. Experiment with different hues of brown, red, and gold, as well as shades of aubergine—and cerise.

There's nothing quite as beautiful as warm beige or cream against dark skin. If you're light-skinned, muted tones like olive green are wonderful, and deep chocolate browns or deep reds are beautiful.

Makeups colors, so called because they are shades commonly found in powders and foundations, add a soft flattering light around the face and make your complexion seem more radiant. Pretty beige, creamy mocha brown, champagne, and pale pinks all fall into this category and are beautiful secondary colors to add to a wardrobe.

Hot colors like apricot and orange and primary colors like red, blue, and yellow look good against dark and medium-toned skin. If you are light you can wear them too, just intensify your makeup. Apply a powder or foundation a shade deeper than you would wear normally and vivid lipstick. Alternatively, you can use a self-tanning lotion to warm up your color so that your skin doesn't look washed out against your clothes.

Black is the safest wardrobe color, particularly if you work in the city, where you're constantly exposed to grime on the street and in the air. In my business most of the women wear black day in and day out. Black clothes hide tailoring imperfections and project an air of sophistication and mystery.

Although pastels are pretty, they are not the best choice as core colors for your wardrobe. Light clothes are high maintenance. They are difficult and expensive to keep clean and hard to match with other shades.

Quality

Quality begins with fabric. Regardless of the climate you live in, lightweight wool is hands down your best choice for your core jackets, pants, and skirts. You can now find clothes made from wool that is as light as cotton. This lightweight wool is good-looking and has a lustrous quality yet keeps you comfortable in eighty-degree weather.

When assessing the quality of a garment, refer to this checklist:

Are the buttons sewn on firmly?

Does the quality of the buttons or other trim on the garment seem to match the quality of the fabric and tailoring, or do they look cheap?

Does the lining pull?

Are there loose threads that could unravel after a few wearings?

If the dress or jacket is unlined, are the seams bound with tape and neatly finished?

Is the lining acetate or silk? Most linings, even in the priciest clothes, are made from synthetics like acetate, but it's good to know that if you are considering clothing with a silk lining, you're considering something special. Hollywood designer Richard Tyler, whose jackets often sell for two thousand dollars or more, regularly lines his clothes in silk.

Good quality doesn't have to be expensive. But you do have to be able to recognize it. It doesn't make sense to pay two hundred dollars for a jacket that falls apart in a year when you could pay the same amount, or two hundred dollars more, for a superior garment if you are able to detect the signs of poor construction.

A good-quality garment will keep its shape for years. The shoulders of a good jacket are softly rounded, not stiff and heavy. If it's already droopy in the store, chances are no amount of ironing or alteration is going to fix it.

Fit

The handmaiden of quality is fit. It sometimes happens that a good-quality garment is a difficult fit. For example, Brooklyn designer Therez Fleetwood designs her clothes for slim, buff women, and the clothes of Austrian designer Helmut Lang are hard to wear if you're not slim and angular. But in general, if you have tried several sizes of a particular style and it still doesn't fit well, most likely the item is poorly made. Walk away from it. The best thing you could do for yourself is make sure your clothes fit properly. Paying close attention to fit can boost your style quotient sky-high.

When you're trying on clothes in a store, be alert to how you feel in the clothes and how they feel on you. Like a pair of shoes, if it's uncomfortable now, it won't feel any better when you take it home. Make a clear-eyed appraisal of how you look in a three-way mirror. If something's bothering you, but you can't put your finger on it, your instincts are probably right, and you shouldn't buy that particular item.

Don't forget to study your rear view in the mirror, where unpleasant surprises can lurk. Assuming you feel comfortable with the surface picture, look more closely, starting with the neckline. If it's a jacket you're considering, are the lapels even? Does the collar lie flat against the back of your neck and around the sides? Does the jacket look as good when it is buttoned up as when it is left open? View yourself again from the back. It there creasing or pulling of fabric across your shoulders or hips, indicating that the jacket is too tight? Fold your arms across your chest. Does the garment pull too much? Do you feel like you're in a straitjacket? Now turn to the side and fold your arms. Is fabric creasing and pulling on the arms? Drop your arms to your sides. Are the sleeves long enough—just covering your wristbone? If everything else is perfect, you can have the sleeves taken up an inch or two or let down if there is enough fabric to cover your wrist.

An investment jacket can be one of the most expensive but most rewarding clothing purchases you make. When looking for a jacket, always look first for fit, says Donna Karan. The shoulder and the neckline are key, and both should fit smoothly. The waist should be gently nipped in, and the jacket shape and proportion should flatter your body. "Buttonholes on the wrist that open, collars and hems that are hand-stitched, and buttonholes that are handmade, not machine stitched" are all hallmarks of a superior jacket, she adds. Jackets that are actually still made this way are rare. But quality jackets that incorporate at least a few of these features are available in stores throughout the country and through custom designers.

If you buy ready-to-wear, don't be

afraid to have adjustments made to ensure proper fit. Most department stores and good speciality stores offer this service. Ask your salesperson. It's a service anyone can use, no matter how much she paid for an item. Usually there's a charge of about twelve dollars for a minor alteration such as hemming a dress. Adjusting the hem of a pant or the sleeves on a jacket so that it is just right for you is a small price to pay for looking your best. If the store does not have an alterations department, inquire about a neighborhood dressmaker or visit your local dry cleaner. Many of them have skilled tailors who will cut and hem pants or change buttons for between five and twelve dollars.

Shape

Build the base of your wardrobe with classic, flattering shapes. A longer jacket ending just below your hips is better than one that stops at the hipbone. Avoid peplums in favor of a classic blazer style—single-breasted, so you can wear it buttoned with matching bottoms or open with, say, a leather skirt for a more casual look. Double-breasted jackets tend to look sloppy when left open. Look for jackets with long sleeves and buttons above the bust so you do not always have to wear a layering piece underneath.

For a skirt, your best choice is a pencil-style, knee-length or two inches above the knee. The slim shape is flattering, and it is a length that suits most women and is acceptable in all offices. For a smooth fit in front, choose a skirt that zips up the back rather than the side. If you must wear skirts or pants with elasticized waistbands, finer shops offer bottoms with waistbands that are flat in front and elasticized in the back or on the sides.

DONNA KARAN'S WARDROBE SYSTEM

Twelve years ago Donna Karan was one of the first designers to pioneer the idea of a wardrobe system, as she calls it. It covers what every woman should have in her wardrobe and should fulfill all her wardrobe needs. "It all starts with the jacket," Donna explains, "and it should feel good on the body."

One jacket
One pair of trousers
A shirt
A coat
A sweater
A skirt
A dress
An evening accessory (like a sequined scarf)
A piece of leather (a jacket, a vest, or a skirt, for example)

A classic trouser should have two pleats in front and be cut straight from hip to ankle. Zip-front styles look good, although a smooth front is more flattering. The pant should have a straight leg and break one inch over your shoe or past your anklebone.

Basic Accessories: Shoes and Handbags

There's no excuse not to buy leather shoes these days. You can get leather shoes for $500 at Saks Fifth Avenue or $29.99 at Payless. Leather allows your feet to breathe and stretch; it's the recognized hallmark of quality footwear. Shoes made from natural fabrics or synthetics can be fun and add dimension to your wardrobe, but choose leather when you're shopping for basic shoes.

The most versatile shoe has a slightly rounded toe and a vamp high enough to cover your toes completely. Anything more adventurous—stiletto heels, low throats, or extremely wide, round toes—will quickly date your look. Choose a heel no more than two inches high. High heels should not be worn every day.

Rounding Out a Basic Wardrobe

Once you have your core wardrobe in place, experiment a bit. The idea of wearing a suit to work every day is antiquated. Add a nicely cut leather blazer to your wardrobe. If you work in an artistic or creative field, a leather blazer in black or brown is quite acceptable.

There are many conservative companies that still prefer female employees to wear skirts and frown on trousers except for on casual Fridays. If you work in one of these unfortunate places, try loosening up with dresses. Buy a beautiful jacket that is what I call a rainy-day-and-Mondays jacket—it works over a ton of things in your wardrobe. It should be black, but this could vary, depending on the color scheme of your wardrobe.

Change a classic look with color. Sweater sets need not match all the time. A cardigan could be black and the sweater beneath it ivory. Try a red sweater and navy trousers. Finish the look with a bold silver sports watch and low-heeled floaters. Play a sherbet-lemon sweater against a mauve skirt. Add a short printed scarf of similar pastels. Fold it into a thin band, and tie it neatly around your neck. Complete your look with small diamond or pearl studs and two bangles.

Vests are great for keeping warm and adding some variety and intrigue to an outfit, but unless it's casual Friday, a vest without a jacket rarely looks sophisticated. Instead of a vest, match a pair of black pants with a black V-neck or crewneck sweater worn over a white shirt. Pull out the collar of the shirt so that it sits over the

sweater's neckline. Add brown or black leather oxford shoes, a wristful of your favorite bracelets (I prefer silver myself), or one big, bold cuff or ring, and you have a look that is sophisticated, professional, and a break from the suited routine.

For a stylish, always current, spectator look, pair your black jacket with a white skirt that's knee length or shorter, pleated or straight. Add pearls and black high-heeled pumps or slingbacks.

Menswear for Women

This classic style, which resurfaces every few seasons, makes women of every size look sexy without being obviously so. The latest combination you should borrow from the guys is a solid shirt worn with a matching tie in dark or pastel colors and paired with a fitted pants suit. If you like to be dramatic and at the forefront of fashion, wear your menswear exactly as the men do—for example, a navy pinstripe suit with a baby-blue silk tie.

If you are a bit more conservative, here's a great variation on the menswear theme. Find a solid silk or cotton scarf in your favorite or most flattering pastel color—mine is pink, yours might be yellow or lavender. Tie the scarf in a band around your neck, or tie it as a loose cravat and tuck the ends inside your shirt. You might also go to the men's department and buy one of those solid-color tie sets. Give the tie away and use the handkerchief in your breast pocket. It doesn't have to match your shirt or your suit but can just add an unexpected flourish.

Every woman should have a pinstripe suit. I prefer it to be trousers, but a skirt suit looks great too. The best colors are navy pinstripe or gray chalkstripe (slightly wider than pinstripes). It's a sleek, dashing look that is appropriate in any environment. A grey pinstripe suit can be worn with almost any color, but it looks great with a white blouse. Be careful wearing gray alone close to your face, since it has a tendency to wash out all complexions. Combine it with white, pink, navy, or sky blue.

A Dress for Success

A wool or linen-blend sheath—a straight fitted dress—is the classic wardrobe staple. Wear it with absolutely nothing except a great bag, high-heeled shoes, hose, and a watch. Or accessorize it with a scarf. Wrap a small scarf in a band around your neck, or wear a bigger scarf boy-scout style—tied in the front with the point in back.

You've heard of the little black cocktail dress, but make sure you have a little black dress for work. Add a jacket, a scarf, jewelry, or a cardigan, or wear it alone. It's the most chic, sensible piece of clothing you can own. When she's not wearing the clothes provided for her in a photo shoot or fashion show, model Veronica Webb finds a black dress to be the best standby for running to and from jobs for designers like Isaac Mizrahi and Giorgio Armani. "Basically, you're having things thrown on you all day," she says. "You're getting powder all over you, you're getting hair spray all over you, but you have to wear one designer piece when you go to work," says Veronica. "Black dresses work very well. You can just put a cardigan, a turtleneck, whatever over it."

Events move so quickly at a fashion show or photo shoot that Veronica's clothes often end up on the floor or balled up in her tote bag because there's no closet in which to hang them. She finds that a black dress made of heavy cotton or a synthetic like rayon can stand up to a lot of wear and tear and still look good. Top model Naomi Campbell always takes a black antique dress and a black suit with her when she travels. "You always have a dinner or a meeting," she says.

If you're wearing suits, add knits in bright colors as underpinnings or change the pace with a shirt of satin, cut velvet, or shiny stretch cotton. When you start mixing different textures and finishes, your style becomes both casual and contemporary: a wool jacket, a chiffon top, and a satin skirt look avant-garde. You can wear a sheer blouse under a jacket to work—but not too sheer. Don't wear a see-through, bra-revealing blouse on the job, no matter how pretty you think it is. You'll look stylish and unprofessional. Save it for after work.

Bundling up

If you live in a temperate climate, your basic wardrobe should include a coat for cold weather and a jacket for spring temperatures. A raincoat comes in handy, but many women prefer to get by with an umbrella. If you travel for business or pleasure, you may still need a coat, even if your hometown has warm weather year-round. The requirements for this coat are different from those for a coat you'll be wearing several days a week.

Choose your basic coat for warmth, long wear, and versatility, in that order. A fur or fake fur coat gives maximum warmth, is lustrous, and works over a career look, a church ensemble, or an evening gown. An ankle-length coat is the most elegant choice. If you are not comfortable with this length, choose one that hits the knee. Anything shorter will not keep you warm enough and is difficult to coordinate with a range of hemlines. A short swing coat a few inches above the knee is sassy, but the proportions are wrong if you are wearing a dress that falls an inch or two below the coat's hem.

Several basic coat styles are versatile and flattering. A military coat is timeless. The cut resembles that of coats worn by military officers, but it is a feminine look that hugs the body with double-breasted buttons and frames the face with a wide collar. A princess coat is similar to a military coat, but the waist is cut higher, and it does not feature two rows of buttons.

More conservative and less feminine is the balmacaan, with rounded dropped shoulders and a straight boxy cut. A car coat—so named because it was originally designed to be short enough to allow passengers to alight from cars with ease—is more useful as a second coat. The typical length, just above the knee, makes a car coat well suited to spring weather.

Bathrobe coats conjure up old-time Hollywood sophistication. They are drapey and plush-looking and tie softly with a cloth belt. If your style is understated, this is a good coat for you. Make sure the coat is ample enough to wrap around you and keep you warm on frigid days.

Stylish coats: balmacaan; military; puff car coat.

As the name suggests, a clutch coat has to be held together by you. That is one disadvantage of this elegant, stylish option. Many fur or fake fur coats are designed as clutches. Clutch coats and swing coats are ideal if you are a big woman, because they give you ample room to move comfortably yet still look fashionable. Cloth clutch coats trimmed with real or synthetic fur around the cuffs and collars will provide you with extra warmth and extra glamour.

No matter what your size, make sure that when you try on a coat you are dressed in the number of layers you will typically be wearing under your coat. Make sure the sleeves are roomy enough to accommodate a bulky sweater if that's how you usually dress in the winter. Do not go shopping in a sweater for your winter outerwear if you are going to wear it over a jacket most of the time.

Jackets often get crushed and tugged by coats that are too small in the sleeves and across the back. Pay particular attention to the area under the arm, where coats tend to be snug. You want to look crisp when you doff your coat, not like you just took a spin in the dryer.

Most coats are sold in dark colors because they have to stand up to daily use and the grime of city streets. A black princess-style or military coat is a wonderful look. Certain styles look stronger in other colors—wear chocolate brown fur or a navy wool balmacaan. A camel coat of any style looks beautiful against brown complexions, but understand that you will have to clean it at least once a month if you want it to remain attractive. Better to buy a light-colored coat as a second piece of outerwear in your wardrobe, to use as a backup or for special occasions.

Much has been written about the classic trench coat, but as long-running acts will, it has lost its snap for me. If you must buy a trench coat, get one in a new color like navy or silver or plaid and in a high-tech fabric like microfiber or nylon. A black patent vinyl trench lined in a fake leopard print for warmth is a stylish wear-anywhere coat.

Puff coats and jackets made of quilted nylon and inspired by sports and hip-hop fashion are now available in a range of electric colors, some adorned with logos. They're fun for the weekends but not the best option on the job, where you want to look ready for work rather than play.

For travel and vacation, your primary criteria for a coat are that it be easy to pack and able to take care of all your needs while you're away from home. Shop for a travel coat in the rainwear section first; you are most likely to find warm, lightweight coats there. Look for something dark—navy, black, or silver, in microfiber or nylon. Microfiber is like a miracle fiber. It's sensuous to touch, drapes wonderfully, is lightweight, and looks like washed six-ply silk. A lot of microfiber coats are water repellent, so they can double as raincoats. Look for one with a hood, and you have protection from light rain and cold. Since temperatures in many cities here and abroad change dramatically from day to night, a lightweight piece that can be worn throughout the day or pulled out of a bag or suitcase with a minimum of wrinkles is ideal.

I love the drama of the shawls worn by the Nigerians, French, and Italians, who throw them over their shoulders even for casual occasions. Anna Getaneh, the Ethiopian model who lives in New York, is often on planes en route to Africa or runway shows in Paris, where she is a favorite of Yves Saint Laurent, Christian La Croix, and Emanuel Ungaro. She considers shawls an essential part of her basic wardrobe. "I wear big shawls in wool or cashmere, in beige, brown, or burgundy," she says. "They're great to sleep with on planes and a good replacement for coats. I always travel with at least one."

Finishing Touches

Carve out a look that people can remember you by. Choose one remarkable thing—a hairstyle, a color, a piece of jewelry—that becomes part of your defining style. Mine is an ear cuff and a short natural haircut.

Set aside time to overhaul your wardrobe at least twice a year. Make a list of what you need—tend to any core wardrobe items that need replacing, and feel free to add some new fun fashions. It is a good rule of thumb to buy the most expensive item you can afford. But did anyone ever stop to figure out what the hell that means?

Financial planners will tell you that common wisdom suggests that your housing, for instance, should take up between 28 and 32 percent of your income. I think fashion and its upkeep should comprise about 4 percent of your income. So if you earn fifty thousand dollars before taxes, you can afford to spend about two thousand dollars on fashion and beauty per year. Black women spend proportionally more on beauty and clothes than any other racial or cultural group. We love dressing up.

Allow the bulk of your style money to go toward clothes that will form the basis of your wardrobe. I also believe in spending good money on shoes and handbags, particularly if you're going to use them for work. Shop around for the best prices for trendy items. They don't have to last long—they'll be out of fashion in a few months.

In pursuit of style, it is wiser to buy that five-hundred-dollar suit and wear it till kingdom come than buy five suits for one hundred dollars each. But there is not much difference between a fifty-dollar white shirt from the Gap and a two-hundred-dollar version. Sometimes the cost is all in the label. Not everything inexpensive is junk, and not everything pricey is built to last. Shop wisely.

Once you have acquired the foundation of your wardrobe, take care of it with gentle cleaning and diligent upkeep. Don't let stains sit. Don't let hems unravel, and don't iron a good jacket without a protective handkerchief or towel between the iron and the garment. Too much unprotected ironing causes wool clothes to shine prematurely. Today, many garments, most notably silk ones, are machine washable. Regardless of what the label says, it is best not to machine wash anything with padding and/or tailoring, like most jackets. The shoulder pads move around, and linings shift and pull in the machine, destroying a jacket's shape.

THE TEN BASIC STYLE RULES

1. Choose clothes that work well on your body and that fit your self-image.
2. Get a little black dress for daytime.
3. Classic styles form the basis of any stylish wardrobe.
4. Seek out clothes that are appropriate for your age.
5. Check clothes for quality as well as style.
6. Don't settle for clothes that are ill-fitting.
7. Figure out the ten essentials you would take on a business trip and begin building your basic wardrobe from there.
8. Don't be afraid to steal good ideas from TV shows, music videos, magazines, or friends.
9. Do an inventory of what you have and what you need before you go shopping.
10. Check your rear view in the mirror before you buy.

Stylish Fabrics: A Guide to African Textiles (and Western Ones, Too)

Much of what we recognize as African or African-inspired clothing can be boiled down to specific textiles and shapes. In the last ten years African fabrics have grown in popularity within the African-American community. Two of the most recognizable are kente and Bogolan. This chapter will give you a quick primer on the most common African fabrics, and a few Western ones. You'll learn to identify what you like—and what works best in your wardrobe.

Perhaps it is the legacy of people who live in sun-kissed climates that African fabrics are characterized by their dazzling use of color—in prints, solids, and resist dyes. A fabric from the Ivory Coast might include a delightful combination of pink, purple, green, and black; another from Nigeria would be emblazoned with orange, green, and chocolate brown; while a Ghanaian kente cloth could broadcast a vibrant mix of tangerine and royal blue.

African fabrics traditionally were made by hand. Patterns are characteristically abstract or draw inspiration from nature and social or political observation. African patterns like leopard, and some batiks, have become so much a part of the discourse of western culture and fashion that they are barely recognizable as African in origin.

The Exotic Leopard

One of the most co-opted elements of African textiles is the leopard print, now a classic of fashion in the West; in Africa, bold-looking leopard skins are still worn in tribal ceremonies.

The leopard is now an endangered species, but wearing a leopard *print* is a chic and modern expression of African culture—just don't wear too much at once. Many stylish women—like Audrey Smaltz, fashion show coordinator and former Ebony Fashion Fair model and commentator—have made touches of leopard print a part of their signature.

The distinctive black dots against a bronze or brown background are available in a range of fabrics, including chiffon, velvet, cotton, and wool. Wear leopard as an accent—in a scarf, a little miniskirt worn with a black turtleneck, a belt, or a leopard-print handbag. Other animal prints, like tiger and zebra prints, denote the rich wildlife of Africa and its respected place in the lives of the people.

Kente

Kente cloth is a rich woven fabric that originated with the Ashanti or Asante people of Ghana. Kente incorporates a popular African textile-making technique called float weave, in which brightly colored threads are floated above the weaving of the main fabric base. For the last thirty years kente cloth has been revered around the world, but only in the last ten have imitations of it become widely available in America. Be aware that many kente prints are imitations—patterns stamped onto light cotton.

Kente cloth often combines jewel-tones of royal blue and gold or red; gold and black; or red, gold, and green; it looks great worn as a shawl, incorporated into a woman's jacket, made into a man's bow tie or cummerbund, or playing another role in evening ensembles. The inexpensive cotton prints make cute sundresses.

Aso Oke (pronounced a-sho-kay)

This larger group of fabrics comprises fabrics woven in strips with a float weave; they are popular in Ghana, Nigeria, and other West African countries. Aso okes often incorporate proverbs in their patterns. Kente fabrics are aso okes that have particular pattern and color combinations from Ghana.

Waxed Prints

African prints are often covered with a light sheen of wax or nonwaxed. Waxed fabrics feel stiff rather than limp. Fancy waxed prints are preferable for clothes meant for work or festive occasions. Many waxed fabrics are patterned with symbols of native West African culture called adinkras. You probably won't find waxed prints used in the African-inspired clothes sold in places like Saks Fifth Avenue, Sears, J.C. Penney, or the *Essence* catalog. The fabrics used by designers

Kente

working on a large commercial scale are usually reinterpretations of African prints and are often made in wool, rayon, or polyester chiffon. The multihued prints that we buy from African dealers are generally waxed prints.

Bogolan

The rugged Bogolan, also known as mudcloth, is identified with the West African country of Mali, and its appeal to westerners lies in its bold black-and-ivory prints. Bogolan is traditionally made of heavy cotton that is first dyed yellow and then immersed in iron-infused mud. The mud is washed out with bleaching agents, leaving behind characteristic graphic patterns. Mudcloth is also made in black with white highlights and in curry brown with black highlights. It imparts a casual air to clothes and is wonderful for jackets, coats, or leisure handbags.

Korhogo

Sister to Bogolan, the finer Korhogo fabric from the Ivory Coast is made in

Adinkra print

square strips that depict artistically rendered animals in black and beige; sometimes a third paprika color is present. Korhogo panels are valued as wall hangings, but this textile can also be used to make vivid handbags, as a motif on the back of a coat, or as a face-framing trim around the collar of a duster.

Damask

Damask, or Guinea brocade, is central to contemporary African style, though, ironically, it comes from Holland. Women of Ghana, the Ivory Coast, and Zaire make their own variation of damask by adding intricate embroidery, which is applied by hand and sewing machine in small dressmaking shops. Damask makes beautiful traditional African clothes suitable for evening affairs.

Lurex

Africans incorporate their love of gold into their fashions with lurex, a shiny fabric shot through with gold threads. The sheen makes lurex ideal for evening wear.

Bogolan

Batik

Also called resist-dye technique, batik is a process developed in many countries, including Nigeria and the Ivory Coast as well as Bali—with which this distinctive textile is often associated. Batik artisans create evocative patterns reflecting daily life by applying hot wax that forms a barrier to the dye when the fabric is dunked in it.

Adire

The Yoruba name adire refers to indigo-colored cottons that are patterned using resist-dye techniques. Nigerian patterns are etched onto the fabric using wax (as in batik) or by sewing small stones into the fabric and then removing them after dying. The result is a dense, blue-black cloth with beautiful patterns in white or varying shades of lighter blue. The batik and adire processes are not to be confused with wax prints, which are industrially printed fabrics with a clear wax finish applied to the fabric's surface.

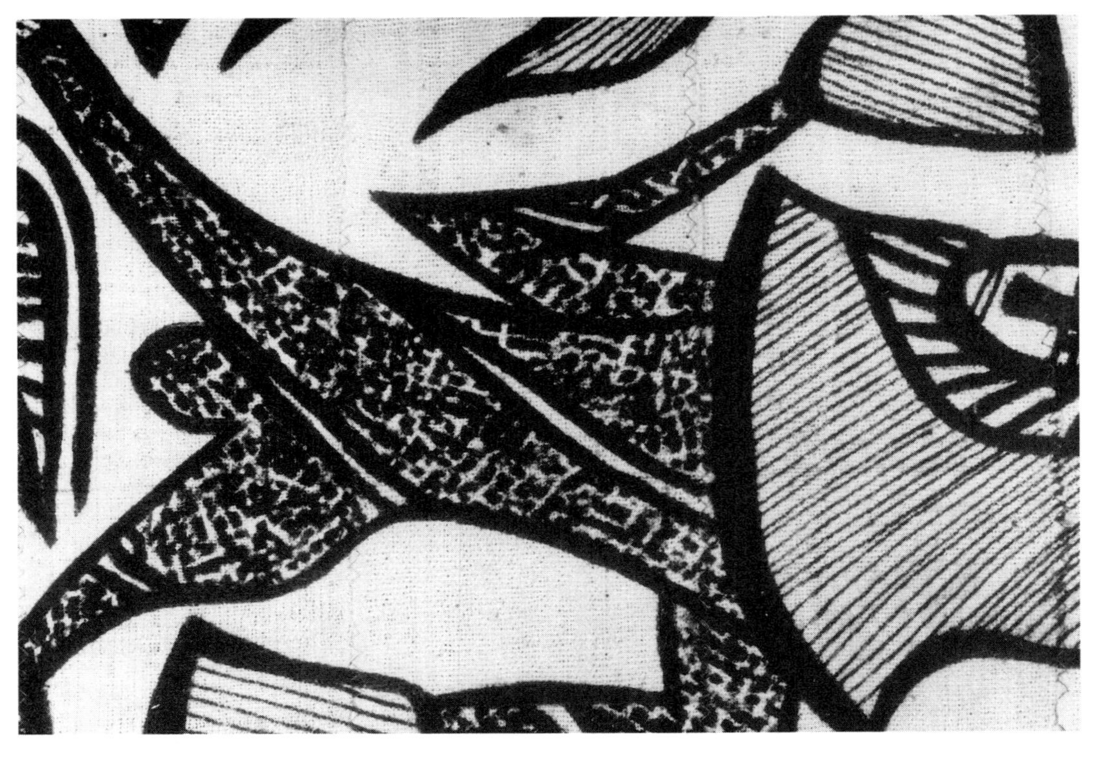

Korhogo

Ikat

Ikat is a simple fabric characterized by light blue and white stripes on lightweight cotton.

Ndebele

Technically, Ndebele refers not to a fabric but to the stunning beadwork of the Ndebele people of South Africa. The Ndebeles apply their techniques in accessories and clothing. A belt may be encrusted with dozens of tiny beads or a cotton skirt entirely covered with red, green, and white beads.

Kanga

Kanga, which means guinea fowl, refers to both a fabric typically worn in East Africa and a style of dress. Light Kanga cottons have bright blocks of color with borders on all four sides; a popular border is the paisley (generally accepted as being of Indian origin), which East Africans probably picked up from their Indian ancestors, with whom they traded and

Batik

intermarried for hundreds of years. As a style of dress, Kanga refers to a wrapped skirt and a second piece of fabric worn as a shawl.

Fancy Prints

Hundreds of inexpensive unwaxed African prints are made in factories. Printed on lightweight cotton—on one side, in harsh colors—fancy prints are not a good investment. The colors often fade quickly. Also known as imiwax or java prints, indicating that they are imitations of resist-dye prints, they are best used when you need inexpensive clothing or home décor.

Some Things You Should Know about Western Fabrics

Cotton

This ubiquitous fiber absorbs perspiration and odor and allows air to circulate

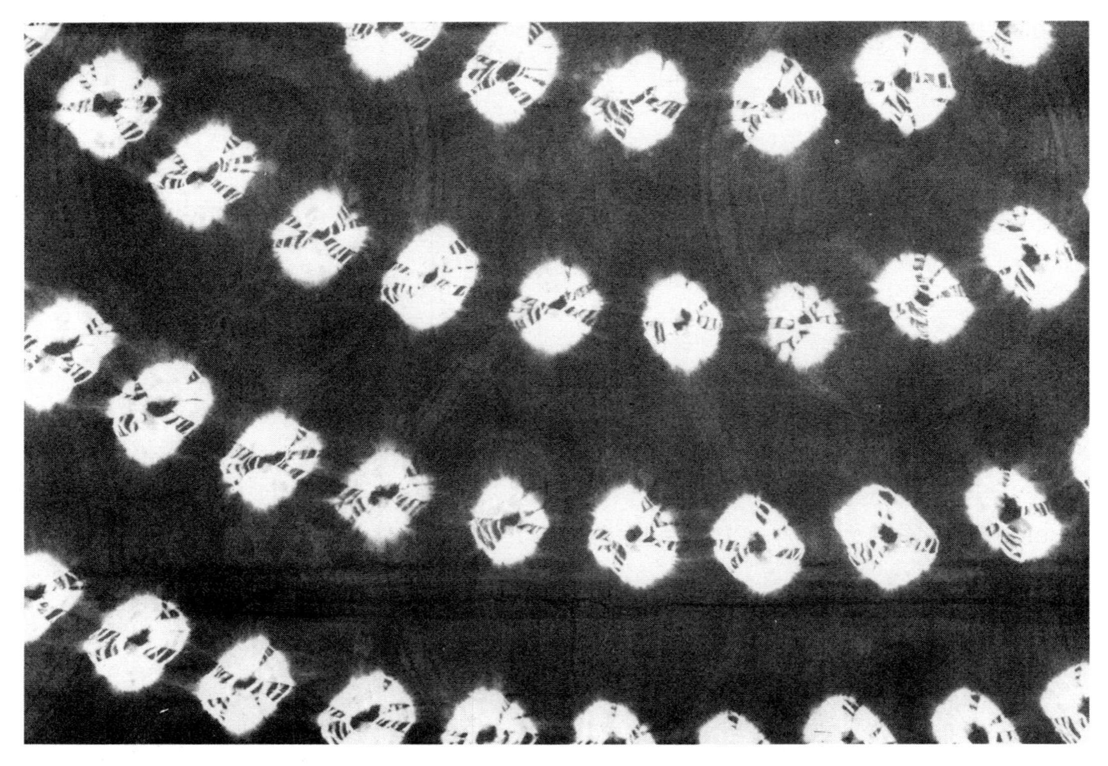

Adire

around your skin. It is one of the most comfortable fabrics you can buy. Cotton garments are usually washable by hand or machine. On the minus side, 100 percent cotton garments do not take color well and usually begin to fade after a few washes. This applies to a dress made of cotton, an African fancy print, or a bright red cotton turtleneck. You may want your blue jeans to fade in the wash, but not your favorite cotton blouse. Look for cotton mixed with other fabrics like polyester, which renders clothes more wrinkle-resistant and colorfast.

Rayon and Viscose

Rayon and viscose are the same thing. A natural fiber, designers often combine it with silk or wool to give drape and a modern, lustrous look to clothing.

Silk Knits

Where have they been all our lives? Sweaters made from silk reflect color beautifully, whether it's a dazzling jewel garnet or a pale wistful lavender. Silk clothes are lightweight, often washable, and feel drapey and sensuous against the skin. When you want less bulk under your clothes, silk knits make wonderful vests, T-shirts, or long johns. Some silk clothing makers claim silk underwear is warmer than long johns made of cotton or cotton and synthetics, but I don't find that to be so. Silk is also used in woven shirts and dresses and combined with other fabrics to make heavier jackets.

Nylon

It's been almost ten years since the Italian fashion house Prada revolutionized the use of nylon in fashion by making hip, faintly militaristic clothes in thick black nylon. And Prada uses this now-stylish fiber to make their popular six-hundred-dollar knapsacks. Since then, every designer worth his or her needle and thread has created clothing in nylon. You can buy a nylon jacket for thirty dollars at Target or one for twelve hundred dollars at Prada. Nylon tailors well, so it looks sharp in jackets. Because of its industrial and sports connotations, anything made in nylon looks immediately cool and youthful.

Most nylon clothes, unless they have some special coating, are easy to clean. They can be machine washed or wiped clean with water. Nylon, because it is nonporous, keeps you warm. The downside is that like polyester, it does not allow the skin to breathe or moisture to escape, so it can make you clammy and malodorous.

Polyester

Remember how we cringed at the sight of polyester? Well, it's back, and it's being used by the most elite designers. You'll be happy to find that a lot of polyester is not the stiff, shiny stuff we kicked it in back in the day. Now you can find polyester shirts that feel as if they are made from silk and fluid, matte jersey polyester gowns as soft as suede.

Then there are a host of polyester-based fabrics influenced by sports. They've had a huge influence on how we dress, and at least one of them will turn up on something you buy or put on this week.

Other Synthetics

Supplex, microfiber, Tencel, and Lycra, the most popular brand name for spandex, are all synthetics. Supplex was first utilized in sports gear and is now used to make more comfortable underwear and weekend clothes. Tencel can look like denim but is soft and fluid. Microfiber makes clothing like socks and raincoats more sensuous to the touch. It's lustrous yet can be easily treated to make it water resistant.

On the Job: Expressing African Culture through Style

In the 1990s, African-American style became a potent fashion statement. To many African Americans, however, it means much more. It's a point of pride, an expression of our culture in much the same way that wearing a dress is a celebration of femininity or a yarmulke is a symbol of Judaism.

For some blacks, wearing an ankh, a kofi, or a kente-trimmed jacket is an opportunity to reaffirm their identity and rich heritage amid negative or nonexistent representations of African-American life. From a style viewpoint, the first thing to think about when wearing African or African-inspired clothes is that you shouldn't give up your standards. Color, pattern, and quality are still important.

It's probably most difficult to integrate our African heritage into our career clothes, since conformity is valued in the workplace and can mean the difference between advancement and stagnation in a career. But a lot has changed over the years. For one thing, we are in the middle of a casual revolution in America's offices, which is broadening the range of clothes that are considered acceptable. Second, there are more African-inspired clothes to choose from. Mail-order catalogs like *Essence By Mail* and big store chains like Bloomingdale's, Sears, and J.C. Penney are making African-American-style clothes more accessible. Several large companies and small home-based businesses now import African cloth to the United States. Nonblack designers and retailers sell African-inspired clothes. Within urban centers like New York, Atlanta, and Los Angeles, our community is producing dozens of talented designers who are inspired to create clothes that evoke the spirit of Africa. (See the Resource Guide at the end of the book for shopping suggestions in all areas.)

Few people feel comfortable going to work in America in head-to-toe African dress, but there are offices that allow it, and it looks fabulous on the women who wear it. The eye eventually adjusts to things that initially look strange. Remember how braids or locks were first looked on?

So what to do? Observe the tone of your workplace and industry. Some businesses are clearly more conservative than others. The fields of television, architecture, teaching, theater, and music allow for more creativity and individuality in appearance than law or accounting. My girlfriend Lois Taylor, a social worker in New York, wears a lot of African clothes and African-inspired jewelry on the job; so does the reggae singer Sister Carol.

If you are self-employed you obviously have more latitude in what you choose to wear. The only boss you have to please is you.

Melding African Style and American Style

Generally, I prefer African prints in western shapes for work. A great way to give an African flavor to your career wardrobe is to wear an African-print vest under a jacket. Any print will do, but you will look best if the colors complement a shade in your jacket. You might blend a traditional black and cream Bogolan vest with an ivory T-shirt and a black suit. Forget the shady-looking imitation kente. Find a vest in a more unusual kente color combination. Stylish women don't dress in clichés. Take an idea, even a commonplace one, and make it your own by applying a little creativity, whether that means hunting down a rarer kente print or wearing something you would normally wear at night during the day.

Don't wear African-print vests, or any vest, without a jacket if you are a midlevel manager or senior executive or an ambitious secretary. It will mark you as a junior employee. But an African-print shirt is cool.

A jacket or dress with African-print trim around the sleeves, on the collar, or down the front placket can be stunning. If you can't find what you want, have it made. Don't let anything stand between you and your style. Take a black linen jacket, purchase a yard or two of black and gold waxed cotton print, and have a tailor add a band of the fabric around the hem of the sleeve, or remove the collar and put on a new collar made from your African cloth. Remember, look for fine fabrics like float-weave aso okes, not just thin cotton prints. Save those for cuter little sundresses when it's time to get a suntan.

Alvin Bell, who created the illustrations for this book, designed a small group of French-style ladies-who-lunch suits. What made them chic and nouvelle was his idea to add large, luxurious, African-inspired carved faux ivory buttons. Take a cue from Alvin and change the buttons on a dress if you need to. (See the Resource Directory for information on how to find African fabrics, trimmings, and accessories.)

Modern dressing is about mixing different cultures and disparate elements. For liberal workplaces, wear a fabulous straight, ankle-length African-print skirt slit at the front or side and paired with a jacket in leather or polyvinyl. Be daring and wrap a shorter skirt over a matching ankle-length skirt from the same material, Nigerian-style, and pair it with a solid jacket. A short indigo batik skirt worn with a navy mandarin-collar jacket is a look that sizzles.

For work, instead of a loose top you can wear an Adinkra tailored shirt with a straight hem and a matching ankle-length skirt for a new-millennium, cross-cultural suit.

I remember that my high school chemistry teacher would wear her buba (African) top and long skirts in incredible African prints. She was a vision as she traipsed across the school yard in her

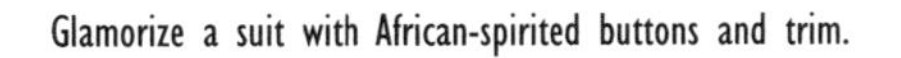

Glamorize a suit with African-spirited buttons and trim.

Pair a sleek tunic jacket with an African-print skirt. Load on African trading beads or pearls. And don't forget your cell phone.

beaded hoop earrings, flat leather thong sandals, and a hobo bag. I, at the impressionable age of sixteen, thought she was divine. But it was the morning that she came to class in her usual African-shape garb, this time made from the same Blackwatch plaid of our school uniforms, that I really knew this woman was fierce!

The point here is that African shapes—bubas, caftans, lappes, and so on—can be reinterpreted through the use of the most traditional Western fabrics. This is precisely what many successful designers, from Yves Saint Laurent to Donna Karan, have done over the years. Yves has beautifully recreated the caftan and Donna the sarong or marasuru skirt.

For added pizzazz, incorporate a leopard-print fur coat into your wardrobe or a leopard-print suede handbag. One of my favorite looks in all of fashion: leopard fur collar and cuffs on a shapely black skirt suit; the fur, real or fake, purrs glamour. For a more understated version of the same outfit, look for a suit trimmed with leopard-print velvet.

African Shapes

Western clothes are a big influence in Africa, and many women there have adapted our mode of dress. But African tradition still runs deep in places like Nigeria, Ghana, and the Ivory Coast, where women wear bubas.

FAMILY UNIFORMS

Couples and families in West Africa will sometimes dress in bubas made from the same print to show their kinship with one another.

The linchpin of African women's wardrobes is the wrap skirt, worn as part of a buba, or as part of a Kanga or lappe outfit—depending on where the woman resides in Africa.

A *buba* (pronounced boo-bah) consists of a drop-sleeve top that pulls on over the head (most traditional clothes from the eastern part of the world do not use buttons or other fasteners), a long wrap skirt, and sometimes two or three extra lengths of cloth used for wrapping the head or the hips or draping over the shoulder like a shawl. A buba can also be a dress, the defining element being the dropped sleeve and loose shape. Yoruba men in Nigeria wear what is called a buba, replacing the wrap skirt with loose pants.

A buba can also be a *Kanga*, which, as noted in chapter 2, also refers to a type of cloth. A Kanga is a two-piece outfit, made from Kanga border-print cloth, worn by women in many East African countries. The ankle-length bottom half is wrapped around the waist, and a matching square of cloth covers the head like a long veil.

STEP 1. Slip on the top of your buba. Standing with your legs apart, position the larger piece of fabric around your hips as shown.

How to Wrap a Buba

Wrapping is an integral part of African style. A buba typically consists of three or four pieces—a top (which can have a dropped sleeve or be sleeveless—as show in the illustration), and two or three squares of fabric at least two by four yards long. One length of fabric can be smaller. You can wear your buba over layering pieces as Lady Mitz shows here, or with nothing underneath. If you're wearing wrapskirts for the first time, you might want to layer a unitard or legging under them until you're comfortable tying and wearing them. Dress it up or down, wear all the pieces together, or break them apart depending on your mood and the occasion. Here Lady Mitz takes us through the basic steps involved in tying a buba.

STEP 2. Bring your left hand over to your right side and tie the ends of the fabric, right over left.

STEP 3. Tie a knot and leave the ends sticking out or tuck them in your waistline.

STEP 4. If you choose, for a dressier look you can at this point tie a narrower width of fabric over the wrapped skirt following steps 1–3. You'll now have a double-tier look that emphasizes your hips (not shown).

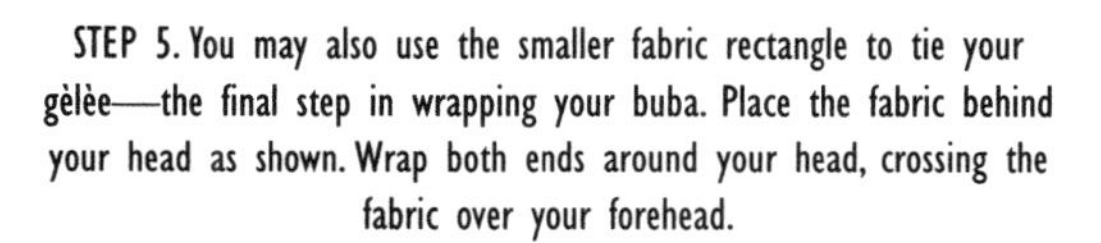

STEP 5. You may also use the smaller fabric rectangle to tie your gèlèe—the final step in wrapping your buba. Place the fabric behind your head as shown. Wrap both ends around your head, crossing the fabric over your forehead.

STEP 6. The ends should now be at the back of your head. Tie the ends securely and position the ends of the fabric to stick out like beautiful fans—as you might arrange a kerchief in a pocket, fanning the two ends of the fabric out so they stand at attention. (To achieve the desired sculptural effect, African women sometimes use stiff fabrics made especially for gèlèes. But they often use whatever is at hand. You can also starch fabric to give it a stiffer hand.) Once you have the basics of tying a buba down, the variations are endless. You can use one piece of fabric as a shawl, you can wear the top with shorts, you can wrap the skirt over a body-hugging T-shirt. Your creativity is your only limitation.

The *caftan* is probably the most widely adapted African shape, worn by both men and women. Was it my imagination or did the fine actor Calvin Lockhart wear his caftan in the seventies with nothing but his altogether underneath? More recently, Jessye Norman has made fabulous caftanlike dresses her signature. Designers in America are always remaking the caftan, and with the renewed influence of seventies style, there are plenty of slinky jersey caftan gowns around.

Djellabas are long tunics worn by men and women throughout Africa and the Middle East. Giorgio Armani bases much of his evening wear on djellabas with their softly androgynous shapes. Worn over matching pants (some Africans refer to djellabas as bubas), they are often decorated around the neck or down the front with amazing embroideries done by sewing machine. Djellabas can be made in almost any fabric, from fine Guinea brocade to casual heavy striped cotton.

Peplums are popular among women from West Africa who favor peplum-shaped tops with huge leg-of-mutton sleeves (not a favorite look of mine). Typically a peplum has a blouson shape that is fitted at the waist and flares out over the hips.

Aprons are worn by many African tribespeople. John Galliano borrowed this look in a stunning show for Christian Dior in Paris in 1996. Aprons made from leather or the intricate beading of the Xhosa, Ndebele, and Kwazulu people of southern Africa often signify social standing or a rite of passage like marriage or reaching womanhood. Put a short African-print apron over pants, then add a jacket that matches the trousers.

Fini-style does not refer to a specific African-inspired shape, but it's a term worth knowing. When a woman mixes two or more prints in her buba it's called fini-style.

Pulling It All Together

When you're putting African-style clothing together, don't overdo it. "Some women throw on too much," says designer Therez Fleetwood, a consultant to Avon's African Boutique and a bridal wear designer. "African prints are so bright and so noticeable, other adornments should be soft jewelry or just one piece of jewelry. Or if you're wearing a print on top and another print in a head wrap, then your bottom should be solid, and your makeup should be soft, too." Prints with black in them are easier to integrate into your wardrobe, she adds. Therez also created the Phe-Zula line of African-American clothing worn by En Vogue at the 1993 Grammy Awards ceremony. "The majority of African clothes are brightly colored, so the woman wearing them has a lot of confidence," she

says. "She has to realize that her garments are going to be noticed."

Select elements of traditional African dress and experiment by mixing them with other items in your closet. You'll have a more stylish wardrobe and have more fun getting dressed in the morning. And isn't that the point?

HOW DID YOU GET THAT LOOK MISS THING? A CHECKLIST FOR PUTTING THE AFRICAN INTO YOUR AMERICAN STYLE

- Start with a little before you progress to a lot—an African-print scarf or a pair of African earrings add subtle African flavor.
- Look for African clothes with a little black for maximum versatility.
- Balance an African top with a Western bottom.
- Know your African fabrics and shapes so you can recognize American interpretations of African style.
- Experiment with soft, fluid dressing in addition to sharply tailored suits.
- If you're wearing head-to-toe African, go easy on the makeup and accessories, so you don't look like you're traveling in costume.
- Mix prints of the same size, the same fabric, and similar color values.
- Learn to distinguish between cheap "fancy" prints and quality products.
- Don't necessarily buy what's easiest to

get. The market is developing, and there are a lot of unusual and stunning African-inspired clothes available from designers who work from their homes or are not well known, as well as big, national retailers.

- Wear your look with confidence and panache.

The New Relaxed Look: Stylish, Casual, and Afrocentric

For those who have been constrained about expressing African style at work, the movement toward more casual dress is good news. It means you can take a more relaxed and open approach to office clothes and they'll still be acceptable in the eyes of your colleagues and, more important, your supervisors. According to the National Retail Federation, more than 50 percent of corporations allow for casual dress, and 80 percent have instituted casual Fridays.

There is, however, uncertainty and confusion about what is appropriate in casual wear as we redefine what it means to look professional or successful. But don't let this transition period throw you. Don't just toss clothes together because your office allows casual wear. You still want to present a professional, stylish image. Remember you're still going to work, not a basketball game. For instance, it's better not to wear a track suit—of any kind; it doesn't matter how much it cost or whose label is on it.

First, follow the cues from your boss. If your boss is dressing more informally these days, it's an opening for you to do the same. You certainly shouldn't be the only one in the office stuck in a rut wearing hard-tailored skirt suits and high-heeled pumps five days a week. On the other hand, if your supervisor is still dressing formally even after your company has decreed casual days, you should feel free to dress in a relaxed way. A more eclectic, diverse approach to dressing is the wave of the future. Dress for success as defined by matching skirt suits, prim blouses, and bland pumps is over.

Many companies, such as Neiman Marcus, Bergdorf Goodman, Target, Lee Jeans, and the Ford Motor Company, offer classes or videos on how to dress for America's newly casual workplace. Ask your employer if guidelines are available. Some retailers in your community will be happy to come to your workplace and run an employee seminar on how to put together a professional-looking casual wardrobe. Inquire through your human resources department.

The best place to start assembling your casual workwear is with a few knit pieces. Knitwear is easy, comfortable, and available in beautiful colors, and it is the basis for a polished but casual career look.

Pull out all the knitwear you own. You may be surprised at how much you already have. Then fill in gradually, buying one or two pieces at a time. There is a range of knit underpinnings available—turtlenecks, cardigans, sweaters, tunics, cardigan jackets, dresses, pants, and skirts. "Women don't have the time anymore," says Randolph Duke, the designer for Halston. "You have to think about what's easy for her, and underpinnings are the most important part of the wardrobe. They're things you can change the look of an outfit with but spend the least amount of money on."

If you don't have one already, get at

Use sleek knits to add fashion and comfort to your wardrobe.

Imaginative combinations—knitwear and African-print wrap skirt.

least one twin set—a cardigan and matching sweater. It's great for work, a classic style that you can wear nine ways till Sunday: Wear the set over a slim skirt or the cardigan like a jacket over a white T-shirt, a V-neck sweater tucked into a tailored pant. Again, the key is to be aware of what you are buying. Does it fit you properly? For work, in particular, you want to have the best casual clothes you can afford. The look you are after is one of casual elegance. "Keep it simple," advises Tommy Hilfiger. "Don't try to complicate it too much. Fit is important. Fit and quality."

Assembling a new look for work may take time, but the thing about casual is that you probably have at least some of the core items already. Don't run out and buy a whole new wardrobe. There are good alternatives available at every price. A decent quality cotton turtleneck can be purchased for $9.99, $19.99, or $99.99. You can buy a wool turtleneck for around thirty dollars or for close to six hundred dollars from a top designer, and if you have a thousand dollars to spend on a fine cashmere turtleneck, you can do that, too. Look for turtlenecks with a little Lycra spandex in them—it helps the neckline keep its shape and prevents snagging. Silk knits, which were once considered luxuries, hold color beautifully. Mock turtlenecks—the collar is not as high as a turtleneck, and there's nothing to turn over—are a sophisticated alternative to turtlenecks.

"Try to make your wardrobe as coordinated as possible," says Tommy. Make it 'coordinator-friendly.'"

Tommy suggests the following lineup as a basis for a versatile, crisp wear-to-work look:

One pair of basic chino pants
One pair of basic jeans
A couple of white blouses
A couple of turtlenecks
Some T-shirts—long-sleeved and short-sleeved
One blazer
One casual jacket, perhaps with an open collar

With this foundation in place, the real fun can begin—you can add fun pieces and items that reflect African-American style. Wear an indigo or navy multicolored shirt, a navy tunic sweater, a striped knit shirt, or an African waxed print with a pair of chinos, and wear khaki or navy suede Hush Puppies or desert boots. A Bogolan jacket would go well with khakis. If you're young or slim—or both—a matching miniskirt or catsuit and knee-high boots look great with the jacket.

Keep in mind that casual in the office does not always mean jeans. If style is your goal, it almost never means blue jeans. If you do wear them, make sure the jeans have a sense of drama, like Helmet Lang's jeans with huge turned-up cuffs or Karl Kani's jeans with topstitching and in an oversize cut. Anna Sui often designs fabulous maxiskirts, cargo jackets, and boot-cut pants in denim, giving the fabric a designer stamp. Calvin Klein has a whole collection called CK Calvin Klein Khakis in beige and olive cotton denim.

Hip-hop Casual

Hip-hop fashion has given America many stylish interpretations of casual to choose from. For example, hip hop has taken classic icons of Anglo-preppy style and created a thoroughly new attitude; use this as inspiration. Many black urban kids prefer design-driven labels like Maurice Malone, Mecca, Calvin Klein, Tommy Hilfiger, Karl Kani, Gianni Versace, and Ralph Lauren as opposed to mass brands like Lee.

Sports-influenced clothes like zip-front tops, racer-style pants with stripes down the side, and hooded sweaters in silk are inspired by African-American hip-hop style. These can be worn alone or under a jacket. If you work in a creative environment, mixing these elements with pieces of tailored clothing is one modern way to dress.

Distinguish yourself from the flock with a tailored white shirt, white jeans, spectator oxfords or loafers, and a narrow golden Masai-style collar or brass bead choker around your neck. You can also wear over-long jeans spilling over high-heeled pumps or open-toed shoes, a very cool look. Or choose oxfords or sturdy shoes that work with the rugged spirit of jeans.

A Dress for Success

Dresses, though not as versatile as separates, offer a relaxed look. The best casual work dress is any version of the safari look. A safari-style dress is a modified shirtdress with a distinctive notch collar and a cinched waist that is usually belted.

The classic safari dress looks right every time.

It can be long-sleeved or short-sleeved. It's fabulous in khaki, olive, or white, with a matching cloth belt or a belt of tan leather. Add tan or brown pumps, heavy-heeled sandals, or espadrilles; a leather and raffia hobo bag from Kenya; smooth hoops or doorknocker earrings, and you're ready to roll. Byron Lars does fabulous shirtdresses with just enough vamp to make everyone who wears them look curvy.

Adinkra print or waxed print cotton dresses in stylish shapes like sheaths and sundresses are pretty and polished and can often be teamed with a little cardigan or a jacket. Look for coatdresses in aso oke or summer sheaths in exuberant waxed prints.

Beware of fabrics with garish colors—widely available in cheaper versions of aso oke cloth, for example. Colors should look bold and crisp and be equally vivid on both sides of the cloth. Cloth of lesser quality is usually bright on one side and much paler on the other side. The cheaper imitation kente print on light cotton, for instance, is not what you should be wearing if you want to project competence and success.

Pretty in Pants

A pair of tailored navy trousers teamed with a white or patterned shirt with an African waxed-print vest is a no-fuss option for casual. Try a simple wool sweater—V-neck or turtleneck—over wide-legged or straight-legged cuffed trousers. Clothes made from Bogolan are great for combining ease with a touch of formality. A Bogolan-print jacket over black trousers or beige linen pants looks relaxed yet exotic.

Consider a batik shirt over a fitted knit top during the summer months or if you live in a warm climate.

Long slim pants in light cottons printed with abstract African designs are great. Take a pink, green, or burgundy skirt with a slit up the side, tuck in a short-sleeved pink shirt, add a brown three-inch-wide leather belt with cowrie shells, and finish off the look with matching brown low-heeled leather sandals or slingbacks. You can achieve the same look with other color combinations. In cooler climates, substitute a body-hugging V-neck sweater worn over the skirt, a leather or nylon motorcycle jacket or golf-style jacket, and knee-high boots.

If your office is more conservative, consider a matching pair of Adinkra-patterned cigarette pants or straight-legged trousers with a twin set that complements one of the colors in the print. On the weekend pair the pants with a ribbed halter top or a georgette tunic suit.

Though we think of African prints as flamboyant mixes of color, there are prints available in muted tones like browns or navy, perhaps better suited to

KENT FREE LIBRARY
312 West Main Street
Kent, Ohio 44240
(330) 673-4414

Hours:
9:00 am - 9:00 pm, Monday-Friday
10:00 am - 6:00 pm, Saturday

CHECKOUT RECEIPT

Materials checked out to:

uthor: White, Constance C. R.
itle: StyleNoir : the first how-to g
E: 07/28/1999

----

some offices. A pencil skirt made from these muted fabrics worn with a black or navy twin set represents a conservative but soft look.

For many women in fields like law, nursing, and finance, casual days mean we can wear trousers to work. Tailored pants may be as far as you can go on the job. Tailored stretch pants offer a sharp look and comfort. But if you can push the envelope, jodhpurs, leggings, and boot-cut stretch pants are amazingly sleek for work as well as the weekend. (Cover your derrière if you're wearing any of these super-tight pants. There are other places more appropriate for showing off your great buns.) Wear a jacket or tunic sweater that stops beyond the hips. You can also add an ankle-length cardigan and cinch it with a big belt. An unbelted hip-length cardigan or big shirt, however, is sloppy. Leggings work best with knee-high boots, over-the-knee boots, or shoes and opaque tights that match your pants. Ankle boots are best left for pants that cover the top of the boot, or dancers in music videos.

Some progressive designers are showing the new look of short trousers. They're really cute if you can pull them off, and if you work in a creative business. They are similar to pedal pushers, but they end at the knee and are tailored like trousers. They look best on a slim body. Wear trousers with a relaxed short jacket and knit top, a motorcycle-style jacket—as shown by the New York designer Daryl K—or with a fitted shirt tucked into your pants. The proportions here are tricky, so keep everything spare and close to the body.

A look popular with young black urban women is a leather jacket, long skirt, and African-print turban. It's not right for every workplace, but I urge you to give it a try; it's very cool. A contrasting solid-color head wrap also looks great juxtaposed with blue denim. Wear a blue denim shirt tucked into a matching skirt and belt it with a standard two-inch leather belt. Now add a red, pale pink, or navy turban neatly tied around your hair (see chapter 7 for how to tie it). Finish with three to six elephant-hair bracelets and small gold studs.

The casual movement represents the best opportunity to integrate African-influenced fashion into your wardrobe and experiment with new modes of dress. It's an exciting chance to express your creativity and individualism while still indicating that you are ready to get the job done.

REMINDERS FOR CASUAL STYLE

- Good quality is still important.
- Make stylish knits the basis of your casual wardrobe.
- Try black or white jeans for a more stylish look.
- On weekends, combine African-print wrap skirts with colorful T-shirts. At work, wear a jacket or shirt with the skirt.
- Avoid faded or ripped jeans.
- Don't wear anything you wouldn't wear to the office picnic.
- At the office, remember that casual doesn't mean sexy.
- Sweatsuits and running suits are out of the question for work.
- If you're dressed casually, carry a casual bag, like a rattan briefcase or nylon tote.
- Ditto for your shoes. Match the spirit of your shoes with the spirit of your outfit.
- Above all, have fun!

Praying and Playing: Your Festive Diva Style

Praying

For many black Christian women, going to church is a chance to celebrate God and celebrate the art of dressing up—a seamless merging of corporeal and spiritual beauty.

If you go to church regularly, you'll want to have a few special outfits. You may have clothes that are versatile enough for church and work, but it is refreshing to be able to slip into clothes that you never wear on the job. I have two dresses that I keep handy for Sunday service. They're not the only things I wear, but if I'm tired or running late, I have these standbys.

Traditional African-American style calls for a brilliantly colored suit (except on white Sundays), a complementary hat, and high-heeled shoes. If this is the style you prefer, a three-piece suit—dress, jacket, and skirt—is a smart choice. Many congregations still consider pants or the lack of a headdress disrespectful. The choice is yours. A two-piece suit, consisting of a jacket and skirt or a dress and matching jacket, can be mixed and matched for different looks over several Sundays.

First Sunday: The dress works with the jacket, a cameo brooch, and a wide-brimmed hat.

Second Sunday: The dress goes alone with a large African-print shawl.

Third Sunday: Jacket, skirt, and bowler hat.

Fourth Sunday: Jacket with black skirt, black lace pantyhose, black heels, and hat that matches jacket.

Don't be afraid to vary your style. Many designers are creating softer clothes that still offer a head-to-toe look but are relaxed. Try a knit top under your jacket, or slip a richly colored striped georgette tunic over your dress. Wear your skirt with a beautiful sweater instead of a jacket. Newer still is the feminine look, a long flowing printed dress in chiffon or rayon worn with a cloche hat. Unexpected color combinations—for example, an orange sweater with a burnt orange African-print skirt, belt, and brown shoes—are pretty and invigorating.

Give a new lift to your suit by wearing it with a gèlèe instead of a hat (see chapter 3). Traditional African dress with its exquisite shades and exotic earthiness is wonderful for church. A suit trimmed with an African print is one option. But consider a dress with adinkra symbols—black and pink, say, with a black gèlèe. A caftan of kente or Guinea brocade with a matching gèlèe looks stunning while praising the Lord. Remember, God don't like ugly.

Playing

For evening, you must have a basic black dress—knee-length or shorter, long-sleeved or short-sleeved—simple in design and cut, preferably in wool, cotton, or silk. It can take you to church, to an afternoon party, to a formal affair, and—in a pinch—to the office. Pearls or a bold gold collar immediately add drama to your black dress. If you attend a lot of formal affairs for work or pleasure, add a black tuxedo to your wardrobe. The traditional tuxedo can be any style—skirt or trousers; but you can substitute a skirt for a more unusual look. Wool is definitely best. Build a whole dressy wardrobe around a tuxedo by considering the tuxedo and your little black dress the bookends.

Bare some skin when the evening calls for formal or semiformal; there's no excuse not to be a diva. A strapless sheath gown or one with thin straps is provocative and festive. Transparency is tantalizing. Reveal as little or as much as you are comfortable with. Sheer can range from a gown with transparent sleeves to a see-through dress of crochet knit or chiffon under which you wear a slip or bra and brief. You might choose to cover up a bare evening dress with a shawl that incorporates an African motif like an embroidered Benin mask.

Evenings should be magical—okay, maybe not those work-related, rubber-chicken evenings, but the personal ones—whether going out with family, your special someone, or the girls. You get to dress up like a Nubian queen, and you should sparkle, literally. Don't be afraid to wear outfits that glitter and catch the light, sequins, rhinestones, shiny satin fabrics, and lurex. The trick is to recognize and choose glittering clothes

that are tastefully done and well executed. Badgley Mischka is a design team that specializes in beautifully sequined and beaded gowns. Their clothes are expensive, but they are a good yardstick for measuring what well-executed beading should look like.

Slim evening dresses are always preferable to full-skirted gowns. Wide skirts make you look wider, says designer Constance Saunders, who has been designing special-occasion clothes for almost twenty years. Choose slimming straight skirts or dresses. Every woman dreams of making a dramatic entrance, and Constance outlines three rules:

Your dress must combine interesting color and texture.
It must fit beautifully.
It must look unique.

Valentino, the Italian couturier, made a name for himself making women look ultraglamorous. He is one of Oprah's favorite designers, and he has helped Sharon Stone, Diana Ross, and Elizabeth Taylor look like divas at night. He has some rules for you:

VALENTINO'S THREE RULES FOR LOOKING GLAMOROUS

- Always be yourself (no insecurity permitted).

- A simple black dress goes a long way—or a red Valentino gown!
- Some color on the lips, always.

> "I always suggest when a woman is trying clothes on, if possible she should do it at home, walking around her room looking at herself in the mirrors, with a drink in her hand and the music playing."
>
> —*Valentino*

African-inspired Evening Wear

A woman who walks into an event wearing a well-put-together African-inspired outfit will turn heads. A gown or buba of Guinea brocade is perfect when the occasion calls for something special. Festive djellabas made with exquisite, lustrous embroidery encircling the neckline are stunning too. Designers Tracy Reese and Byron Lars once wore fabulous matching djellabas they had bought in the Ivory Coast to a black-tie affair in New York City. You should have seen the flashbulbs go off.

These traditional styles can be worn with flat metallic sandals, velvet slippers, or high heels. For ultra glamour, add a matching head wrap.

Inspired by the Masai, in 1997 Ralph Lauren created exquisite multicolored gowns with tiny beads forming chevron patterns down the length of the dress. Beaded belts, necklaces, or an incredible beaded apron from South Africa look beautiful against jersey gowns.

Batiks are a more subtle alternative to waxed prints for evening. A tie-dye gown or buba looks amazing in dusky colors like clay, earth, or indigo. Nigerian women wear bubas made from embroidered georgette, white metallic lace, and gold-edged cutwork lace for festive affairs. The layers of rich cloth, one over another, make for a luxurious look.

A white djellaba trimmed in gold makes a stunning evening gown. Wear one without the trousers—you may need a short nude or black body slip or unitard, as many of the white djellabas are semitransparent. Again, sheer metallic stockings and matching high-heeled sandals complete the look.

DON'T GIVE ME THAT HYUNDAI

Nigerians have pet names for especially luxurious fabrics they use to make their festive bubbas—the fabrics are named after cars. Mercedes and Cadillac are two popular top-of-the-line fabrics; the names denote the richness of the cloth.

Right, Therez Fleetwood's sexy combination of "George" and Guinea brocade.

If you dare to stand out—a sexy man's-style djellaba.

Bubas come with matching pants, but you can substitute your own pair of trousers or a long skirt in a contrasting color. Pair an emerald-colored djellaba with purple satin pajama pants. Accessorize with metallic skin-tone stockings and gold strappy high-heeled sandals.

Your clothes are the focal point of your evening wear, but don't neglect the accessories. African-print clothes, authentic and inspired, look great dressed up with an amulet necklace or a wristful of brass bracelets. Complete the look with high heels or dressy flat sandals.

When your evening includes a sit-down dinner, remember that you want to shine even while seated. Don't be too plain on top, leaving all the action below. Wear beautiful jewelry—earrings with stones that catch the light and make your eyes twinkle, or a dramatic necklace, perhaps of hammered silver, that draws attention to your too-fabulous eyes.

For a last sensuous touch and an extra secret glow, dust your neck, shoulders (if bare and décolletage) with bronzed eyeshadow, gold-flecked dusting powder, or a thin dab of metallic bronzer.

Choose small handbags like clutches, minauderies (small jewelry bags), or bags with pearl or chain handles. Turn a pretty cosmetics case into an evening bag, or even remove the powder from a large compact case and carry it with your money and a tissue in it. Don't ruin your evening look with a large handbag.

Before you go out for an evening, relax in a warm bath sprinkled with your favorite fragrance. Light a candle in your room or your bathroom, creating your own boudoir. Put on your favorite Marvin Gaye or Toni Braxton CD and sip some chamomile tea as you unwind and get ready for the night ahead when you'll make your grand entrance.

AN AFRICAN-INSPIRED REVERSIBLE EVENING WRAP IS THE PERFECT ACCOMPANIMENT TO A BARE EVENING DRESS. HERE'S HOW TO MAKE YOUR OWN.

Select about three yards of a lustrous fabric: a lurex, Guinea brocade, or aso oke. Choose a solid piece of acetate or silk of equal size, and sew them together. (Use a machine, or have a dressmaker do it.) If you are wearing, say, a red gown, choose at least one fabric that has a hint of red in it or a shade exactly opposite, like navy or purple.

One side of the stole can be velvet, fake fur, or quilted acetate—all readily available in your local fabric store. If you like, trim your stole with tassels from the upholstery store, cowrie shells, or coins you've collected from Africa (have holes drilled in them at a jewelry store).

The great thing about a stole is it can keep you warm yet looking elegant if the room is too chilly; when things warm up, just drape it over the back of your chair. Wear your stole folded lengthwise and draped over one shoulder, draped over both shoulders, or in the middle of your back with the ends of the stole in the crooks of your elbows.

Fabulous Full-figure Dressing

For any woman, the road to looking appealing is to emphasize her best points. This holds true whether you are a size 8 or size 28. Take a long look at yourself. Do you have large, shapely legs? Smooth, full arms? A great chest? You can learn how to use color and pattern to play down some characteristics and highlight others. This chapter is not a pep talk on the virtues of being large-bodied; it's about making the most of what you have by trying new ideas, applying time-tested formulas, and experimenting with more modern notions of how to look your best.

Most of the suggestions throughout this book apply to women of all shapes and sizes. There are, however, some styles that large women should avoid if they want to look their most stylish, just as there are clothes and combinations that do not flatter someone who is short or very tall.

The emphasis should never be on looking smaller but on looking your best. Professional models know if they strike a certain pose for the camera, they look phenomenal. Turn the head slightly, and they don't look so great. Each top model learns what's best for her. And you should, too. It's a question not of looking perfect but of understanding what brings out your best features.

Luckily for us, body image is not as big an issue for black women as for white women. A variety of body types are accepted and considered attractive by both men and women in our culture. Big hips, full breasts, and sturdy-looking thighs are coveted by many in the black community. Since black girls and women do not see themselves fully integrated into the images of attractiveness in popular culture, they may have opted out of the system. When it comes to our bodies, at least, many of us have long ago stopped looking—or perhaps never did—to white America for affirmation or criteria of what kind of body qualifies as beautiful.

Several of our most admired women over the years have worn a large size, including the late blues singer Bessie Smith, U.S. Representative Barbara Jordan, Jessye Norman, Aretha Franklin, Dr. Jocelyn Elders, Maya Angelou, and Coretta Scott King.

On television, a range of glamorous, attractive—even cool—women with meat on their bones fill the screen, from Queen Latifah, Jackee Harry, and Kim Coles to Nell Carter and Isabel Sanford. It would be naive to think that the mammy syndrome does not play a role here; nevertheless, the one large-sized white star on TV, Roseanne Arnold, is equated with homeliness.

Though Oprah has agonized about her weight, for most blacks, I would venture to say, it has been a nonissue. The pounds were incidental to her intelligence and talents as a talk show host, actor, businesswoman, and philanthropist.

For women of our culture, the real issue of weight concerns health. Organizations like the Black Women's Health Project in Atlanta have encouraged us to pay attention to weight-related health issues. If your weight is causing or is an indication of ill health, then you need to take action.

There are fashion rules that have developed regarding big women. Though it seems popular to throw them out in the new mood of "there are no rules for large-sized women," I beg to differ. There are no rules—if you don't care how you look or how others perceive you. But the truth is, if you are interested in style, some time-honored observations still hold. Your goal is to look good and big, not big and bad.

More than half the women in the United States now wear size 14 or over, and as the population ages, that number will increase rapidly in the next two decades. The average bra size has already gone up to a 36C from 34B a few years ago. This growth is a boon for women who have been frustrated by the lack of well-made plus-size fashions. Several elite designers still do not offer their clothes above a size 14, but more are beginning to do so (see the Resource Directory). Perhaps by the next century, special sizes won't be so special anymore.

The Basics

One piece of wisdom we were all once familiar with is that large women should wear one color. This is true. When you dress tonally, you look more sophisticated and fool the eye into seeing one long line of color. Tonal dressing elongates the body. It looks better than throwing on a sweater, a skirt, shoes, and pantyhose in different shades.

Every plus-size woman should own a set of basics in black. Nothing elongates, slims, and hides better than the shade of night. You won't always want to wear black—although I come pretty close—so vary your wardrobe with different colors to suit your mood and add some spice. But gather some black basics that make you look terrific no matter what, offer versatility, and are chosen with your body in mind—as follows:

One pair of straight tailored trousers.
A V-neck or surplice T-shirt tunic, long- or short-sleeved.
A vest to midthigh, if you're petite; a bit longer is okay if you're taller.
A cotton shirt, again to midthigh or longer, to go over trousers or black leggings.

These constitute basic flattering shapes for large sizes. Wear your surplice top over the trousers to work. On another day add the waistcoat. On casual days, wear the shirt over your trousers and finish with a long simple chain pendant, amber beads, or three or four strands of colored African beads. If you're going to the movies, the shirt goes over black leggings. An African-print scarf can be worn inside the neckline, or a short brass and bead necklace can top it all off.

Proportion

Proportion is one of the least-discussed components of style, but it is one that can make a significant difference in how you look, particularly if you have a big frame. Proportion is the relationship between objects or lines; it refers to how each element balances with another.

Short tops over long bottoms are generally not attractive combinations for plus sizes. Wear any length of skirt, trousers, or dress with a long jacket that ends at about your fingertip or an inch or two above.

You don't have to drown yourself in bulky sweaters all the time. For work, layer a finely knit silk or wool tunic sweater under a matching wrap or belted cardigan.

Full skirts make you look wide. Choose slim skirts that taper toward the knee. Don't get caught wearing a jacket with shoulders the size of a quarterback's, a long tunic over a long full skirt, and a long scarf. We've seen that look before, and it's not flattering: it's too much. The proportions are wrong. Keep things skimming—but not hugging—the body. Seek balance from shoulder pads, but do not wear big ones like those popular in the eighties. If necessary, pull out the pads and replace them with smaller ones you can purchase at a sewing store.

Boxy jackets over full pants will make you look shorter and thicker. Instead, choose sweaters that extend beyond your hipbone and elongate your torso to "match" the length of your body from waist to feet, so you don't appear excessively top-heavy. The fact that a larger woman can and should carry a large rather than small handbag is also a function of proportion. A small handbag magnifies the size of the body next to it. Select a bag with either a handle strap or a shoulder strap that puts the bag at waist length and no lower. A handbag swinging below your hip is not helping you achieve your pulled-together look.

Designers do their final balancing of proportion when they consider what footwear to match with a specific outfit. Don't wear chunky-heeled shoes or boots with a tapered skirt, leggings, or cigarette pants, for example. To balance the eye, these styles require slimmer lines and more delicate heels and details. A heavy shoe anchors ankle-length skirts or wide-legged pants. There's a reason bell-bottom pants are worn with platform shoes!

Hems

Hemlines that graze the ankle or hang one or two inches above the knee are the most flattering. Big women often have shapely legs—show them off in skirts above the knee and long skirts slit up the front, back, or side to just above the knee. Wear dark, sheer tights and shoes with medium-height heels.

In casual settings, reveal long shapely legs in stylish pieces like fitted jodhpurs and leggings with racing stripes down the side. A long shirt makes an easy topper. Add a choker of beads or a small African-print scarf around your neck.

The V-Neck Story

Stock up on V-neck sweaters, V-neck dresses, and surplice or wrap styles. The V shape, pointing downward and revealing some skin at the neck, helps give you a more dynamic and thin look. Make a V-neck by opening the top two or three buttons of your shirt, whether you are wearing the shirt alone or with a jacket. One of the ways designer Tom Ford made those ultralong-looking models who stalked the runways of Gucci in 1996 look so tall and sleek was by showing everything with shirts that broke open at the neck, very high heels, and trousers that ended an inch or so below the anklebone.

Patterns

Should large women wear patterns? It's a long-debated question. The answer is definitely yes. We need look no further than the range of well-endowed native African women who shroud themselves in glorious patterns every day to see that beautiful prints need not be just for size 10s or smaller.

Choosing a pattern is a very personal decision—let your instincts guide you. Do you really like it? Is there something in a particular pattern that draws you to it? The second consideration is size. Choose smaller patterns over large ones, unless the pattern features one bold graphic against a solid background. A small, dense pattern does not emphasize expanse the way a large print does.

Avoid mixing different prints. If you combine a print with a solid, turn conventional wisdom on its head and wear the print on the bottom and the solid on top. This combination is more flattering to large women, perhaps because most women are larger on top and taper toward the bottom. For print bottoms, I'm referring to one thing and one thing only—ankle-length skirts. Do not attempt to wear a short printed skirt or patterned trousers. Disaster. A soft, straight skirt in a paisley, a bold floral, an African waxed print, or a Bogolan or aso oke cloth can be pretty and lyrical. Combine a black-and-white print with your black shirt; a burgundy, olive, and chocolate wax print with a burgundy Mao jacket; a paisley with a leather jacket. A head wrap or hairband made from the same African-print cloth is fun and makes your outfit look regal.

Shapes

Many African styles, because of their loose shapes that skim the body or fall away from it, are well suited for women with large hips and busts. Take advantage of the wrap tradition, purchase lengths of fabulous fabric, and wrap your skirts for maximum comfort and panache on weekends, at festive occasions, or at work, if appropriate. Buy an ample amount of fabric. If your hips measure about forty-five inches, choose a length of fabric about three yards wide. Versions of the djellaba—the slim-fitting, long tunic that

A buba, also called a djellaba, is easy yet exotic.

falls just below the hip or to the ankle—are beautiful for lounging. Dress them up for an evening out.

If you're larger than size 16, steer clear of peplum jackets. Peplums are severe and exaggerated; you need a softer, more tailored look. Alvin Bell's exclusive designs for the Mosaic line at Sears emphasize soft, fluid tunic shirts over matching languorous pants. It's a feminine and sophisticated look that suits a variety of body shapes. The clothes are shapely but still skim the body. Alvin further refines the traditional tunic look by accessorizing it with hip-or waist-length chain belts with African-inspired brass accents.

I can't say enough about adding a chain belt to a long tunic look to show some shape and vary a look. Chain belts are chic and versatile and give a quick sizzle to any outfit. Use one to give shape to a hip-length sweater worn over trousers to work. (Don't tuck sweaters or blouses into pants. It looks uncomfortable.)

Many large women may go through three different sizes in the course of three years because they are dieting. Don't get complacent and wear jackets that are too tight because you're waiting to lose weight. It looks unprofessional and calls attention to your body, which in a professional setting is not where you want your emphasis to be. Instead, buy a blouse or knit top that can be worn under the jacket, allowing you to leave it open.

For special evenings slip into a buba of lustrous Guinea brocade.

Consider Custom

If you're spending upwards of three hundred dollars for a suit or dress, consider having your clothes custom-made. This will ensure a better fit that caters to your body's natural shape. There are many good tailors around. Ask for recommendations at local bridal shops, who must often do custom work, and your local department store. Post a notice at your church or attend some local fashion shows, where you're sure to ferret out some local talent. In most black communities there are skilled neighborhood tailors and dressmakers who are professionally trained, or schooled on the job. Many are also designers in their own right. Working from home or a small design studio with low overhead, they can afford to make clothes at prices that compete with the good ready-to-wear items sold in fine department stores.

Whether you have clothes made or you buy them off the rack at a store, begin with the best fabric you can afford. Don't scrimp. Think in terms of buying two basic tops and bottoms for the year, if necessary. Select a high-quality worsted or superfine wool in a classic shade like navy, black, or brown. When you consider that you will be able to wear this suit for at least five years, it does not become so difficult to spend five hundred to a thousand dollars for an outfit. Offset the initial outlay with underpinnings that are value priced: V-neck sweaters, crisp white shirts, or stretch satin shirts for thirty dollars or so.

Dresses

Dresses are excellent options for plus-size women who want the polish and class of a suit. In fact, when you want to look your best for work or church, a dress is preferable for several reasons: The dress skims the body, and it's one piece, so it's easier to deal with. Overall, it creates a cleaner, easier line. You can always retain the option of adding a matching jacket that falls below the hip. A wardrobe of four or five dresses in different colors, including one in black, is a good investment for any plus-size woman.

A sheath is a simple dress cut straight and slightly away from the body. A shift is straighter and not as fitted. Also flattering are chemise and empire dresses—both fall downward away from the bust. A chemise gives you more room from bust to hem and is almost a trapezoid shape, like the tent dresses of the 1970s. Elegant or casual, it may have buttons down the front and feature a bateau neckline. Essentially, an empire has its waistline below the bust; it may or may not be fitted under the breasts. A coatdress or jacket dress, as it is sometimes called, is, as the name suggests, an elongated jacket. It is tailored, with shoulder pads, a notch collar, and buttons down the front.

For evening or church, a chemise or sheath with a jewel neckline—so called because it forms an ideal backdrop for necklaces and brooches—can be glamorized as much or as little as you like. For work, add the standard pearls, a black cameo brooch, or an Egyptian-collar necklace of flat hammered gold (imitation is fine). Drape a brightly colored African-print scarf around your neck and tuck the ends into the neckline of your dress.

Finishing Touches

Don't spoil a great outfit by neglecting the details. It's often harder for a big woman to look the way she would like because of the relative scarcity of fashionable, good-quality clothes. Ironically, poor quality shows up more readily in a size 18 than a size 8.

Whatever you're wearing, keep things neat and pulled together. Keep the spirit of your outfit from head to toe. If your look for day is tailored and clean, be consistent: A gray pinstripe sheath dress and a matching long jacket should be teamed with black, gray, or chocolate brown hose and matching low-heeled pumps; a pair of smooth silver earrings, large or small; and a good-looking chrome-colored sports-style or Timex basic watch. You might do your hair in a clean bob, a French braid, or unadorned goddess braids. Don't look sloppy by mixing it up. For, instance, in this case, it would be a mistake to pile on necklaces, strappy shoes suitable for an evening out, or a delicate antique watch.

Here's another example. Let's say you start with an African waxed-print dashiki and a pair of blue jeans. You've box-braided your hair and added a bunch of brass bangles, drop earrings, and toe sandals. *Don't* all of a sudden replace your sandals with serious flat oxfords.

Shoes

Shoes are the finishing touch of any outfit, and if you are full-figured, you usually require a larger size shoe with a wider fit. Though it is not always easy, it is not as difficult as it once was to find comfortable, stylish shoes. You can now find sizes 10 through 14 in a wide range of stores, from Bergdorf Goodman and Stuart Weitzman to Nordstrom and Payless.

The ideal basic shoe for a large woman who wears over size 10 is an elegant pump with a medium-width square toe, two-inch square heel, and a square vamp. Suitable for a variety of occasions from work to church to a dressy affair, they are comfortable and stand up to lots of wear. Avoid slingbacks if you have wide feet.

Your feet will slip around in them, and the shoes will quickly lose their shape.

High- to medium-heeled sandals with rounded or square toes are sexy and fresh-looking on any foot. Add bright red vixen nail polish, or buff your nails if you prefer the natural look.

Bags, totes, alligator-print doctor's bags, messenger-style bags, and hobos are larger-scale styles that look good on big women. African-print knapsacks or totes and straw baskets woven in Senegal and other East African countries are whimsical touches for warm weather.

Underpinnings

Pay particular attention to your lingerie. Be sure items fit comfortably and give the support or control you require. Wear control underwear to give yourself a smooth fit under pants and evening wear in particular. "No matter how you're dressing for evening, look for a foundation," says Randolph Duke, the Halston designer. "Evening has to have a foundation, whether it's built into the dress or it's something you buy that lifts and separates."

Queen-size hose for dark skin tones is widely available at specialty stores, drugstores and department stores. Make your hose do double duty; choose control-top hosiery when you need a smooth line but not necessarily a reduction in size. Wolford, Donna Karan, DKNY, and Ralph Lauren hosiery are four good brands that seem to last a bit longer and offer more shaping than many others on the market. They are expensive, but the extra expenditure may be worth it.

Any woman wearing a size 38 or larger bra should give her bustline extra attention. As mentioned in the lingerie chapter, it is worth it to seek out a store that fits brassieres. Before putting on your bra, dust your shoulders and under your breasts with dusting powder to cut down on chafing. Make little pads to tuck under your straps so that they do not cut into your flesh. And choose brassieres with the widest possible shoulder and chest bands. Again, the new sports bras are definitely worth trying. And remember, a satin cup will give you a smoother finish under sweaters than a lacy bra.

The girdles our mothers wore were punishing. Thank God for spandex and elastin. You can now get a girdle that looks just like a full-cut brief but has all the control of the old-time stiff girdles.

New Style Aids for Plus-size Customers

Midway between custom-made clothes and ready-to-wear is a new area of fashion that in the long run should prove a blessing to women who have difficulty finding clothes that fit well: computerized custom design. You can now buy, in a handful of Levi's stores, computerized custom-fit jeans. It works like this. You go into the store and choose the color and style of jeans you wish to buy. A computer scans your body with your clothes on and registers your measurements. The measurements are then sent by computer to a Levi's factory, where a pair of jeans are cut and sewn to your size. The finished item is shipped to the store for you to pick up about three weeks later.

Using a similar idea, a new company called Utilities Design Match offers the customer a chance to put together her own version of a basic black dress and to choose elements like hem length, neckline, and basic shape. Currently, the company only offers sizes 2 to 14, but it's an encouraging development for women whose bodies don't conform to mainstream sizes and shapes.

The same thing is happening with shoes. The Custom Foot sells made-to-order footwear at ready-made prices. Visit the store, and they will take measurements of your foot, which will be sent to the factory, where a shoe will be made especially for you using the dimensions of your foot. Prices average around one hundred dollars and you must choose among the styles offered in the store.

Big women can carry off dramatic hair and strong, beautiful makeup. Many have extraordinary-looking hands, with none of the knobbiness of slimmer women's hands. Keep your hands moisturized and your nails the length of your fingertips or longer; finish them with clear polish or a French manicure. I also like our style of adding brilliant eye-catching nail polish in glistening red, metallic white, or blazing orange to long nails. But remember, claws are inappropriate if you want to be taken seriously at work. Accessorize with one bold ring with a large stone or three or four smaller rings like the rows of copper and brass Ivoarian rings or gold signet rings.

Final Thoughts

If an outfit looks fabulous on you, buy two; the second can be the same color or a different shade. Great clothes for big women are hard to come by, so don't waste the opportunity. If a particular combination makes you look your best, do not hesitate to use variations of it time and time again. People may say you're wearing the same look over and over, but your goal is to look good, not necessarily different, every day. Leave that to the fashion models.

Here are some additional ideas for style-setting looks that work for plus sizes:

Try a purple or black surplice dress. Purple is a powerful and elegant color. The color of royalty and the surplice neckline—a V-neck wrap—give you that elongating V, forcing the eye to travel downward. Add nothing but a pair of small gold earrings, perhaps with a small purple tone.

Wear a buba of waxed print or batik. Accessorize with clean, bold gold or brass jewelry. Take a black cardigan jacket or shawl-neck jacket—remember, it should reach below the hips—and add black pants, a white or ecru shirt or tank top, and a matching white or ecru man's silk evening scarf with fringe. This look is sleek and sophisticated for work or evening. The scarf covers up, while it also softens and flattens the neckline and chest.

A cheongsam, or Mao, jacket should be in every plus-size woman's wardrobe. They are exotic and flattering. Team a cheongsam with an ankle-length batik skirt or small waxed-print skirt. It's a proven classic, so you can wear it no matter what the prevailing style. It so happens that right now it is at the height of fashion.

Try pairing a black, navy, or gray sweater with matching tailored pants. Wear a white shirt (some stores sell collars and cuffs) with the collar pulled out over the neck of the sweater. Add a triple strand of pearls, matching socks, and your pumps, and you're ready for the executive meeting.

PLUS-SIZE REMINDERS

- Don't hide your body in a muumuu.
- Dress tonally.
- Keep the spirit of your outfit from head to toe.
- Choose hemlines that fall to the ankle or an inch above the knee.
- Don't wear tops that stop at or above your belly button.
- Cover your derrière whenever you can.
- Remember, your goal is to look good, not small.
- Identify your assets—you do have them—and play them up for all they're worth.

Adding the Flourish: Making African-inspired Accessories Work for You

Accessories are the most efficient way to individualize a look and the least expensive way to expand your wardrobe. Scarves, bracelets, shoes, necklaces, and brooches can all breathe new life into a tired outfit. And accessories offer an easy, exciting path to style with an African flavor. Concerned about wearing overtly African or African-American clothes to work? You can express your heritage in accessories. African accessories add a dramatic flourish to Western-style clothes and give black style that extra snap.

Our first consideration about a fashion item should be whether it looks good, but when it comes to African-inspired clothes and accessories, we often want to know their symbolism in our culture. We wear them to celebrate our heritage as well as to exhibit our style.

In countries like Senegal, the Ivory Coast, and Kenya, many accessories convey spiritual, religious, or social meaning. Little beaded necklaces with rectangular beaded pendants called ucu, or love letters, are made by young Zulu women in South Africa to give to their boyfriends as an expression of love. Westerners once thought ucus contained actual words, but the meanings conveyed in the graphics are symbolic, not literal. Among the Masai people, mothers and lovers give men exquisitely beaded belts to show their affection and respect for them. Nomadic desert dwellers in North Africa view accessories as an easily transportable means of artistic expression. They create bangles, armlets, and beadwork to wear around their necks or waists. You may wish to wear African-influenced jewelry this way, or its role in your wardrobe may be purely decorative. Regardless of your motivation, the variety is endless. African flourishes include earrings and hair beads, arm bracelets and ankle cuffs, gold teeth caps, and ivory bracelets that can be as wide as a watch or stretch from wrist to elbow. Now that's style!

Early development of iron tools allowed Africans to carve spectacular jewelry in ivory and glossy metals like gold and brass. In his brilliant 1965 book *Facing Mt. Kenya*, Jomo Kenyatta points out that the Kikuyu tribe of Kenya has from time immemorial used iron tools. Ironsmiths, particularly those working with brass, were believed to be mystics.

Cowrie shells decorating earrings, anklets, and chokers were once used as currency in some African countries. European glass beads, especially those imported from Venice, served the same purpose in the early nineteenth century in Kwazululand, ruled by great leaders like Shaka Zulu. Glass beads were sometimes used as a means of exchange for livestock. Today glass beads are now replaced by plastic ones, as women make intricately beaded belts that rival the work done in exclusive French ateliers. They construct necklaces and clothing for themselves and their men using thousands of tiny colorful beads applied by hand.

It's not just the design but the choice of materials that often sets African jewelry apart. In Zimbabwe, African soapstones are carved into smooth, amorphous objets d'art and fetish symbols that look wonderfully modern as pendants suspended from a leather cord. Coarse, black, shiny elephant hair is shaped into multistrand bracelets that blend seamlessly with modern Western clothes as well as African fashions.

Some rappers—who look like they were about to keel over under the weight of their several gold chains—will tell you they're sporting an African look. There's a lot of truth to what they're saying. As the source of most of the world's gold and diamonds, Africa has an old tradition of artisanship in these precious stones and metals. Huge gold collars and chains and finely carved, heavy tubular bracelets have been made in West African countries like Ghana, Liberia, and Nigeria for hundreds of years. Gold has been utilized not only in jewelry but in the amazingly luxurious garments embroidered with gold worn by tribal leaders.

Ivory has been so widely used and was in such demand among Europeans and Africans to make flamboyant jewelry and home decorations that its trade is now tightly regulated to prevent the slaughter of elephants—its main source. But inspired imitations abound.

The important thing to bear in mind with African-inspired accessories is the wide variety available. There's something to suit every taste.

Adorning the Ears

The most essential pieces in your accessories wardrobe are earrings. I don't know about you, but I won't go anywhere without my earrings. Earrings draw attention to your face and reflect the sparkle in your eyes. Doorknocker earrings—the heavy hoops with grooves and designs carved into the metal that are popular with African-American women—are traceable to African style, though they are uniquely African American. Many doorknockers encompass the Egyptian ram's head symbol.

The Jenne women in Africa wear humongous gold earrings called kwottenai kanye, passed down from generation to generation and valued at over a thousand dollars. The descendants of these earrings are the giant doorknockers. It's not a style I recommend, but it is fun to look at. Even smaller earrings can tear delicate ear lobes and result in keloids, the thick scars to which black women are prone. For work, choose doorknockers not much bigger than a quarter.

Multiple piercing of the ear's outer edge, including the ear lobe, is not unique to Africa but is a characteristic style of many African women. If you pierce your ears more than once, wear small earrings above the ear lobe—tiny rings in gold or silver or diamond studs. If you desire the multiple-earring look without the holes, wear ear cuffs. Since they are sold as singles, you can create your own pair. Cuffs fit over the upper part of the ear, hugging the ear to stay in place. Look for them in stores that sell Indian or African jewelry or cater to the young, like the stores in the East Village in New York City.

Smooth, thin gold or silver hoops are also very chic and classic and can be twice as big as what you might choose in the heavier doorknocker style. When you're hanging out, you can be more adventurous. Try hoops big enough to go around your wrist or drop earrings of colored beads or cowrie shells.

Adorning the Throat

Beaded necklaces with tiny square pendants are associated with South Africa. Throughout Africa, small leather or brass pouches are worn around the neck by Muslims, who carry verses from the Koran or a talisman in them to ward off bad luck. You can adapt these necklaces to your wardrobe. They're a funky and attractive addition to a casual outfit or a semiformal dress. Combine a pouch with a contrasting top or dress, so the necklace is set off against the clothing.

Dramatic chokers are also characteristic of African style and are sexy and arresting. Think of Miriam Makeba, the fabulous South African singer, in chokers so high they all but cover her throat. The

West African–style earrings of gold, silver, gold plate, and cowrie shells.

Masai wear spectacular beaded chokers or collars incorporating four or more bands of colors like white, blue, red, and green. The effect is beautiful and dramatic. Egyptians are often depicted in drawings and museum exhibits wearing gold collars. The women of Benin, an area famous for its influential sculpture, suffered for their beauty. These were women who didn't mind being fashion victims; they willingly wore bronze collars that weighed several pounds because the collars represented prestige.

You can achieve the same stylish effect without the pain. Casual chokers of cowrie shells or a knitted band of red, green yellow, and black are great with a shirt or T-shirt or under a jacket. For formal occasions, play up the drama of a strapless gown or one with décolletage by wearing a beaded choker. Jazz up a plain jewel or bateau neckline with a gold or silver collar necklace.

Gold looks best with strong warm colors like red, deep green, orange, and purple, as well as black. Silver or platinum (much rarer and terribly expensive) are particularly pretty with black and complement colors like mint green, pink, pale blue, and lilac. Masai women shave their heads to highlight the beauty of their jewelry; you don't have to go that far. You can get the same effect with short cropped hair or by wearing your hair up, swept off your neck.

You are probably familiar with the popular style of necklace made from several twisted strands of tiny beads. These necklaces, often available in freshwater pearls, are copies of the twisted strings of beads called pound necklaces worn by the Tutsi women of Rwanda. They offer a pretty way to soften and add color to an outfit.

Religious Symbols

An African cross worn as a pendant on a necklace or dangling from a chain belt adds immediate flair to your wardrobe. Crosses are icons. They are imbued with such deep meaning in our culture, and visually they possess such symmetry that they can change the whole attitude of an outfit. Crosses are worn by Africans to protect the wearer from evil spirits. They are common in the jewelry of Ethiopians and other northern Africans, who still wear them primarily for religious reasons.

Fasten a large silver cross to a black velvet ribbon and wear it around your waist or on your hip over a long slinky black dress. Wear a small delicate chain with a gold cross (many stores in Hispanic neighborhoods carry them, or try a children's jewelry department) around your throat during the day or with a low-neck gown slit high up the leg at night. This mixing of sexiness and innocence is interesting and provocative.

Both Rastafarians and the Falashas, or

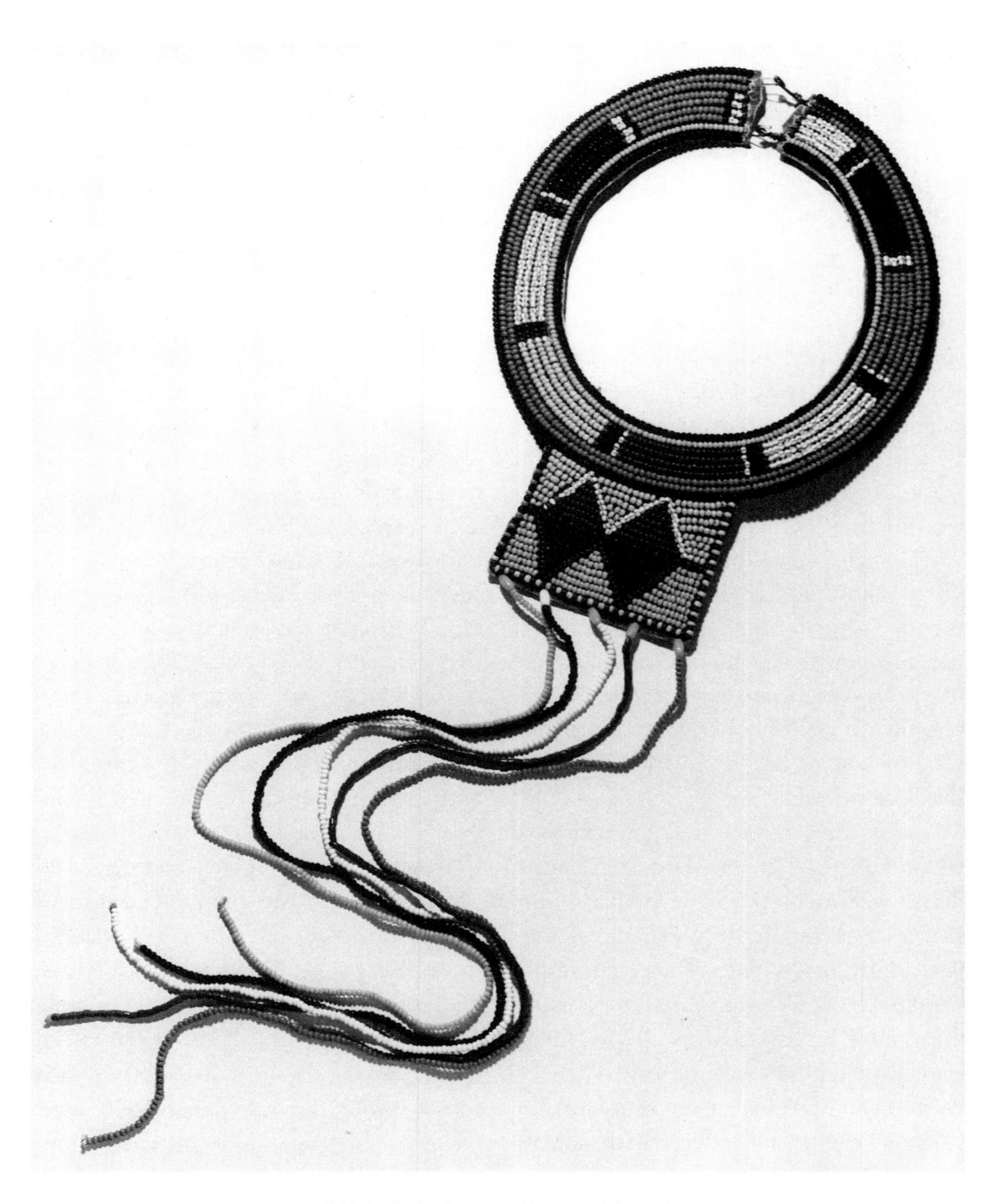

Multicolor Masai collar made of hundreds of tiny beads.

Gold-plated "bead" necklace made by West African lost wax process.

black Jews, in Ethiopia wear the Star of David, symbolizing their status as Jews or the lost tribe of Israel. An intricately carved silver cross called the cross of Agadez is popular with the Berbers of North Africa and the Niger people. Many designs for the cross of Agadez resemble the Egyptian ankh, which became popular here in the 1960s and is the most easily obtainable African cross. In Egypt, the ankh stood for life. Usually made in silver (in some parts of northern Africa, silver is more precious than gold), these crosses are sold as rings and pendants by African-American jewelers and street vendors and in alternative jewelry stores.

Bracelets

Brass bracelets are popular in East Africa. Some are flat bands about an inch wide with fanciful decorations; others coil around the wrists in a spiral.

Wear thin bangles in groups of two to six. A bunch of silver bangles and a silver ankh pendant against a black sweater or dress are breathtakingly chic.

Though most trading in ivory is now illegal, there is good fake ivory jewelry out there. Fashion just saw a revival of tortoise shell (it too has to be fake, because of bans on hunting tortoises), so a revival of ivory isn't far behind. You can start it off. Ivory is timeless and appropriate for the office, for kicking back, or for black tie.

Ivory bangles with lead or silver beads are worn in Zaire and Nigeria, and some ivory bangles were believed to encourage the conception of a male—so find out what's going on if your man suddenly starts giving you ivory jewelry. Ivory is also associated with protection from bad spirits and, like gold, it signifies the wearer's wealth.

For purely casual wear, the red, green, and yellow costume craft jewelry inspired by Rastafarians is unbeatable. Wear the brightly colored leather pendants with blue denim. Finish a casual black outfit with Lucite bangles painted in red, green, and yellow with black stripes, as is the style. Wear one big bangle or combine three smaller ones.

Crosses of Agadez in silver, star of David on left.

Egyptian women often wore arm bracelets high on the upper arm. Paintings in Egyptian pyramids depict Cleopatra and other Egyptian queens like Nefertiti with these armlets. I love them with a long, sleeveless dress for evening or with a sleeveless fitted sweater and jeans for weekend days.

Anklets

Once associated with ladies of the night, sexy anklets are popular again—with everybody. In ancient times, they adorned the feet of men and women liv-

Right, a silver ring depicting an Ankh, an ancient Egyptian symbol of life.

Copper arm bracelet.

ing in warm climates in Africa and Asia, where inhabitants often went barefoot.

A delicate gold anklet worn under your hose is appropriate for work or evening. Anklets made from colorful beads, cowrie shells, or leather add panache to beachwear, relaxed drawstring pants, or a sexy summer dress. Make your own anklet, using crystals or colored beads and some nylon string, available at the fishing store or craft shop.

Hats

African Americans have inherited from their African ancestors a love of hats and a fondness for adorning the hair with intricate ornamented hairstyles.

In African society both men and women still wear hats for religious and ceremonial reasons. Many groups carry on the earliest tradition of wearing wigs or added horsehair to create spectacular hairstyles. Egyptians wore heavy horsehair wigs, as did Nubians living in Egypt and other Africans living south of the

Sahara. Here in the United States, blacks probably wear more hats than anyone else for cultural and religious reasons. Sure, we now go to church hatless, but for generations of black women, covering the head for church has been a sign of respect and piety. Hats are also an opportunity for us to look festive and promenade our beauty.

Just as African-American women have friendly competition to turn it out at church—the hat being the ultimate style weapon—Nigerian women vie with each other in their skill at tying a gèlèe. (See chapter 3.) A creatively wrapped head is valued and admired. Nigerian women's spectacular gèlèes are traditionally worn with bubas.

African hats can provide a wealth of inspiration for milliners here. In South Africa, women wear a high, brimless, cylindrical hat that resembles one worn by the pharaohs in Egypt. Women wear it pulled down on the forehead, with a band of Shembe beads applied around the entire circumference of the hat. Shembe refers to a pattern of mostly white beads and is named after Isaiah Shembe, a South African who was called the black messiah.

Kofis are growing in popularity in the United States. Made from fabric, this soft bowl-shaped hat is often worn with a matching suit or dress. But a kofi can be a nice contrast to a non-African weekend outfit. Try wearing one as a finishing touch for a pair of jeans and a crisp white shirt.

African Americans have strongly influenced African headgear, as more Americans have begun visiting the motherland and immigrants from countries like South Africa, Ghana, Senegal, and Nigeria have made their homes in our cities.

In African cities you can find baseball caps—as American as apple pie—made from kente cloth. In a similar funny twist, migration from the Caribbean has brought tams or knitted berets in red, green, and yellow or red, green, and black to the United States, and no one sells these tams more aggressively than brothers from Senegal. At one point in the early 1990s, a popular novelty in New York City was a tam with attached imitation dreadlocks. Peter Tosh wigs were a fad in Zimbabwe in the 1980s after he toured there.

Wearing a hat these days requires a certain amount of pride of presentation and style, two things black women do not lack. African Americans and their kinfolk across the Atlantic inspire headdress designs around the world. "A quick review of some of these [African-American] hats reveals affinities with Egypt, African Islam, Senegal, Jamaican Rastafarianism and Swahili and Ghana in combination," writes Christine Mullen Kreamer, an expert on African headdress, in her book *Crowning Achievements.*

Show-stopping hats

"This eclectic mix may suggest the extent to which actual African forms (as well as the notion of Africa) have captured the imagination of clothing designers and their clients."

Scarves

No stylish woman's closet should be without three or four scarves. They are useful for covering your hair in a light drizzle, keeping your head or neck warm, covering up by the beach or pool, or adding some color around your face.

"The scarf is one of the number one accessories," says designer Alvin Bell. "You can turn a dark suit into more than just a plain dark suit by putting a bright scarf around the neck and tucking it into your collar or wear it flowing down the front of your jacket."

Avoid the one-armed-bandit scarf—the scarf draped over one shoulder—at all costs. It's passé. Instead, follow Alvin's advice, or fold your scarf into a thin band, wrap it around your neck twice, and knot it in front, tucking the ends into your collar.

Check your wardrobe color scheme and add scarves accordingly. It's better to buy a generously sized scarf—at least eighteen by eighteen inches—than a small one. You'll get more mileage.

Rayon challis, silk chiffon, silk satin, polyester, or lightweight stretch wool are the best fabric choices for scarves because they are lightweight and drapable. Make sure at least one of your large scarves picks up a color in your swimsuit; it will come in handy as a pareo.

You may want to cover your head with a turban made from an African textile. If you use a solid rather than a print, choose a fabric with some stretch to it like cotton jersey. The turban will fit more snugly and give a cleaner line.

Your turban can be a towering mass above your head, or it can be worn close to the skull. Select a piece of fabric that is approximately two feet wide and three feet long, or longer. More fabric will make a bulkier turban. No need to sew the ends—the edges will be tucked in. Follow these simple guidelines:

HOW TO TIE A TURBAN

1. Lay the length of fabric out on your bed and fold it along one long side, creating a hem about two inches wide. Keeping this hem in place, face your mirror and place the cloth on your head like a mantilla. The hem should lie flat on your forehead, and equal lengths of cloth should fall on each shoulder. You may have to lean your head back slightly to prevent the cloth from slipping off your forehead.
2. Grab the two ends and cross your hands in the back as if you are about to tie a scarf at the back of your head, but then bring the two ends of fabric around to the middle of your forehead.
3. Now crisscross the fabric in the front (just as you did in the back) but this time just above your forehead. Pull the ends of the fabric toward the back and around your head again if you have enough fabric to do so. When you only have two short ends of fabric remaining, tuck the ends in.
4. Now grab hold of the extra fabric sticking out in the middle of your head, gather it to the back or to the side, and tuck it into the bands of

crisscrossed fabric at the center or back of your head. Voila! You should be turbaned and ready to go. Practice a few times until you get the hang of it. The turban may be low on your forehead. You can wear it this way if you wish, or you can firmly place your palms flat on the front of the turban and gently slide it back an inch or so to reveal more of your forehead or some of your hair. Check to make sure that all the raw ends are hidden and the turban is secure. Tuck any raw edges up into the layers of fabric.

Here's another sharp look you can adapt to your wardrobe for work, church, or downtime.

HOW TO TIE A CHIGNON TURBAN

1. Follow steps 1 and 2 for tying a turban. (You can tie a chignon turban using a shorter length of fabric, too.)
2. When you cross the fabric in the back, instead of bringing the ends forward, twist them as if you were twisting a ponytail at the back of your head. Make sure the twist of fabric is taut.
3. Now, holding the turban in place at the back of your head with the left hand, use your right hand to twist the "ponytail" in a clockwise direction so that it forms a small bun at the nape of your neck. Tuck the end under the twisted bun you have created. The tension will keep the bun in place.

If you don't feel like creating a turban, tie a scarf flat on your head, knot it at the back, and leave the ends flowing down your back. Wear it with smooth hoop earrings or doorknockers and a T-shirt and jeans or a T-shirt tucked into a long skirt.

Fold a scarf into a triangle and wear it like a cravat, with the knot in the back and the pointed ends tucked into the neck of your blouse or jacket.

How to tie your own chignon turban: (1) ponytail; (2) bun.

THE NEW CLASSICS

Classic accessories should be a part of every wardrobe. It makes life simpler and eliminates stress, because classics can be worn in a variety of settings and with a variety of looks. When you're running out of time, fumbling around for just the right pair of earrings to go with a particular sweater or beaded gown, classics will spare your nerves.

Here are the classics you should not be without—and the African-American counterparts that should be designated classics for every well-dressed woman's wardrobe:

Anglo-American Classic	African-American Classic
Two- or three-strand pearl necklace	Tutsi triple-stranded Pound necklace
Smooth gold hoop earrings	Small gold doorknockers
A cameo brooch	Corinne Simpson's black cameo
A paisley-print scarf	A leopard-print or kente scarf
A gold signet ring	A gold ankh ring
Accessories and clothing combinations of red, white, and blue.	Accessories and clothing combinations of red, green, and yellow or red, green, and black.

Handbags

Your primary bag for work should be leather and roomy enough to hold a few office papers and the daily paper. I don't like the look of dragging around two bags. Occasionally it is unavoidable, but if you routinely need loads of space in your bag, consider a larger handbag instead of carrying two. Backpacks, totes, stylish briefcases (many of which now look more like big handbags), and zip-top totes in nylon or leather are snappy and hold a lot.

You'll need at least one compartment for holding small items like keys and pills. A good leather hobo bag, like those made by Coach, or a Prada nylon bag and its imitators are attractive options. They look modern and are lightweight, sturdy, and easy to clean. Just as there are different qualities of leather, there are varying grades of nylon, so be careful to choose a bag made of the thick sturdy type. Be

Corinne Simpson's black cameo brooch.

aware that when bags are too soft they can become misshapen. Look for a bag that gives you the option of both a hand-held strap and a shoulder strap.

Keep your work bag in good repair by rubbing it with a soft damp cloth every few weeks to remove invisible dirt and debris. Then buff with a soft towel and rub any hardware to an attractive shine. Avoid applying polish or mink oil to your handbag, as it may eventually rub off onto your clothes. Your bag is often in your lap or rubbing against you without your realizing it.

Bags made of burlap, African cotton prints, and Bogolan can make interesting summer handbags for those of us who work in liberal offices. Otherwise, they are best saved for the weekend. They are too casual for a professional setting, except as that annoying second tote to carry extra paperwork or gym clothes.

Check out small purses and cosmetic bags made from quilted African waxed prints or Bogolan—they make great handbags for evening or the weekend. Shaped as cylinders or rectangles—some with a cute handle on top—they are big enough to hold your purse, makeup, sunglasses, and keys. These bags come in a variety of prints from the Ivory Coast.

Shoes

You should have at least four pairs of shoes in your wardrobe: a medium-heeled pump; a black faille evening shoe with a slender heel; a pair of flat loafers, and a pair of sandals or sneakers. "If you're wearing a beautiful pair of shoes, you can wear almost anything," says Tom Ford, head designer for Gucci. "I find if I wear an old pair of shoes in a photograph, no matter what I'm wearing it doesn't look as good as when I'm wearing new shoes. Shoes are absolutely key."

High heels, more than two inches in height, elongate the leg. The crook of the ankle is straightened somewhat and the calf muscle stretched. A woman in high heels looks sexy because the shoe forces her to adjust her center of gravity and tilt her hips forward into a position of tottering vulnerability. Some women just like the added height of heels, but because these kinds of shoes throw off the body's natural alignment and force our feet into hurtful positions, I don't recommend them for everyday wear. If you're uncomfortable, it's going to be difficult to look and do your best.

If you can't give up your high heels for work or casual wear, look for shoes with wide toes—round or square. Top designers, from Tom Ford to African-American Scott Rankin, have been designing footwear with wider toe boxes. There are many stylish options available. Choose a stacked heel over a stiletto (a very thin heel like a pencil) to give your body a wider base of support.

If the long-legged look is what you crave, it's healthier to shorten your skirt and wear matching hose with lower shoes, all in the same color. These tricks will elongate your form and make you appear slimmer and taller.

Throwing Shade

Alvin Bell's advice on why we should always keep extra sunglasses in our desk at the office: "You never know when you'll need a pair. One, your boss might yell at you. Two, it's six-thirty P.M. and your boyfriend didn't show up for your date. Three, your ex-husband calls to say the check is not in the mail."

No woman should be without a pair of sunglasses. I love racer-style glasses, inspired by racing car drivers and skiers. They wrap around the eyes and project a sleek, modern look. Speng-type glasses—wire frames with small round lenses—will make you look cool, intellectual, and slightly androgynous. These frames suit a small face. If you have a broad or fleshy face, thick, wide-rimmed glasses will flatter you. Think Jackie Kennedy Onassis, who always adorned her wide face with big, round chic shades. Black sunglasses are standard and work for every complexion. But brown frames with brown lenses look great, and matte silver frames with black lenses, or black frames with navy or purple lenses are divine. Brightly colored frames look cheap—they merely keep the sun out of your eyes, when they could do so much more.

TEN ACCESSORY RULES TO LIVE BY

1. Use accessories to update your wardrobe.
2. Always have a scarf and a pair of sunglasses in your office drawer for emergencies.
3. Use earrings and scarves to draw attention to your face.
4. Sometimes one big, bold ring is all you need.
5. Match the scale of jewelry you're wearing—Don't wear delicate earrings with a big, rugged bracelet.

6. You can pile it on, but choose one focal point like necklaces or bracelets.
7. When you pile it on, keep your clothes simple.
8. Remember that bold buttons function like jewelry.
9. Let your hat frame your face but not obscure it.
10. When it comes to gifts, you're allergic to fake diamonds, fake pearls, and gold plate.

Multicolored Senegalese straw bracelets

Lingerie: Creating Style from the Inside Out (Plus Rules for Buying Flattering Swimwear)

Lingerie has evolved from body protector and shaper to a source of sensual pleasure for women. What's most important about lingerie, however, is comfort. Let's face it: Great style doesn't always mean maximum comfort. Who among us has not worn shoes that pinched our pinkie toes, a bra that cut too deep, or braids that were killing us, all in the name of looking good? For awhile the physical pain is numbed by the rush of adrenaline we get from feeling that we look our best. But this should be an occasional lunacy. Discomfort is impractical when you need to concentrate and be in top form. Thank goodness, the days are long gone when a woman could be lashed so tightly into her corset she would need the smelling salts.

Choose lingerie with three purposes in mind: (1) to mold and enhance your body; (2) to help clothes fit their best; (3) to provide sensual pleasure. Purchasing beautiful lingerie is a treat to yourself and a means of privately expressing your individualism and sexuality.

The field of lingerie has grown exponentially in recent years. Sales of brassieres alone totaled more than three billion dollars in 1996. The fitness boom and Madonna's conical bra, designed by Jean Paul Gaultier, have helped women become more aware of lingerie. Several top designers—including Donna Karan, Valentino, and Bill Blass—design lingerie collections, and sales of control garments have taken off. We all want to be a little slimmer and a little shapelier. The addition of fibers like spandex, which adds stretch, and Coolmax, which helps keep moisture away from the body, have expanded the range of comfortable underwear.

Your innerwear wardrobe falls into two categories: (1) your basic panties and bras; (2) control garments. Naturally, your foremost needs are in the first area.

Panties

For a smooth fit under trousers and revealing skirts or dresses, choose seamless full panties with flat waistbands and legbands. Bras and panties made of microfiber give a smooth finish, and they feel great against the skin.

Many models on the job wear thongs to avoid panty lines if they have to go down the runway in tight-fitting or transparent clothes. For most women, however, thongs may not be the most comfortable option.

Bras

A good, comfortable fit is essential when selecting a bra. Victoria's Secret has a new bra called Perfect Silhouette that it claims molds to the size and shape of your breasts after you've worn and laundered it a few times. Many stores will now allow you to try before you buy. A few have professionals, called cotiseries, who will help you fit a bra. Among them are Bloomingdale's, Terminal Lingerie in Jamaica, New York; Sara's Lingerie in Ancien, California; and Ripplu in New York City.

A bra should lift your breasts up, contain your entire breast in the bra cup, and feel so comfortable that you forget you're wearing it. A well-fitted bra not only makes you feel great but ensures that your clothes fit better. Sweaters lie more naturally, and blouses and jackets have a smoother fit. The new sports bras are good bets for seamless support under sweaters. They are generally more comfortable than traditional bras because they have wider straps and feel less rigid under the breast. Skip the cotton bras with the matching panties—these are generally no more than cropped merinos and provide little support, even for an A cup.

If you have a small bust, you can wear a wider range of clothes more easily than your larger sisters. But we sometimes want to augment what nature has given us. A padded bra can round you out under a sweater, and increase your bust size from 34B to 36C. Inspired by the demands of women who have had to undergo mastectomies, several lingerie companies have begun to manufacture bra inserts, or explants, as they are sometimes called. Made from silicone, they slip into your bra to give natural-looking added fullness. Curves, a line of breast enhancers produced by Bodylines, now offers brown-toned Mocha Curves for black women. Breast inserts are expensive, though. They cost between one hundred and two hundred dollars.

Black is still the best color if you're

concerned that your underwear might show through—it disappears under semi-transparent clothing. Skin-toned lingerie is better for completely see-through clothes. Big stores like Saks Fifth Avenue and Caldor and large brands like Calvin Klein and Warners are great sources for purchasing brown underwear that matches our complexions.

Shapers

Control lingerie has grown with advances in fabric technology and the needs of millions of body-conscious babyboomers reaching middle age. Just as the demand for plastic surgery has increased, so has the demand for this type of bloodless plastic surgery. You'll want to take advantage of what's available, but the range of products and the names can make a woman's head spin: Smoothie's Tummy Terminator, Nancy Ganz's Bodyslimmer, Donna Karan's control hosiery, Va Bien's La Fanny Fabulous are just a few of the great products on the market. The following list will help you sort out what to expect when you go shopping:

YOUR BODY SHAPER DICTIONARY

Control briefs or panty girdles: A painless alternative to liposuction, these undergarments can make your hips look smaller.

Braslips or control slips: These full and half slips have built-in bras. They create a smooth line if you are wearing a clingy dress. Many control slips come with a built-in panty for further control, eliminating the problem of panty lines.

Bodyshaping unitards or all-in-ones: For some women these may be preferable to control slips, which sometimes ride up the leg.

Unitards and bodysuits: Be careful not to confuse these with body shapers, which may look the same. Unitards offer coverage under diaphanous dresses or skirts, much like your everyday slip, but they do not provide control. Make sure that you are getting what you need.

Control-top hose: These lifesavers slim and shape the tummy and thighs. But shop around—some of them are so tight you'll feel like you're wearing jaws of steel.

Merry Widow: Around for at least as long as the corset, this item is most useful for shaping the torso. It is traditionally made from lacy fabrics.

Longline bras and bustiers: These shapers extend from chest to navel and offer control for jiggly breasts as well as puffy stomachs.

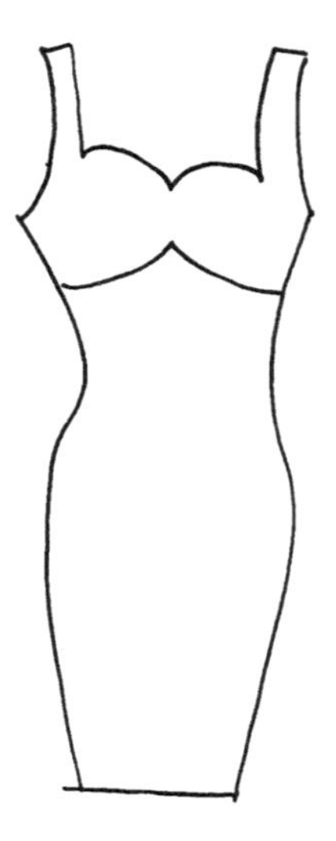

Braslip or Hipslip

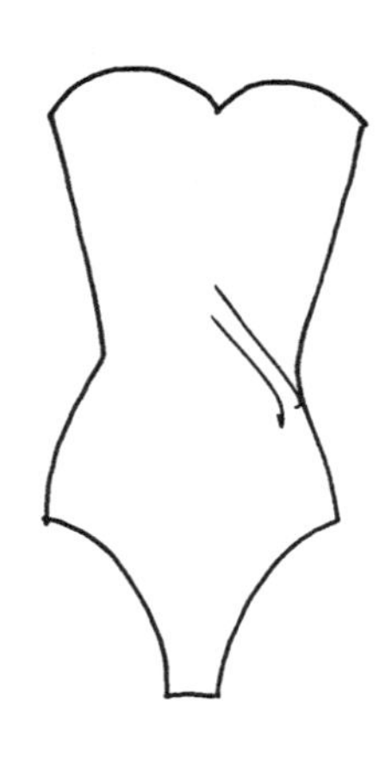

Merry Widow

Longline bustier

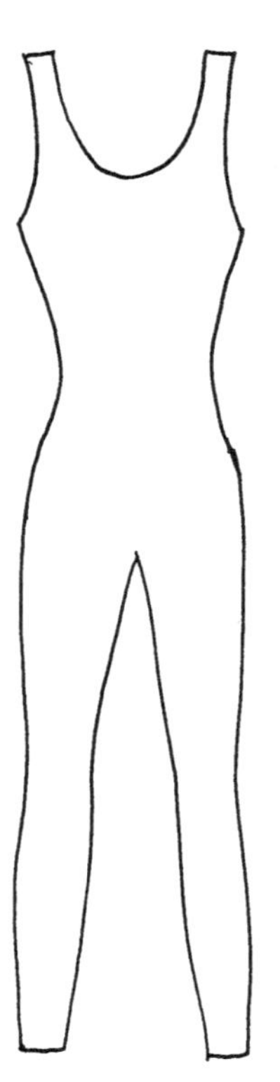

Unitard

Mold your body with lingerie.

Taking It to the Street

The innerwear-as-outerwear trend is part of a larger movement toward more casual dress. Some styles are especially attractive on younger women or those who are in great physical shape. There is, however, lingerie for the street that can be worn on all types of bodies. Don't think of it as lingerie. It's a modern, stylish way to dress that will look great on you and, in the process, save you money.

Shop the lingerie departments for street clothes and beat the high prices you'd have to pay for a similar garment in the ready-to-wear department. In lingerie, you can find clothes suitable for a party or hanging out, and with prestigious labels. Donna Karan has an extensive sleepwear line, with slipdresses and lounging pants that range in price from one hundred to a few hundred dollars. You can wear these clothes anywhere. Donna's regular dresses and pants would run you several hundred dollars more. Valentino Intimates always has fabulous little lace slips and nighties. Buy one, and you have a sexy Valentino dress for a couple of hundred dollars instead of a couple of thousand. A Calvin Klein heather cotton slipdress from his innerwear collection costs under a hundred dollars. Try buying a Calvin Klein ready-to-wear dress and be ready to write a check with three zeros.

A black bra under a white mesh T-shirt

A QUICKIE LINGERIE STYLE GUIDE

- If you're wearing innerwear as outerwear, make sure it looks deliberate—for example, wear brightly colored underwear under a completely see-through T-shirt.
- Keep bra straps in place under a bare evening dress with double-sided sticky tape, available at the drugstore or office supply store.
- Look for the appropriate bra for today's simple, bare evening wear. Halter bras, one-strap bras, and strapless bras are excellent options.
- Instead of wearing hose and a tummy controller, buy hose with built-in thigh and tummy control, like those from Donna Karan, or Wolford.
- Care for lingerie by hand washing it in Woolite or dishwashing liquid. Or put delicate items in a lingerie bag before tossing them into the washing machine. Your underwear will last longer. Air dry it—heat from the dryer can damage delicate items.
- Avoid looking trashy—finish lingerie looks with delicate jewelry or one bold piece.

or a fucshia bra under a lime yellow T-shirt with blue jeans is racy and fun. Put a lace-bordered slip under a cardigan and add flat or high-heeled sandals for a modern, feminine look.

Prowl lingerie boutiques for great buys in:

- Stretch satin T-shirts
- Silk lounging pants
- Silk nighties—short and long—that double as slipdresses
- Satin or velvet smoking jackets that can be worn as chic evening jackets over a sheath gown or long skirt

Choosing a Swimsuit

Many of the fabrics that have made lingerie so much fun have come out of the swimsuit arena. Today swimsuits come with built-in underwear, which means a more flattering silhouette and more comfortable fit.

Don't expect to look your best in a swimsuit if you don't put any thought into shopping for a swimsuit. Before you buy, decide what feature you want to draw attention to and what you want to play down. Do you want to show your great cleavage? Take the emphasis off your thighs? Draw attention to your beautiful skin tone? Hide or show off a stomach? There are swimsuits on the market that can help you accomplish all this. They don't provide miracles, but they are helpful in fooling the eye.

Don't base your decision about a swimsuit on your old one, though it may be just fine. Strip down and make your assessment. Then try on some swimsuits at a store. Start by trying on suits a size larger than your regular clothing size. A suit that fits properly should not ride up the crotch. You should be able to easily slide your fingers under the straps and your breasts should not spill out of the sides of the straps.

There are two basic types of swimsuit: two-piece and one-piece, also called maillots (pronounced my-ohs). There is also something called a monokini, which is a one-piece swimsuit with thin bands of fabric joining its bra to its brief portion.

A bikini or a monokini are both great options if you have an extremely curvy figure. String bikinis—they fasten with strings around the neck and on either side of the brief—are sexy and revealing. If, however, you plan to dive, swim in choppy waters, or horse around, you could emerge from the water minus your suit. Save the string bikini for when you're sunbathing or just taking a languid dip in the pool. The latest avant-garde style in two-piece swimsuits is the boy-cut brief, a bottom that is cut straight across like Daisy Dukes shorts or a boy's brief. It's a great stylish look for a young angular body or for women who want coverage over hips and tummy but still want a two-piece.

If you want to minimize breast size or cover scars on the chest, look for suits with a high neckline. Halters or racer-back swimsuits often have a high neck in front, which lengthens the torso and covers up cleavage.

Check out one-piece suits with built-in bras for control and coverage. One-piece suits are a smart choice for large women. Maillots (and two-piece suits with high-waist briefs) can flatten the stomach using a tummy-control panel, which works like a girdle. Many swimsuit manufacturers, including Gottex, Jantzen, Oscar de la Renta, and Anne Cole offer pretty suits with this feature. You can also minimize a belly of jelly with a swimsuit that features shirring—tiny pleats—across the stomach.

Want to hide your thighs or skip the bikini wax? There are two stylish options: a boy-cut suit or a bathing dress—a one-piece suit with a little skirt attached that will not impede recreational swimming. Adrienne Vittadini makes some adorable ones. She also designs some 1940s and 1950s-style maillots that are cut below the hipbone. For women who like and can wear a leggier look, most swimsuits today are cut Brazilian style, that is, high on the thigh—in some cases above the hipbone.

One of the best things to happen in swimwear recently is that more companies are allowing women to buy their swimsuit tops and bottoms separately. Land's End, the Gap, Victoria's Secret, and Spiegel are among these companies. None of us are built symmetrically, and in a bathing suit it becomes more apparent. You may have a 38CC bust and size 10 hips.

Swimsuit manufacturers have also recently started to attach a tag to swimwear to tell you how it's designed to shape your body. If it is labeled (1), it means it has a built-in bust minimizer. If it's labeled (2), it will enhance your bust size.

Water Colors

There are colors you can wear in swimsuits that you might not wear on a daily basis. Dark-skinned women look fabulous on the beach in hot pink or white—and there's no need to shy away from white in swimsuits anymore. With the advances in fabric technology, you can find white suits manufactured by companies like Gottex that do not suddenly become transparent when you go for a dip. In addition, many white swimsuits are now lined. Shop carefully.

Hot pink, orange, or orange red are also smart choices if you have a golden bronze complexion. The effect of the sunlight hitting your skin and setting these colors aflame is unbeatable.

If you are light-skinned and stay that way even in the sun, hot shades will make you look washed out. In general, avoid intense shades. Instead, wear black, which can be a very sultry look in a swimsuit. Cooler shades like lavender, pale yellow, light blue, or seafoam green will look pretty on you. And dare to experiment with neutrals, like beige, champagne, and light mocha brown. They're unusual and very sexy. There are a lot of metallic swimsuits coming out now, but be careful—for the most part, if you're over twenty-one, you should pass on them. They tend to look tacky on everybody but teenagers.

Prints in swimsuits should be small. Big suit, big flowers, big woman: I don't think so. Tiny floral prints, abstract African prints, and small ginghams work well. Leopard prints are wildly exotic on any shade of skin—just choose the intensities of color that work best for your complexion. (An all-over leopard or animal print is too wild if you are size 16 or over. If you love the look, find a suit that uses an animal print as a trim. If you're dark brown, choose a leopard or tiger pattern with more beige and white than black and brown, and if you have a light complexion, do the reverse.

I love hardware on swimsuits—little silver or gold metal rings, called grommets, or a small gold-colored clasp at the hips or joining the breast yoke of a bikini. Recently, Hermes showed a collection of fashionable, sleek swimsuits with small gold and leather buckles.

The stylish swimmer or sunbather always has a cover-up handy. Most designers create matching cover-ups—little skirts, shirts, or robes. You can also make your own to go over your swimsuit. A couple of years ago Gottex introduced one collection of swimwear inspired by Josephine Baker and another inspired by Egyptian culture. Generally, though, it is hard to find swimsuits incorporating African or African-American motifs. Cover-ups offer a great opportunity to express African-influenced style.

TO TIE A PAREO

Stand with your feet about twelve inches apart. Hold one end of the fabric in each hand at waist height, with the opening to the front. Bring your left hand to your right side, wrapping the fabric tight over your tummy and toward your back. Now do the same with your other hand, making sure that the first wrap is one or two inches above the second. Tuck the end of the fabric down into your waist. (If you've attached strings, wrap them around your waist and tie them securely in a little knot or bow.) You can also just tie your pareo to one side like an African buba.

Lengths of African tie-dyed fabric or waxed prints make beautiful pareos (skirts that are wrapped and tied). To create a pareo, choose enough fabric, about two yards, to wrap around your body once with an overlap of at least six inches. For a halter wrap, measure at least three yards. Choose a print that picks up a color in your swimsuit. Your final outfit will look more pulled together and fashionable. You might also attach two strings, each twelve inches long and made from the same material, to either end of the fabric. This will help you tie your pareo more securely if you are going to wear it off the beach, say to go shopping or to a poolside cocktail party.

In tropical places temperatures drop at night, and you may require more coverage. A slim caftan is an elegant choice for poolside cocktails or après swim. Even in the evenings, it's quite acceptable to have your swimsuit show through if your caftan is made from semitransparent material. The top piece of a buba, which is often made from a diaphanous, lightweight cotton, makes a beautiful caftan. For daytime parties, a terrycloth dress over a terrycloth swimsuit is an adorable combination for a woman of any age.

TO TIE A HALTER COVER-UP

Hold square of fabric behind your back, above your breasts. Cross the two ends of the fabric over your chest and tie in a small neat knot behind your neck. There will be an opening down the front.

Getting Married—African Style

Weddings in the United States and throughout the Diaspora are joyous events filled with pomp and grandeur. A wedding is a special affair for the bride, groom, and extended family, and every couple wants to make their day as memorable as possible. There are two ways to do this—by adding stylish touches or sentimental ones.

A wedding with an African spirit can be both stylish and sentimental. The African touches can be expressed in the clothing of the wedding party, in décor, or in ritual. The wedding can be authentically African or just vaguely Afrocentric.

Dressing up

When the designer Lady Mitz returned home to Nigeria to marry, the whole village got involved in the celebration. For the first half of the wedding, she wore a white buba and a spectacular white headdress that fanned out like bird's wings and was trimmed with gold. Her husband wore a handsome calf-length buba of deep indigo.

A buba or djellaba in rich, white cut lace or a colorful aso oke makes a beautiful wedding dress. Replace the traditional trousers of the man's buba with a skirt of the same matching fabric as the top of the buba or a different dressy fabric like silk georgette. Make a soulful wedding gown by rendering a fit-and-flare ballgown shape in a beautiful African waxed print. Guinea brocade, lace, or gold-threaded aso oke are popular fabrics for African-inspired wedding dresses. Gold and white are traditionally used in Nigerian and East African weddings. Once you select a fabric, you can have it made in any shape you desire.

A traditional Ethiopian dress, a Yabesha Kemis, makes a simple, romantic wedding gown. The white dress is embroidered around the hem, zips up the back, and has an elasticized waist. It is traditionally worn with a matching shawl. You might put the shawl over your head or rest it on your shoulders.

As a bride, focus on enhancing your best features. Don't do a Dr. Jekyll and Mr. Hyde on your wedding day and suddenly try to totally change your look. If you tend toward a clean, minimal style, don't go baroque and pile on layers of tulle, lace, and beading.

Wedding gowns can be divided into two basic shapes—the columnar sheath and the full-skirted dress. The sheath will give you a modern, sleek look. A big-skirted gown is more traditional and romantic. Whatever direction you choose, make sure the interest is around your neckline. A bare neckline, a high neck, or a decorative detail like beading or embroidery can draw the eye to where it should be—on your face. Think about the rear view, too—brides show a lot of their back while exchanging vows, and you want to look beautiful from every angle. A bridal gown with a long train, a kick pleat, or a godet with a lace inset is appealing.

Fashions in wedding dresses change slowly. Don't let that scare you out of being adventurous. Most brides marry in white, but in reality almost any color is acceptable for a wedding dress. Pastels are prettiest for Western-style gowns. Ivory, off-white, champagne, cream, and antique yellow are all popular colors that flatter dark complexions. A gown with a high neckline, huge puff sleeves, and full skirt looks old-fashioned. Show some skin around the neckline, or have your arms in short sleeves. A slim gown lends itself to a slit up the leg. The question is—demure or daring? If you want to be demure, show a little leg up to the knee; to be daring, take it all the way up your thigh.

If your wedding is a Miss Diahann Carroll affair—you're getting married for the second, third, or fourth time—a curvaceous fitted suit in white, ivory, or even red satin is perfect. The skirt can be just above the knee or to the ankle. Finish with a turban, a kofi or a brimmed hat.

If you're expecting a little one, princess or empire gowns that are fitted over the bust and then loose below are best. Tracy Reese designed an African-inspired white silk apron to go over the wedding dress of a very pregnant Margot T. Lewis, a New York special events planner, a few years ago. The gown's creator, bridal-wear designer Christopher Hunte, took inspiration from a Valentino dress, at Margot's request.

An African hairstyle is a refreshing way to incorporate part of your heritage into your wedding and give yourself a regal air. Create an upswept hairstyle with goddess braids or twisted Senegalese braids. Dot your hair with a spray of fresh white flowers, pearls, or gold balls. Combine a traditional African gown with a Western-style headdress like a tiara or veil. An African-inspired headpiece or hairstyle can be the compromise that heals a wound between daughter and mother over what to wear. (Try telling her it's not her wedding!)

Designer Therez Fleetwood, who designs African-American and Anglo-American gowns for regular and plus sizes, says: "The mothers come in, particularly from the South and the West Indies. They say, 'I'm not no African.' It's very generational. For some of the younger folks, black consciousness is at the forefront of our minds now, but some of our parents equate African style with something negative. The mothers sit there mumbling, but eventually they come around."

Even if the bride opts for a Western-looking gown, the groom or bridesmaids can still adopt elements of African-American culture. The bridesmaids' clothes need not bear any relation to the bride's dress, and today women in the wedding party welcome a dress that can be worn again. For your bridesmaids, have a seamstress make a short halter dress in a pretty navy, sky blue, and black waxed print, which can be worn with a jacket of transparent navy chiffon or organza. The effect is simple and discreet yet elegant. Here's another popular idea: a short or long sleeveless sheath in blue cotton sateen or satin—or you might ask each bridesmaid to wear her favorite color—with an ankle-length apron skirt, with a slit up the side, to go over it. Have the bridesmaids sew blue and gold beads into their hair, which they can wear in a chic, upswept style.

For a morning wedding or small affair, bridesmaids can wear a long, solid-color jacket paired with an ankle-length wrap made from an African textile. Each bridesmaid can choose her own print. Give each bridesmaid a small bouquet of bright multicolored flowers that picks up some of the colors in her wrap skirt.

A buba of rich Guinea brocade makes a beautiful dress for the mother of the bride. She might also wear a simply styled jacket and ankle-length skirt, a broad-brimmed hat, and an African-style choker or waxed-print scarf that wraps around her neck.

If you or anyone in your party is wearing a wrap and is not an expert wrapper, consider cheating a bit by stitching the skirt to hold it firmly in place. If you live in a large city, you might want to hire an African woman who is experienced with wraps to help you get dressed on the big day.

Don't wear a lot of jewelry on your wedding day. A head wrap or headdress

African-inspired satin and organza gown with gold African embroidery for the bride and Afrocentric pants suit for the groom from Nigerian Fabrics and Fashion.

of any kind can balance large earrings, though smaller pieces work better. A simple dress will offset a bold necklace, but generally wedding gowns look best with thin, delicate necklaces. Bracelets are always distracting.

Put the emphasis on your hair and makeup. Makeup should be applied lightly or at least look that way. Use an oil-free moisturizer, foundation, and powder; powder foundation will give your makeup staying power. Don't hesitate to powder your nose before you enter the church and before taking photographs—these pictures are forever.

I asked Harriette Cole, author of *Jumping the Broom: The African-American Wedding Planner*, for some further valuable tips for the prospective bride.

- Make sure you have your final fitting several days in advance of the wedding date to allow enough time for necessary alterations.
- The wedding day is always long. Have a bridesmaid or maid of honor keep a comfortable pair of shoes ready for you to change into after the ceremony.
- African doesn't mean you have to conjure up images of ancient African history or slavery. It can mean copying a wedding dress worn by an elder in your family or wearing bright colors from the Caribbean. Examine which aspects of your cultural heritage are important to you when you begin planning your wedding.

The Groom

The groom will cut a handsome figure in a traditional black tuxedo worn with a royal kente-cloth bow tie and matching cummerbund. He can also opt for a more informal look, which might include a tunic shirt with a Nehru collar, matching pants, and a band of aso oke fabric draped around his neck like an untied necktie.

A djellaba makes a fantastic wedding outfit for the groom at the ceremony or at the reception. (If you really want to make your wedding memorable, you and your groom can wear matching bubas: you in the female version and he in the male.)

The groom and best man can wear matching waistcoats of batik, kente, or other African fabrics. The same principle can be applied to the ring bearer—the print need not be exactly the same, but it should be clear he is mimicking his elder, the groom.

A tuxedo over a kente vest is great. Use a collarless tuxedo, or one with a Nehru collar, for an avant-garde effect.

Décor

It gets hot in church, so give guests fans covered with inexpensive kente cloth as they enter the house of worship, or place one on each guest's seat. This is a sentimental reminder of your African heritage and a useful keepsake from your wedding.

Decorate the pews with exuberant sprays of flowers tied with strips of kente or with ribbons of red, green, and yellow. At the altar or in the reception area, arrange a cluster of African sculptures—if you don't have your own, borrow some from a friend or request them as wedding gifts.

Drape tables in inexpensive African prints or layer them with imitation waxed prints and solid-color toppers. Centerpieces can be inspired by any African motif—tiny sculptures, a bunch of tiny brooms made with sticks and straw and painted gold, or a little book saying what getting married means to you. Do some research and use your imagination—there are many possibilities.

Ritual

At Lady Mitz's wedding, guests threw money at the bride and groom, tucking dollar bills into their clothes and trying to stick it onto their foreheads as the couple moved through the crowd of well-wishers. How come no one told me about that ritual when I got married?

In some African tribes, guests are adorned with beads provided by the bride and groom; the beads show that each guest is part of the celebration. Then there's the tradition of jumping the broom, in which couples actually leap over a broom after exchanging vows. It is not clear if this folkway was actually brought over from Africa or was a creative innovation of our slave ancestors, who were often denied the right to be married legally or by the church.

Star of the Show

As you make your decisions about what to wear, your hair, and your makeup, remember that your wedding is one big drama, and you're the director—and the star. Start organizing months or a year ahead, giving yourself enough time to make your wedding exactly the way you want it at the lowest possible cost. Be sure to ask for and get help from your mother, your fiancé, girlfriends, or a professional wedding planner. Even the simplest wedding can be a pretty complicated affair. Good planning will help you to be more relaxed on your wedding day.

Champagne silk and cowrie shells in African-inspired motif wedding gown by Therez Fleetwood.

10

Fast and Fabulous Hair and Makeup

A great hairstyle and a healthy complexion can go a long way toward looking great. Invest in a good haircut, and take care of your skin. African-American women may have inherited their attitudes toward hair from their African sisters; in Africa, hair is treated with loving attention. Women think nothing of spending several hours creating spectacular coiffures, incorporating human hair or synthetic hair extensions to achieve the desired effect.

Senegalese hair-braiding shops have become a familiar part of our urban landscape, as more Africans from Senegal, the Ivory Coast, Nigeria, and Ghana have immigrated to the United States in the last few years. When these stores began mushrooming a few years ago, they allowed American women to make the next step in braids beyond the cornrows (or canerows, as they are also called in the Caribbean) of the 1960s and 1970s. Staffed by women who are often supervised by a man, the shops offer intricate braided hairstyles, one more fantastic than the next. Braids not only reflect black women's pride in their culture but offer the convenience of a hairstyle that can remain in place for several weeks. Among the popular styles are goddess braids—thick, raised braids, usually about an inch wide, that coil around the head and end with a knot on the crown. Senegalese twists resemble taut drop curls. For box braids, the hair is parted into tiny squares and plaited. Microbraids, tiny braids no bigger than a string, can be done by anyone with the time and patience. If you add strands of extra hair, the plaits will stay neater for a longer period. There are many variations of the basic cornrow, in which hair is plaited flat against the scalp in narrow or wide bands. Some of the cornrows done by the Senegalese are remarkable, and the result can truly be called a work of art. These styles, which cost between fifty and one hundred and fifty dollars and take several hours to execute, are widely popular.

Some women who would love to go natural are reluctant because they are afraid it will convey a negative image at work, says Diane DaCosta, a natural hair specialist who owns Dyaspora Salon and Day Spa in New York. "A lot of women tell me that. I tell them it's OK to go natural. What's important is to take proper care of your hair."

Diane recommends a conditioner once a week and a warm oil treatment at home or in a salon once a month.

To maintain your hairstyle and minimize damaging split ends, short hair should be trimmed every two or three weeks. If your hair is longer, cut it every two to three months. Braided hairstyles can be quite flamboyant, but it's best to choose a more conservative style if you are an executive or work in a conservative office. Opt for styles close to the head, preferably off your face, and shoulder-length or shorter. The braided bob worn by Erika Alexander, who plays Max on the television program *Living Single*, gets my vote as a great look for work.

Adornment of the hair is an important part of African culture, but on the job,

BRAID CARE

To keep braids neat and scalp healthy, oil between your braids at least every other day. Black women's hair tends to dry out, especially in the winter, so a regular routine of moisturizing the scalp with a hair pomade or oil is a good idea, whatever your hairstyle. Use a light lubricant like baby oil, olive oil, or bergamot. Gently oil between the braids, being careful not to disturb the hair. Tie your head with a light scarf at night to maintain neatness. To cleanse the scalp between salon visits, wear a stocking cap made from old pantyhose and wash your head under a gentle shower stream, applying shampoo and water with the stocking in place. Blow the hair dry. This procedure allows you to wash your hair and still keep your braids. You can also wash your braids without the stocking cap—but recognize that there will be some displacement, and you might have to remove your braids a little sooner.

An alternative is dry cleaning. Mix about two ounces of alcohol with four ounces of witch hazel. Dip two cotton balls in the solution, squeeze them out, and wipe your scalp between the braids and around your hairline from front to back. Repeat the process with fresh cotton balls until done. Allow your scalp to dry out, or use a hair dryer to speed up the process. This routine can be done once a week to freshen up and keep oil and residue to a minimum. Synthetic braids should stay neat 6 to 8 weeks, said Diane DaCosta, longer than natural braids. It's also a good idea to have your braids professionally washed and steamed every two weeks.

keep the hair accessories low-key. Small beads, cowrie shells, or gold balls are attractive options. On weekends and festive occasions you can be more creative. If you're getting your hair done with lots of decoration, which you will want to remove for Monday morning, be sure to let your hairdresser know. She can attach adornments so that they can be easily snipped off, leaving braids intact.

Ideas for African-inspired hair adornments include coins, cowrie shells, colored or metallic beads, semiprecious beads, like those made from crystal, for special occasions, and colored ribbons or string—to wrap braids.

Natural Style

Your best bet for a natural cut may be your barber. Since more women process their hair than wear it natural, fewer black hairstylists are adept at cutting fades or close-cropped naturals. Short hairstyles for natural hair include a Makeba—shaved close over the entire head—and the fade, where the hair is cut angularly into varying heights. You need not have a small face to wear your hair short.

Afros are making a mini comeback. For the nineties version, wear your hair three to five inches long and slightly uneven. Plait moist hair the night before, then moisten it again in the morning with water or moisturizer before fluffing hair out with a pick or wide-toothed comb. The point is to keep some waves. This is not the high, sculpted Afro from back in the day.

For variety, pull your Afro back with a two-inch-wide hairband made of plain fabric or an African print. Since black hair tends to be springy, use a band that ties, so you can tighten it as needed to keep your hair back.

I've used a ton of concoctions on my natural hair. Like many women, I'm constantly trying new beauty products. One of the best I've sampled recently is Wella's Liquid Hair Polish. Glycerin-based products, like those designed for curly perms (don't make me say Jherri curls) are also good for moisturizing natural hair. Gels work to sculpt not only chemically straightened heads but also low Afros. Be careful, though, they are drying. Liv, that old standby in the red-and-white jar, is great for moisturizing all types of African hair, permed or natural.

Locks require a lot of moisture and products that won't stick to the hair. Apply light oil—baby oil, jojoba, and olive oil are all fine—to your scalp and hair. Work it through the hair. Once a month, warm the oil and coat your scalp and locks, leave it on for an hour or overnight, and shampoo twice. Locks pick up dust easily, so always remove any fluff clinging to your hair at least once a week.

Chinese bumps are a cute hairstyle for young women, and they are a good overnight set for an Afro. Mothers often put bumps or plaits in their daughters' hair as an at-home style for casual days. The growing popularity of "chini bumps" for street style is typical of how blacks have often taken the humble tools of everyday life and made them into something stylish or exotic. Locks and braids are ideal for fast-paced lives. They help you get out of the house quickly, because they don't require much care and styling once they are set.

Straightened Hair

Chemically or mechanically straightened hair is, in essence, hair that has been weakened, and it should be maintained properly—as should bleached or colored hair.

Black hairstyles of the 1990s are strongly influenced by the street—the hip-hop and ragamuffin styles—for example, the three-hairstyles-in-one look: bangs, kiss curls, fingerwaves, and a fade all in one head. More power to you. Whatever your style preference, a program of care and styling for your hair is essential to looking polished.

"It's so kinky, it's so nappy, all that negative stuff is because we view our hair as a problem; we don't know how to take care of our hair," says Leslie Louard-Davis, owner of Supreme Satisfaction in Hempstead, New York. "We shouldn't be too busy to take care of ourselves. One difference I've seen between black women and white women is that white women will go every week or couple of weeks and take care of their hair, especially in corporate America. Black women will wait till the last minute to come in for a touch-up."

Leslie recommends visiting your hairdresser every one or two weeks. In between visits, wash and condition your hair at least once a week, and treat it with extra virgin olive oil. Choose products with a water-soluble base rather than a grease base, she says; she suggests Sebastian products and Nexus Therapy shampoo or Humectres conditioner.

I still have mixed feelings about weaving but I have had to step back from my strongly held position against it. I know too many together sisters who are proud and comfortable with the African in them, who straighten their hair and artificially lengthen it.

If you are putting a weave in, invest in having it done properly. Your stylist shouldn't be putting Crazy glue in your hair—which happened to Naomi Campbell when she first started wearing weaves years ago. Today, Campbell says that weaving, when done professionally, helps to protect her hair from all the abuse it gets on the job.

Here are two chic styles for permed, textured, or natural hair that you can do easily when you haven't had time to visit your hairdresser.

For longer hair, make a French braid. Brush your hair back, making it as smooth as possible around the hairline. Working from the front, gather up three clumps of hair—you're about to plait your hair. Now begin plaiting down the center of your head, adding lengths of hair as you work your way down to the nape of the neck. Tuck the end of the plait under at the nape of your neck and brush up any loose strands along the sides.

For short or medium-length hair, part the hair into small sections, add gel to each little square of hair, and comb it through. Roll each section of hair tightly between your fingers. The result will be a head of small drop curls that lie close to the head.

Facing Yourself

Skin Care

The most important thing to remember about your skin is that it is sensitive and tends to spot and scar easily. The basics of skin care involve cleansing and protection. Cleanse your skin twice daily. Dermatologists recommend a superfatted soap like Dove, Neutrogena, or especially formulated face washes. Regular bath soap, they say, is too harsh and dries out facial skin.

Steam your face once a week or once a month for about fifteen minutes: Lie down and cover your face with towels warmed in the oven or dunked in hot water and wrung out. You can also fill a basin with steaming water (add some chamomile tea bags, or peppermint or lavender if you like), cover your head with a towel, and let the steam open and clean your pores for about ten minutes. Don't hold your face too close to the water. Steam can burn.

It's a myth that all black skin is oily. It can be both oily and dry. Whatever your skin type, use a moisturizer.

A cool matte look has often been coveted by blacks. Shine, I think, was subliminally associated with sweating and working in the fields. A cool skin tone was more often found among house servants or, better yet, the masters' wife—considered the epitome of beauty. A more modern approach is for us to accept that moist, glowing brown skin can look sexy and attractive, too. It can be enhanced with some natural-colored lip gloss and highlights around the eyes.

Not all cosmetics that are suitable for white skin are useful if you're a black woman. Try a product before making an investment. And, of course, don't assume a product will do exactly what it says.

Makeup

Use makeup to enliven your face and protect your skin. Cosmetics now claim to have environmental protection features, but even the most rudimentary face powder provides some defense against grime and weather conditions.

Black women have a hard time finding the right foundations for their skin tones, since our complexions vary so widely. However, the situation has improved in the last few years. There are now some cosmetic lines created with black women in mind (see the Resource Directory) and others with a wider range of colors that cater to African Americans, Asians, and Latinas as well as Caucasians.

Makeup for black women should have a yellow rather than a pink base. Pink used to be the basis of most, but now cosmetic manufacturers realize that yellow-based colors look more natural on most complexions. According to makeup artist Lanier Long, who works with celebrities such as M.C. Lyte, Aretha Franklin, and Connie Chung, a lot of products being offered for black women are formulated for white skin and then darkened. As a result, they leave the skin looking ashy. Iman, MAC, and Black Opal are three of the lines he prefers. "I don't think that dark-skinned women put enough time and effort into developing their look," says Long. "It's hard to find just the right colors. Often it's necessary to mix two or three together."

If you want to always look your best, have a few makeup tricks ready in your bag. You can do a lot with the following:

Powder compact with a mirror
Lip liner
Lipstick or lip moisturizer
Hand cream

Keep at home or add as you wish mascara, foundation, eyebrow pencil, eyelash curler, eye shadow, and a manicure kit, including nail-whitening pencil and clear nail polish.

I haven't come across a lot of black women who look good in tons of makeup. Load it on when you just want to have fun for evening, but you won't necessarily be looking your best. "Overdone makeup, overdone hair, overdone clothes, we all know what that looks like," says Tadree Copage, a makeup artist who has worked for *Black Elegance, Elle*, and *Essence*. "Less makeup and softer makeup is better."

Makeup artist Lanier Long applies plenty of eyeshadow to bring out Roshumba's eyes.

Often it's hard to find the time to create perfect hair and makeup, but if we're organized and have done our homework, great style doesn't have to be time-consuming.

Hair and Makeup Fit for a Diva—In Fifteen Minutes!

I asked Leslie Louard-Davis and top makeup artist Roxanna Floyd to recommend a hair and makeup routine that is quick and guaranteed to make you look good.

Diva Hair in Ten Minutes

The easiest, most flattering style is the bob, says Leslie. A bob is a blunt cut, clipped evenly straight across the ends. It can stop just below your ear lobes or at the shoulders.

Evening: Before you go to bed, rub a light hairdressing into your hair, brush it back gently for ten seconds, and tie on a silk scarf or bonnet. Also, because cotton absorbs your hair's natural oils, says Leslie, you might want to switch from a cotton to a silk or polyester satin pillowcase.

Morning: Blow-dry your hair for a few seconds, or longer if necessary. Using a heating or curling iron, pull the iron smoothly down your hair, turning the ends inward toward your neck and chin. This softens and smoothes the hair. (You're not trying to curl your hair, so you don't have to roll the hair in the curling iron and hold it there.) You're ready to go.

Diva Makeup in Five Minutes

Roxanna travels from coast to coast for assignments that can begin early in the morning and go late into the night, so not only does she have fifteen years of experience in the makeup business but she understands the demands of a busy life. Her work has appeared in numerous magazines, including Essence, Vibe, *and* Harper's Bazaar, *as well as in films and music videos. She has worked with stars like Queen Latifah, Maya Angelou, Molly Ringwald, and Mick Jagger. Roxanna created the makeup for Whitney Houston in* The Preacher's Wife *and* Waiting to Exhale*—for which she also made up Angela Bassett.* For your quick makeover, you'll need blush, mascara, and lipstick. Use a foundation if you want to even out your complexion.

Apply a moisturizer, then your foundation. Roxanna recommends a cream-to-powder foundation, but liquid is quicker. Use a damp makeup sponge and blend lightly. Don't forget the jawline and hairline.

Apply blush or bronzing powder. Choose a shade that is close to your skin tone. Use a big, fluffy brush and dust lightly. You want to warm the cheek but not *color* it. Add a sweep to the eyelids.

Always make sure the eyebrows are well groomed. Fill in sparse brows with a pencil or brow powder. Apply eyebrow gel (clear mascara works well) to smooth unruly eyebrows and direct them into their natural arch.

Add plenty of mascara to the eyelashes to bring out your eyes. Black works for everyone.

Line the lips with pencil, then apply sheer lipstick or a clear lip gloss.

If you're going out after work or don't want to spend a lot of time on your makeup for a festive event, add shimmery or frosted color to eyelids or cheeks or paint your lips a deep ruby. Play up one feature. You can also experiment with a smoky look, using deep, rich shades of eye shadow like chocolate or blackberry. Line eyes with black eyeliner, top and bottom. Pay close attention to blending. It's the key to beautiful makeup.

Remember, makeup does not have to be applied with a dumpster to be effective. The right products, correctly applied, can go a long way to making you look beautiful. Take advantage of free demonstrations offered by salespeople; often you can pick up some tips, and you don't have to buy anything. It gives you a chance to see how different colors and ideas work with your features. The idea really is not to make up but to make better. Have fun with it.

11

Women We Love: Case Studies in Style

We all know women who are well put together. Working in the fashion industry, I'm exposed to stylish women all the time. You can always pick up tips from other women whose style you admire or who have something in common with your look.

This chapter looks at some shining examples—nine women who have developed their own great style—and offers tips we can pick up from observing them. I've chosen celebrities, because these are women we are all familiar with. Yes, they are wealthy and can afford some of the most expensive clothes, top hairstylists, and makeup artists, but being rich doesn't make it any easier for them. In fact, their wealth and prominence make it all the more difficult for them to maintain their appearance, because they are constantly in the limelight and being judged by how they look. Like we're doing now.

Oprah Winfrey

Through thick and thin, Oprah has kept the style faith; she has taken the cookie-cutter news anchor look and added flair to it by not being predictable. She is not afraid to wear vibrant colors, favoring deep shades, mostly in the jewel family, like ruby red, burgundy, and topaz.

Tailored suits and dresses are her trademark. Her look is classic and conveys power. She favors a monochromatic color scheme for her tops and bottoms and often a jacket to pull together a look.

Oprah uses jewelry well—bold earrings call attention to her face. Her makeup is always flawless, as befits someone who is

Oprah Winfrey

on television all the time. Make note of the emphasis on her eyes—she applies a lot of dark, smoky color to bring them out and make her look more energetic.

Lesson: A jacket is still the quickest, easiest way to go on a power trip. She could try a more modern look in a simple sweater and skirt or a sexy suspension dress.

Diana Ross

It's always a surprise to me when Diana Ross is not included in books or awards programs for stylish women. Few contemporary stars can match her interest in clothes and ability to put herself together. Let's forget the hair nightmare of the last few years; Diana has continued to shine as one of the most stylish women in the world for more than three decades. She has often said she did not have the best voice of the Supremes. She might have added that she was not necessarily the most statuesque—but she has certainly shown an eye for fashion.

Diana is the epitome of style, whether she is wearing a white shirt with slim black pants, her hair tied back in a chignon, and black Jackie O–style sunglasses or is making an appearance with one of her favorite designers, Thierry Mugler, in a flamboyant corset and shiny black leggings that he designed for her.

Diana's emphasis has been on European design; her look expresses the chic elegance of well-tailored clothes that do not overwhelm her small frame. She is experimental and remains contemporary by keeping up with changes in the fashion world.

Lesson: Make sure your clothes work for you. If they don't fit well, have them altered to fit your body. Diana is petîte and therefore not easy to fit, yet she is always well turned out.

Toni Braxton

Here's someone who took a leaf out of Diana Ross's book. Toni, or someone in her camp, decided that there was room for a young female singer to develop a fashion profile. Because she wears a size 2 to 4 and is not very curvy, Toni is careful about what she puts on. Her style is sexy and adventurous; she wears revealing designs that show off her well-toned physique. Her clothes are relatively simple—jeans and T-shirts, unadorned gowns—but they fit her closely or they feature flattering cutouts or transparency.

She carries the sultry look into her makeup, emphasizing her lush lips with natural browns and adding lots of eyeliner and mascara to her eyes to make them look larger and more soulful.

Lesson: You don't have to have beauty-contest measurements to be sexy. Wear clothes that fit you closely but are not

Diana Ross

tight. Choose dresses that bare your arms, legs, or back when appropriate, and keep your makeup soft, in natural colors. Avoid too much glitz in your makeup and your clothes or you'll wind up looking trashy, not sexy.

Toni Braxton

Jessye Norman

This opera star has capitalized on her strong features and ample size and made them grander. She cleverly favors clothes that skim the body, and her preference is for lustrous fabrics in Eastern shapes reminiscent of Africa or Asia. She often accessorizes with a headband pulled over her curly mane, or she covers her head with a turban. The headdresses make her appear taller and more regal. The look is classic diva, which works perfectly with her otherworldly voice and exotic features.

Lesson: You don't have to dress meekly if you're a large woman. You can put together a fabulous look that relies on your size to pull it off.

Susan Taylor

Susan's look is African-American corporate. As editor-in-chief of *Essence* magazine, she must not only project a polished image for readers but be ready for a public speaking engagement one minute and a meeting with corporate executives the next.

She wears her hair in long lustrous braids away from her face, a style that emphasizes her strong cheekbones. For

Jessye Norman

work, Susan tends to choose dark colors that travel easily, though in the warmer months she'll lighten up. She might wear a knee-length duster coat, a turtleneck, and a fitted skirt to the knee. Susan's skirts are never short, and she balances their length with chic high-heeled shoes, sometimes created by African-American designer Scott Rankin. She favors a classic fur coat to ward off winter chill.

Her outfits often include an African motif such as a cameo brooch, a scarf, or a draped and tied skirt worn under a jacket. She favors bold jewelry and small multiple rings, one of which she wears on her thumb.

Susan opts for strong makeup to emphasize her sharp features. She boldly wears bright red polish on her long, poetic fingers, creamy brown foundation, burnt red lipstick, and black eyeliner.

Lesson: Braids can be a part of a styl-

Susan Taylor

ish, corporate look. Keep them neat and relatively conservative.

Tina Turner

Designer CD Green was thrilled when Tina chose one of his dresses, a white, crystal-covered mini, to wear in her 1997 concert tour. The dress, he was told, must be fourteen inches from waist to hem. It's this kind of attention to figuring out what works best for your body that helps women like Tina consistently look their best.

Tina emphasizes her hair and her legs. Her carefully tended blond or highlighted wigs, high-heeled shoes, shirts worn over leggings, and short dresses are all designed to keep the focus on her best assets. She has a short, thick torso and beautifully shaped, feline legs. For this reason you rarely see her in a suit—it would cut her already short waist in half. Instead, she gravitates toward little trapeze dresses that skim her body and draw attention to her amazing legs.

Notice that in her performances, or in her advertisements for Hanes, she wears little shorts or minidresses. When she does cover her legs, she generally chooses leggings, so the great silhouette remains.

Tina likes to work with designers who create feminine, hip clothes, like CD and French designer Azzedine Alaïa, who also dresses Grace Jones and Naomi Campbell.

Lesson: If you are short-waisted or have a thick middle, take the emphasis off your waist with chemises, trapeze-shaped dresses and tops, tunics, and sheaths. And remember, some black women can look great as blondes.

Naomi Campbell

All the top models look fantastic in magazines, advertisements, or on the runway. Their hair and makeup is done for them by the best hands in the business, their clothes are provided by top designers, and skilled stylists put the look together before they set foot in front of the camera. Off work is another story—models become part of the regular population. Some of them have style, most don't. Naomi Campbell is an exception. She obviously really cares about looking great, and she knows a thing or two about clothes and makeup.

Her look is high-maintenance glamour puss. She has fun with fashion. Other models latched on to grunge or the dreary Salvation Army look—Naomi never fell for it. She is most often seen in tight clothes that emphasize her small frame or pretty, feminine dresses.

It's important for Naomi to be seen in the latest fashions, and she gravitates to designs by Alaïa, Tocca, Gianni Versace

Tina Turner

Naomi Campbell

and vintage clothes. She loves high-heeled shoes, even though she's close to six feet tall. We can also presume she'll soon be wearing a lot of Ralph Lauren, since she's the star of two of his spring 1997 advertising campaigns.

Naomi's hair, which she has worn short above her ears, almost to her waist, and shoulder length, is always sleekly done. She has it colored a shade or two darker than her bronze skin, highlighting her beautiful complexion. Naomi plays around with her eyes with colored contact lenses, but they are not so light that they look fake and scary. And she emphasizes her already lush lips with a lip pencil and earthy lipstick colors like cinnamon or plum.

Lesson: Nothing beats high heels for conveying glamour. To emphasize full, lush lips, first outline them with a lip pencil. My mother used to use an eyebrow pencil, and that works fine, too. Antique stores and flea markets can be a great source for unusual jackets or pretty feminine dresses.

Patti LaBelle

When you first think of LaBelle, you think of flamboyance. Although she once wore overdone, wacky clothes, these days Patti tends to dress more conservatively. In one sense, her approach to style is very Afrocentric: She wears fitted, tailored suits, then she goes all out with her hair, jewelry, and nails.

She's been a fan of Donna Karan—and Donna a fan of hers—since the designer opened her company in the late eighties. Donna creates the kind of curvaceous suits that fit Patti's body well.

Patti believes in big hair, and she's made it her signature. She's not afraid to experiment with extremes, from her famous spiked sculpture hairstyle to a relatively demure, teased coiffure.

Lesson: Develop a signature for yourself that will help you stand out. Make this signature the anchor around which you build your style, whether it's wearing a scarf or an interesting hairstyle.

Whoopi Goldberg

Whoopi gives you the feeling that she is nonchalant about her style. Don't buy it. Her style is too consistent, too unconventional, and fits her personality too well to be an accident. This is a woman fully aware of how she looks and how she wants to look.

Her relaxed, men's-style suits, jackets, and baggy pants are understated and androgynous. The idea is to make you think not man or woman but Whoopi, the person.

Whoopi balances the anonymity or understatement of her clothes with attention-getting dreadlocks and dark black-

Patti LaBelle

Whoopi Goldberg

berry-colored lipstick, a bold African-American statement.

Since she is in the performing arts, Whoopi's locks can also be read as yet another expression of her creativity. Her clever molding of a unisex but feminine, breakthrough style has doubtless helped her transcend some of the obstacles of sex, age, and race that afflict so many Hollywood actresses, particularly black women. Her style doesn't recognize boundaries, and when you consider her acting roles, you can assume that her style has helped persuade producers and casting agents not to consider boundaries for her either.

Lesson: Understated clothes can make a strong statement. Dreadlocks can be an attractive part of a creative Afrocentric style.

There are other women who can serve as style models. Young people are strongly shaped by television actors and singers. The singer Erykah Badu is developing an arresting Afrocentric style. Monica, Aaliyah, and Lauryn Hill of the Fugees are popular fashion role models. Before this, Janet Jackson and the members of TLC were setting it off with their baggy pants and overalls and skinny minitops. On television, Erika Alexander's braids and too-cool lawyerly suits have found a following.

Remember to adapt ideas to your own personality, body, and circumstances. For instance, few people in corporate America can get away with dreadlocks as long as Whoopi's, but many women are beginning to wear shorter versions to the office. And teenage role models are fine for a trendy idea here and there, but for real style you have to look to women who have staying power. How do they do it, day in, day out, year in, year out? No one has time to reinvent great style every day. After all, we have work to do.

Erykah Badu

Giving Your Man Some African Style

Black men have always had a stylish bent. Think of Miles Davis, Jimi Hendrix, Jesse Jackson, and Michael Manley. Or Geoffrey Holder, LL Cool J, Maxwell, and Prince. Men are as passionate as women about expressing the African side of their culture, and the present mood of men's fashion, which is becoming more avant-garde, allows for more liberal expression.

It is most difficult to integrate African-inspired style into career clothes, but it can be done. An African-print tie is one option. A vest under a suit jacket is a good idea if your man works in a creative environment. A pair of dark trousers and a matching shirt with a contrasting band of African print around the collar or on the pocket is elegant and stylish.

Popular in some African countries and the Caribbean is the shirtjac, which is ideal for warmer climates. Also called a Cuban-style jacket, it is a lightweight, softly tailored jacket, often short-sleeved with no shirttails, sometimes worn with matching pants. Some of more enterprising men accessorize the shirtjac with a cravat.

In casual offices or on casual Fridays, hip-hop fashion can be an expression of your significant other's African-American heritage. If he's under forty, he can wear whatever's in vogue. If he's older or just prefers more classic clothes, advise him to go for subdued colors in baggy jeans and tops that fit close to the body but are not too tight. Logos are okay. Be aware, though, that the bigger they are, the more juvenile they look. Many sports companies have switched to symbols rather than large words on clothes, which is good news for him.

If your man is doing the urban look, let him do it all the way. He shouldn't wear jeans with his tasseled loafers or wingtips. Choose refined designer hiking-style boots or shoes instead of the kind of thermal construction boots made popular by Timberland. Save those for the weekend.

In his off time, he can also try teaming a dashiki with jeans. The new dashikis are more tailored than those that were popular in the sixties and seventies, and they come in a variety of prints. Wear old dashiki prints only if you are going for a deliberately retro look. For festive casual affairs like an evening barbecue or going to the theater, the dashiki works well over a pair of tailored wool trousers, the kind he probably already has in his wardrobe. Another sleek style is a Bogolan vest with relaxed linen trousers.

When it comes to evening, black tuxedos look fabulous with kente bow ties or cummerbunds, or he might drape an African-print scarf around his neck. A print vest, with or without a jacket, is interesting. Even sharper is a vest that is cut away in the back, like the waistcoats worn by saloonkeepers.

Some African-American men wear the djellaba for daytime as men do in Africa, but in America it's also a great alternative for formal and semiformal affairs, where it provides a note of drama. The djellaba or buba consists of a tunic that falls to the hips or lower, and it's worn with matching drawstring pants. Get one made from rich cotton brocade and trimmed with lustrous embroidery around the sleeves, the neckline, and the hem of the pants.

African men have a tradition of wearing jewelry, and they are seemingly more comfortable with it as adornment than the men of some other cultures. Many West African males in Nigeria and the Ivory Coast wear a thick bangle of rolled gold around the wrist. Gold indicates wealth and prosperity. It's okay to wear this kind of bangle to work, even with a conservative pinstripe suit. More casual would be three or four brass bangles or dark leather bracelets, all of which are available in African stores. Since the 1960s, love beads and Egyptian ankhs, the symbol of life, have been a popular motif in African-American men's jewelry. A thick ankh ring or pendant adds flair to an outfit.

Kofis, Ntampos, and fulans are brimless hats made from African prints. They add a flourish, whether worn as a counterpoint to Western dress or to complement a head-to-toe African look. The hat should sit one or two inches above the eyebrow.

African men often wear hats in daily life. In countries like Cameroon, it is improper for a man to appear in public without his head covered. For some time, wearing an earring was associated with gay men, even though males in ancient societies in Africa and Asia decorated their ears. Now an earring in one ear and a closely shaved head make a definitive African-American statement, as do dreads, Afros, twists, and cornrows.

Make Sure the Man on Your Arm Looks Good

For a stylish, sporty look on the job or in a casual setting, think Billy Dee Williams in *Mahogany* or Ron O'Neal in *Superfly*. What do they have in common? The turtleneck. In cool or cold weather, nothing works better to casually define a suit or a sports jacket.

Tell the man on your arm to make sure his clothes fit well. Naturally, you can help him with this simply by saying, "Yes, honey, you look real good." Or "No, sugar, don't even think about wearing that." I know he asks you. So don't be stingy with your free advice.

Black men have trouble finding clothes cut to suit their bodies, says menswear designer Shaka King. This was news to me. (I always thought my husband was just being his usual persnickety self when he would drag me from store to store in search of trousers that flattered his physique.)

"Men of African descent—we curve out. I call it the S-shape. We need a different fit for our butt and thighs," says Shaka. "Every black man I know buys his suits too big because of this. No matter how slim a brother is, it's all the same. Brothers will sometimes tell you they wear a size 46 jacket when they really wear a 38. They've been buying their suits big to get the fit they need in the pants."

If this sounds familiar, as it did to me and my husband, it's a good idea to have your clothes custom made. Shaka also recommends shopping for Italian suits. "Italian men are built wider," he said. "The reason Italian-made clothes like Armani and Hugo Boss are popular with a lot of black men is not the name but the fit."

Shaka advises his customers—who include Malik Yoba, Alonzo Mourning, Branford Marsalis, Lou Gossett, Jr., and the members of Dru Hill—to put a wardrobe together for longevity.

Here's his basic list:

A good black suit
A good pair of dark pants
A nice sweater—a turtleneck or mock turtleneck—of wool or cashmere
Two shirts—one sporty, one dressy

Tommy Hilfiger adds these suggestions for must-have casual clothes:

Basic chinos
A pair of jeans
A white shirt
Two T-shirts, long- and short-sleeved
A blazer or casual jacket

HOW TO KNOW IF YOUR MAN IS HAVING A STYLE EMERGENCY

- He's matching the shoes to the shirt to the jacket to the ring on his finger. Let him break it up a bit or it looks forced.
- He'll wear brown shoes with black socks in a New York minute. Tell him to always match his shoes to his socks.
- He's wearing too many patent leather slip-ons. Make him invest in a good pair of simple leather shoes.
- He's wearing a suit with a baseball cap. I don't care if Arsenio Hall wears it. Don't mix elements.
- His jacket sleeves are stopping a couple of inches short of his wristbone, and his pants are hugging his crotch and thighs like nobody's business.

—*Shaka King*

It is often difficult to locate black-inspired fashions and beauty products, or black designers. They are not usually widely distributed. I've created this directory to help you find them and plan your wardrobe more effectively. Some of the beauty companies mentioned do not cater to black women exclusively but have created their products with dark as well as light skin tones in mind. For your convenience, there are five categories: Western fashions by black designers; designers of active and urban wear (or hip hop); designers of African-inspired fashions; African-inspired accessories; and plus-size fashions. I've indicated those designers who also create menswear.

WESTERN FASHIONS BY BLACK DESIGNERS

The Alain Moore Collection
7707 Woodside Ave., #1E
Queens, NY 11737
(718)205-0797

Alex Rapley
1428 Master St.
Philadelphia, PA 19121-4333
(215)765-7676

Amsale
625 Madison Ave. 2nd Fl.
New York, NY 10022
(212)583-1700

Angela Slate Couture
at Freedom
7428 S. Vincennes Ave.
Chicago, IL 60621
(773)488-FREE
(for men only)

Anthony Mark Hankins Studio
3913 Prescott Ave.
Dallas, TX 75219
(800)789-4AMH

Aubrey Designs/Aubrey Lynch
321 W. 47th St., #1C
New York, NY 10036
(212)586-8639

Baseline Sportswear
7266 Melrose Ave.
Melrose, CA 90046
(213)937-3232
(for women and men)

Biba Bis
724 N. Wabash Ave.
Chicago, IL 60611
(312)988-9560

Bobby Joseph
155 Lafayette Ave., #3B
Brooklyn, NY 11238
(800)213-1803
(for women and men)

Bramer Leon Couture
4822 Cannon Hill Farm Rd.
Atlanta, GA 30329
(404)321-4117
(for women and men)

Brian Cifone (Converse and
Perry Ellis
Outerwear)
475 Fifth Ave.
New York, NY 10017
(212)686-5050

Brian McKinney
9223 5th Ave.
Englewood, CA 90305
(213)757-8258

The Bridal Path for DiWillis
Fashions
306 W. 38th St., 10th Fl.
New York, NY 10018
(212)868-0626

Byron Lars
at Wheaton PR
29 W. 57th St., 11th Fl.
New York, NY 10019
(212)355-3232

Cassandra Bromfield
1353 Fulton St.
Brooklyn, NY 11216
(718)398-1050

CC Unlimited
627 St. Lawrence Ave.
Bronx, NY 10473
(718)542-4875
(for women and men)

CD Greene
58 W. 58th St.
New York, NY 10019
(212)317-1418

Chez Jackie
231 Peachtree St.
Atlanta, GA 30303
(404)523-1325

Christopher Hunte
306 W. 38th St., Ste. 1604
New York, NY 10018
(212)244-0420

Class Secrets
5326 W. Bellfort St.
Houston, TX 77035
(713)721-3435

Cristina Natale
232 Bryant Ave.
Floral Park, NY 11001
(516)437-3503

Darryl's
492 Amsterdam Ave.
New York, NY 10024
(212)721-2709

Dawn Ebony Martin
110 Thompson St.
New York, NY 10012
(212)334-6479

Diahann Carroll
at J.C. Penney
Call your local J.C. Penney

Drop Dead Collection
4900 West Adams Blvd.
Los Angeles, CA 90016
(213)737-3331
(for women and men)

Douglas Says
P.O. Box 268
New York, NY 10014
(201)435-2736

Duende
342 Park Place
Brooklyn, NY 11238
(718)230-5201
(for men only)

Ela Boutique
1625 Grand Ave.
Baldwin, NY 11510

Eric Gaskins
202 W. 40th St., Ste. 601
New York, NY 10018
(212)575-5692

Esteem
26 5th Ave
Brooklyn, NY 11217
(718)622-9093
(also feature African-inspired
clothing and accessories)

Exodus
The E Shop
771 Fulton St.
Brooklyn, NY 11217
(718)246-0321
(for women and men)

Evonne Price
2303 Alfred Drive, Apt. B
Yeadon, PA 19050
(610)623-1725
(for women and men)

5001 Flavors
2541 7th Ave., 6L
New York, NY 10039
(800)943-2329
(for women and men)

Felicia Farrar
307 7th Ave., #307
New York, NY 10001
(212)307-1140

Freedom
7428 S. Vincennes Ave.
Chicago, IL 60621
(773)488-FREE

Furs by Elaine
350 7th Ave.
New York, NY 10001
(212)868-2525

G III
512 7th Ave., 33rd Fl.
New York, NY 10018
(212)403-0500

Harriet Jackson
509-01 North Masher
Philadelphia, PA 19120
(215)927-1645

Harold Clarke Couturier Atelier
1528 Jackson Ave.
New Orleans, LA 70130
(504)522-0777

If It Aint Ruff Don't Wear It
3830 S. Broadway
Los Angeles, CA 90037
(213)235-0000
(for men only)

Island Trading
401 Lafayette St., 6th Fl.
New York, NY 10003
(212)477-9066
(for women and men)
Also Miami Beach

Jamila's
315 Flatbush Ave.
Brooklyn, NY 11217
Ph: (718)398-6463
(also features accessories)

JCO Clothing Inc.
742 Ponce de Leon Place
Atlanta, GA 30306
(404)875-7406
(for women and men)

Jeffrey Banks
15 E. 26th St.
New York, NY 10010
(212)889-4424

Johnathan Behr
134 S. Robinson Blvd.
Beverly Hills, CA 90048
(310)275-7764
(for women and men)

Kara Saun
1331 ¾ S. Mansfield Ave.
Los Angeles, CA 90019
(213)939-5662
(for women and men)

Katsumi & Malcolm
35 W. 57th St.
New York, NY 10019
(212) 688-5165

KD Dance
339 Lafayette St.
New York, NY 10451
(800)443-1371

Khismet Wearable Art
1800 Belmont Road NW, 1st floor
Adams Morgan, Washington, D.C.
(202)234-7778

Knottitude Designs
50 W. 34th St.
New York, NY 10001
(212)239-4117

Linda Lundstrom Ltd.
33 Mallard Rd.
Toronto, Ontario
CANADA M3B154
(416)391-2838

Linda's Unique Fashion Design
4427 Wesleyan Pointe
Decatur, GA 30034
(770)987-1882
(for women and men)

LSO Designs
20010 Calvert St.
Woodland Hills, CA 91367
(818)883-9138

Magic NY
823 Friel Pl.
Brooklyn, NY 11218
(718)436-0020

Malachi Enterprises
P.O. Box 3199
Grand Central Station
New York, NY 10163
(718)671-5715

McQuay by Dreana Furs
345 7th Ave., 17th Fl.
New York, NY 10001
(212)279-1273

Michael NY
202 W. 40th St.
New York, NY 10018
(212)620-9014

Michele Dudley Knitwear, Ltd.
Riverside Commons
700 River Ave.
Pittsburgh, PA 15212
(412)441-2621

MKO Man
3221 N. Alameda, #K
Compton, CA 90222
(310)537-1122
(for men only)

Nigel Nits
10 Lexington Ave., #27
Brooklyn, NY 11238
(212)642-8156

NOXS
80 E. 7th St.
New York, NY 10003
(212)674-6753

Onyx Noir
231 W. 29th St.
New York, NY 10001
(212) 268-8168

Pat Jacobs
435 E. 14th St., #9A
New York, NY 10003
(212)477-2747

Patrick Robinson
55 Great Jones St.
New York, NY 10012
(212)529-2476

Positive Wear
37–34 W. Century Blvd., #1
Inglewood, CA 90303
(310)672-7192

Rochate
P.O. Box 1145
Midtown Station
New York, NY 10018
(888)ROCHATE
(for women and men)

Ron Wilch
6143 Germantown Ave.
Philadelphia, PA 19144
(215)849-9622
(for men only)

Rubin Chappelle
150 W. 25th St., Ste. 500
New York, NY 10001
(212)367-8061

Rude Boy Stylee
8101 Orian Ave, #2
Van Nuys, CA 91406
(818)994-6644

Shaka King
207 St. James Pl. #3L
Brooklyn, NY 11238
(718)638-2933
(for men only)

Sharon Sherry
1250 Fifth Ave, #4N
New York, NY 10029
(212)534-3297

Simply Greta
401 W. 45th St.
New York, NY 10036
(212)586-4402

Sir Benni Miles
1466 Broadway, #221
New York, NY 10036
(212)869-5729
(for men only)

Stephen Burrows
at Grandview
11 South Broadway
Nyack, NY 10960
(914)353-4189

Steven Cutting
1359 Broadway
New York, NY 10018
(212)875-7944

Toni Whitaker
2437 University Blvd.
Houston, TX 77005
(713)520-8555

Total Image Custom Clothing
P.O. Box 148188
Chicago, IL 60614
(800)995-IMAGE

Tracy Reese
238 E. 36th St.
New York, NY 10016
(212)679-1429

Troy Artis Studio
405 11th St.
North East, WA 20010
(202)610-2802

Venusian Galleria
4332 Degnan Blvd.
South Central, CA 90008
(213)298-9229

Vincent Falls New York
138 W. 25th St., 8th Fl.
New York, NY 10001
(212)642-8156
(for women and men)

Wilbourn Exclusive's
International Designs
Galleria Specialty Mall, 1
Galleria Parkway
Atlanta, GA 30339
(770)541-7200

Youngblood Collections
143 W. 119th St, #4B
New York, NY 10026
(212)749-2136

ACTIVE AND URBAN SPORTSWEAR

2B1
230 W. 39th St, 11th Fl.
New York, NY 10018
(212)391-1988
(for women and men)

20 Below
1299 Louis Nine Blvd.
Bronx, NY 10459
(718)542-6666
(for men only)

4U11 Wear
446 Mertle Ave.
Brooklyn, NY 11205
(718)522-5795

Billy Brown
P.O. Box 483
Bronx, NY 10461
(609)877-1993
(for men only)

DLO
499 7th Ave, #22 South
New York, NY 10018
(212)631-9200
(for men only)

Dolce
3900 Gramby St.
Norfolk, VA 23504
(757)622-7488

Enyce
119 W. 23rd St. #803
New York, NY 10017
(212)271-4200
(for men only)

Exodus
The E Shop
771 Fulton St.
Brooklyn, NY 11217
(718)727-3722
(for women and men)

Fat Joe
560 Melrose Ave.
Bronx, NY 10455
(718)665-6030
(for men only)

Five Spot
230 W. 39th St, 11th Fl.
New York, NY 10018
(212)869-3996
(for women and men)

Fubu
350 Fifth Ave, #4820
New York, NY 10118
(212)564-2330
(for women and men)

Her Game 2
(212)946-2636

Holly Hood
3400 Around Lenox Dr., Ste.
B400
Atlanta, GA 30326
(404)848-9030

Karl Kani
1411 Broadway, 17th Fl.
New York, NY 10018
(212)382-3900
(for women and men)

Maurice Malone
at August Bishop
300 E. 42nd St., 4th Fl.
New York, NY 10017
(212)681-7191
(for women and men)

Mecca
1466 Broadway, #217
New York, NY 10036
(212)695-8866
(for women and men)

Nappy Sportswear
580 Broadway, #604
New York, NY 10013
(212)431-6684
(for women and men)

Naughty Gear
106 Halsey St.
Newark, NJ 07102
(201)642-3910
(for men only)

NY LUGZ
155 6th Ave., 9th Fl.
New York, NY 10013
(212)691-4700

No Names Designs
60 Poplar St.
Atlanta, GA 30303
(404)584-9655

Northpeak
at August Bishop
300 E. 42nd St., 4th Fl.
New York, NY 10017
(212)681-7191
(for men only)

Oddity
Rio Mall, #C105
595 Piedmont Ave.
Atlanta, GA 30308
(404)685-9573
(for women and men)

Phat Farm
129 Prince St.
New York, NY 10012
(212)533-PHAT

PNB Nation
133 W. 19th St., 2nd Fl.
New York, NY 10011
(212)989-3650
(for men only)

Refugee Camp
146 W. 29th St., 4W
New York, NY 10001
(212)244-7400
(for men only)

Shabazz Brothers
462 Seventh Avenue
17th floor
New York, NY 10018
(212)967-5980

Sista Series
325 Clinton Ave., #14D
Brooklyn, NY 11205
(718)789-9818
(for women and men)

Soul Brothers
191-08 120th Rd.
St. Albans, NY 11412
(718)481-8510

Spike's Joint
1 South Elliot Place
Brooklyn, NY 11217
(718)802-1000

Spike's Joint West
7263 Melrose Ave.
Los Angeles, CA 90036
(213)939-7823

Too Black Guys
2 Follis Ave.
Toronto, Ontario
CANADA M6G1S3
(416)538-3451

Urban Gear
5205 5th Ave.
Brooklyn, NY 11220
(718)492-5044

Vons
106-11 Northern Blvd.
Corona, NY 11368
(718)898-1113
(for men only)

WuWear
61 Victory Blvd.
Staten Island, NY 10304
(718)720-9043
(for women and men)

WuWear
509 Peachtree St.
Atlanta, GA 30308
(404)249-1738
(for women and men)

AFRICAN-INSPIRED FASHIONS

Abraham Pelham
104 E. 34th St, #3B
New York, NY 10016
(212)586-6983

Ademola Mandella
Simply Greta
401 W. 45th St.
New York, NY 10036
(212)586-4402
(for women and men)

The Afrikan Colour Scheme
4341 S. Degnan Blvd.
Leimert Park Village, CA 90008
(213)298-9837

Ahneva Ahneva
3419B W. 43rd Pl.
Leimert Park Village, CA 90008
(213)291-2535

Akiba Kiiesmira
113 Sea Pines Rd.
St. Helena, S.C. 29920
(803)838-7246
(features accessories also)

Bemo Collection
29 Holly St.
Pasadena, CA 91103
(818)796-4747

Brenda Brunson Bey
4 W. Circle of Art and Enterprise
704 Fulton St.
Brooklyn, NY 11217
(718)875-6500
(for women and men)

Craft Caravan
683 Greene St.
New York, NY 10012
(212)431-6669

Densua's African Treasures
2841 Coreen Briar Pkwy.
Atlanta, GA 30331
(404)346-2637

Di Willis
New York, NY
(212)868-0626

Eden Collection
4 W. Circle of Art and
Enterprise
704 Fulton St.
Brooklyn, NY 11217
(718)875-6500

Epperson
The E Shop
771 Fulton St.
Brooklyn, NY 11217
(718)727-3722
(for women and men)

F.A.I.T.H Designs, Inc.
1410 Broadway, 7th Fl.
New York, NY 10018
(212)221-8600

4 W. Circle of Art and
Enterprise
704 Fulton St.
Brooklyn, NY 11217
(718)875-6500
(features accessories also)

Fulany Fashion
700 Fulton St.
Brooklyn, NY 11217
(718)834-0861

Homeland Fashions
122 W. 27th St., 8th Fl.
New York, NY 10001
(800)AFRICAN

House of Oosala
Brooklyn, NY
(718)638-2871

Ibaka
4 W. Circle of Art and
Enterprise
704 Fulton St.
Brooklyn, NY 11217
(718)875-6500

Januwa Moja
1464 Belmont St., N.W.
Washington, D.C. 20009
(202)387-4741

Jene Originals, Inc.
Kongo Square Gallery &
Gifts
4334 Degan Blvd.
Leimert Park Village,
CA 90008
(213)291-6878

Lady Mitz
120-44 164th St.
Jamaica, NY 11434
(718)949-4298

Lola Faturoti
209 W. 29th St., Ste. 215
New York, NY 10001
(212)564-7252

Melonie Lynn Designs
at House of Ujamaa
154 Vanderbilt Ave.
Brooklyn, NY 11238
(718)857-4411

Moshood
698 Fulton St.
Brooklyn, NY 11217
(718)243-9433
(for women and men)

Mosaic by Alvin Bell
(call your local Sears store)

Moshood
217 Mitchell St.
Atlanta, GA 30303
(404)523-9433
(for women and men)

Nefertiti Collection
1407 Broadway, #3701
New York, NY 10018
(212)354-9090

Nigerian Fabrics and Fashions
701 Fulton St.
New York, NY 11217
(718)260-9416
(for women and men)

Nubian Nation
133 W. 111th St.
Chicago, IL 60628
(773)488-1197

Therez Fleetwood
13 South Oxford St., The Garden Apt.
Brooklyn, NY 11217
(718)330-0237

Tony Williams
11815 Chesterfield Ave.
Cleveland, OH 44108
(216)761-0574

Twain Revell
145 W. 138th St., Ste. 8
New York, NY 10030
(212)281-4285
(features accessories also)

Woza Cephas Designs
(718)638-5371

AFRICAN-INSPIRED ACCESSORIES

Ahnenoi Designs
116 Willoughby Ave., #1
Brooklyn, NY 11205
(718)622-7446
(jewelry)

Akosua Bandele
123 Cedar Landing Rd.
Windsor, NC 27983
(919)794-9764
(jewelry)

Amethyst
555 Edgecombe Ave., #13B
New York, NY 10032
(212)568-3167
(jewelry)

Audrey Weaver
324 E. 74th St., #2D
New York, NY 10021
(212)772-3504
(scarves)

The Black Cameo by Coreen Simpson
4 W. 37th St., 5th Fl.
New York, NY 10018
(212)736-6188

Blackmen Jewelers
260 W. 121st St.
New York, NY 10027
(212)864-5870

Dabanga
304 5th Ave.
New Rochelle, NY 10801
(914)636-7107
Out-of-state: (800)732-0142
(jewelry)

Diva Creations
97 St. Paul's Ave.
Staten Island, NY 10301
(212)816-7303

Dorian Webb
54 Greene St., 4th Fl.
New York, NY 10013
(212)463-7757

Essence Eyewear/Essence Hosiery
(800) ESSENCE /(800)327-2300

ETU Evans
431 Convent Ave., #4A
New York, NY 10031
(212)862-3757
(jewelry)

Fort Smith
837 E. Drexel Square
Chicago, IL 60615
(773)978-5734
(jewelry)

Funky People
470 Broadway, 2nd Fl.
New York, NY 10013
(212)226-5197
(hats)

Geacommetti Neckwear
3967 Flad, #1W
St. Louis, MO 63110
(314)865-2422

House of A Million Earrings
169-17 Jamaica Avenue,
Jamaica, N.Y. 11432
(713)297-7950

Harris Hat Designs
283 Grand Ave.
Brooklyn, NY 11238
(718)636-4537

Imani Jewelry
163-15 130th Ave., #6E
Jamaica, NY 11434
(718)528-6240

Jacqueline Lamont
470 Broadway
New York, NY 10013
(212) 226-5197
(hats)

Jay Sharpe
1812 W. Main St., 2nd Fl.
Richmond, VA 23220
(804)353-4733

Karen R. Roache
516 Willow Dr., N.E.
Orangeburg, SC 29115
(803)531-0154

Kwame A. Ross
116-30 168th St.
St. Albans, NY 11434
(718)712-5509

Lea
(202)232-2860
(jewelry)

Look From London
347 Fifth Ave., 6th Fl.
New York, NY 10018
(212)213-2656
(hosiery)

Marvin Sin
123 Cedar Landing Rd.
Windsor, NC 27983
(919)794-9764
(handbags)

Monifa Designs
36 Plaza St., #7F
Brooklyn, NY 11238
(718)398-3122

Omo Misha
(212)969-0606

Pursevere
200 3rd St.
New York, NY 10009
(212)614-0341

Sesheni
at Esteem
26 5th Ave.
Brooklyn, NY 11217
(718)622-9093

Shimoda Accessories
25-72C 8th Ave.
New York, NY 10030
(212)491-6726

Sun Gallery Goldsmiths
2322 18th St., N.W.
Washington, D.C. 20009
(202)265-9341

Uniqua Designs
171 Eastern Parkway, #C10
Brooklyn, NY 11238
(718)398-4855

Venus Dennison
311 Washington Ave., #C1
Brooklyn, NY 11205
(718)857-4292

Yancey
P.O. Box 76
Pratt Station
Brooklyn, NY 11205
(718)622-1024

PLUS-SIZE FASHIONS

Ashanti Bazaar
872 Lexington Ave.
New York, NY 10021
(212)535-0740

Ashley Stewart Stores
(800)338-2327

Bloomingdale's
(Shop for Women)
(800)537-0228

Carmen Marc Valvo
530 7th Ave., 23rd Fl.
New York, NY 10018
(212)944-7370

Carnival Creations
180 Madison Ave, Ste. 901
New York, NY
(212)532-0810

Chadwick's of Boston
(800)525-6650

Daphne Larger Sizes
467 Amsterdam Ave.
New York, NY 10024
(212)877-5073

Daphne Lingerie
473 Amsterdam Ave.
New York, NY 10024
(212)579-0479

Dana Buchman
(800)522-3262

Danskin
(800)288-6749

Elisabeth by Liz Claiborne
(800)555-9838

Enna
1127 South 60th St.
Philadelphia, PA 19143
(215) 471-6277

Glitz to Grandeur
727 E. 79th St.
Chicago, IL
(773)488-3400

Inside Out Lingerie Inc.
2531 8th Ave.
New York, NY 10030
(212)234-1456

Just My Size
(800)978-FITS

Kilgour & Sweet
343 Milburn Ave.
Milburn, NJ 07041
(201)376-5358

Lane Bryant
(800) 477-7030

Lord & Taylor
American Women Shop
(800)223-7440

Macy's Woman
Call your local Macy's

Maxine's
1613 E. 87th St.
Chicago, IL 60617
(773)221-8308

MMCF by Mary McFadden
525 7th Ave., 9th Fl.
New York, NY 10018
(212)398-6670

Mosaic by Alvin Bell
at Sears
Call your local Sears

Saks Fifth Avenue
Salon Z
(800)347-9177

Simply Greta
401 W. 45th St.
New York, NY 10036
(212)586-4402

Toma
at Grandview
11 South Broadway
Nyack, NY 10960
(914)353-4189

Wilson Harris III
at Freedom
7428 S. Vincennes Ave.
Chicago, IL 60621
(773)488-FREE
(for women and men)

HAIR PRODUCTS

Affirm
(800)332-8566
(Complete hair care system)

Aveda
(800)328-0849
(Pomade, Brilliance, Malva Shampoo and Conditioner)

Infusium 23
(800)252-4765
(Complete hair care system)

Khamit Kinks
(212)965-9100 or (404)607-9805
(Natural hair oils)

Mane & Tail
(610)882-9606
(Shampoo and conditioner)

Mizani
(800)621-6143
(Complete hair care system)

Motions
(800)997-4336
(Complete hair care system)

Nexus
(888)265-3748
(Shampoo and Conditioner, Emergencee, Humectress, Detangler)

Phyto
(800)55PHYTO
(Phyto 7 Phyto 9)

MAKEUP PRODUCTS

Anna Bayly
1 Fifth Ave.
New York, NY 10003
(212)505-8245
(lipstick)

Bobbi Brown Cosmetics
600 Madison Ave.
New York, NY 10022
(212)980-7040

Clinique
(800)567-9157

Fashion Fair
820 S. Michigan Ave.
Chicago, IL 60605
(312)322-9444

Francois Nars
(888)903-NARS

Iman Cosmetics
(800)366-4626

M.A.C.
(888)232-9622

Origins
(800)723-7310

Prescriptives
767 Fifth Ave.
New York, NY 10153
(212)572-4400

Revlon (Shades of You)
(800)473-8566

Acknowledgments

A book requires more than an author if it is to see the light of day. I'm thrilled that Perigee approached me to do this project and that they agreed to include the history of African-American style in this book. It's been tremendously gratifying yet unbelievably backbreaking work. But my way was made a bit smoother by the support of many people: The Perigee team, including my patient and clearheaded editor, Suzanne Bober, and publisher, John Duff. Darlene Gillard Jones took on the amazingly arduous task of coordinating shoots and gathering photographs for the book. Thank you so much, Darlene. Veronica Jones, my soul sister and fellow Libran and Danite, gave support both practical and emotional, as did Elyse Feldman and Sandra Graham. I appreciate the cooperation of my colleagues in the fashion industry, from the designers and models to the skilled workers behind them who make them look good. Thanks to Natascha at Marion Greenberg, Lynn Tesoro at Ralph Lauren, Lionel Vermeil at Jean Paul Gaultier, Bernard Danillon de Cazella at Christian Dior, Lisa Sheik at Gucci, Erica Johnson at Tommy Hilfiger, Melissa Comito of Fairchild Publications, the Fashion Outreach family, and everyone who gave me suggestions and encouragement. I am truly grateful.

I am unbelievably lucky to have sitting a desk away from me one of the most nimble minds in the business, my editor at my day job, the director of fashion news for the *New York Times*, Claudia Payne, who graciously read through parts of my manuscript, giving me her helpful reaction. Thanks also to Cassandra Harvin for getting me on course with the first few chapters.

Because so little has been written on this subject, it was a gold mine, and there were many interesting directions we could have gone in—one we touched on was assembling the work of some of the top black fashion and portrait photographers working today. Matthew Jordan Smith, definitely someone to watch. George Chinsee, Joe Grant, Anthony Barboza—still kickin' it. Marc Baptiste—I swooned when he pulled out his trove of fashion pictures and photos of Miss Thing—Erykah Badu. Frenchman Gilles Bensimon, also creative director of *Elle* magazine, who showed Americans how to photograph black models as well as they photograph white models, was exceedingly generous in sharing his work. Thank you, Gilles, I officially name you an honorary black fashion photographer for *StyleNoir*. Daniela Stalinger's beautifully lyrical shot of Audra is groundbreaking. And Alvin Bell pulled out the stops to create the fashion illustrations that appear throughout this book: the beautiful, fashionable black woman with some attitude.

These acknowledgments would not be complete without saying thanks to my mum for her lifetime of exemplary guidance in melding intellect and compassion.

Unbelievable support, again both practical and emotional, came from my sweetie pie, Denrick. The best part was, I was not surprised. Thanks so much for your encouragement and stimulation, Denrick, for picking up the slack with Nefatari and Kimathi (thanks, Nefatari and Kimathi), for picking up the clothes from Lady Mitz, and for much more.

COVER:

Makeup: Tadree Coppedge; Hair: Leslie Louard Davis and Tadree Coppedge. Calfskin Jacket: Patrick Robinson; Turtleneck: Yeohlee; African mask necklace of platinum and laser-cut crystal: Paola de Luca for Unoerre; Earrings and earcuff: Lester of House of a Million Earrings. Photographer: Anthony Barboza

Page 8: Romeo Gigli: Photograph by Gilles Bensimon.

Page 10: Dinka women in beaded corsets: Photograph by Robert Estall.

Page 11: Christian Dior Couture by John Galliano, Fall 1997: Courtesy Christian Dior.

Page 11: Jean Paul Gaultier collection, Fall 1997: Photograph by Frederique Garela. Courtesy Jean Paul Gaultier/AEFFE.

Page 12: Byron Lars collection, Fall 1994: Photograph by Gilles Bensimon.

Page 13: Tracy Reese Collection, Fall 1994: Photograph by George Chinsee. Courtesy *Women's Wear Daily.*

Page 13: Chanel does hip hop: Photograph by Cedric Dordevic. Courtesy *Women's Wear Daily.*

Page 16: Member of the Akuffo family of Ghana: Photographer unknown. Photograph and Prints Division of The Schomburg Center for Research in Black Culture. The New York Public Library. Astor, Lenox and Tilden Foundations.

Page 18: Mary Todd Lincoln: Photograph from the Meserve-Kunhardt Collection, Schomburg Center for Research in Black Culture.

Page 21: Bessie Smith: Photofest. Schomburg Center for Research in Black Culture.

Page 22: Josephine Baker album cover: Photographer unknown. Courtesy Columbia Records.

Page 24: Randall White: Photographer unknown. Courtesy White family.

Page 25: Cab Calloway: Photographer unknown. Photographs and Prints Division of The Schomburg Center for Research in Black Culture.

Page 26: Wedding of Jacqueline Bouvier to John F. Kennedy: Photographer unknown. PhotoFest.

Page 27: Dorothea Towles: Photographer unknown. Courtesy Dorothea Towles.

Page 30: The Supremes: PhotoFest.

Page 31: Diana Ross: PhotoFest.

Page 33: Naomi Sims: Photograph by Abner Symons. Courtesy Fairchild Publications.

Page 34: Jimi Hendrix: PhotoFest.

Page 36: Miles Davis: Photograph by Anthony Barboza.

Page 38: Arthur Ashe and model in Dashiki: Photograph by Anthony Barboza.

Page 39: Black Seventies Soul Style: Photograph by Anthony Barboza.

Page 40: Arthur McGee: Photograph by Bert Andrews. Courtesy Arthur McGee.

Page 42: Stephen Burrows: Photographer unknown. Courtesy Stephen Burrows.

Page 43: Jon Haggins: Photographer unknown. Courtesy Jon Haggins.

Page 44: Scott Barrie: Photograph by John Aquino. Courtesy Fairchild Publications.

Page 45: Constance Saunders: Photograph by Fadile Berisha. Courtesy Constance Saunders.

Page 45: Willi Smith: Courtesy Fairchild Publications.

Page 46: Peggy Dillard: Photograph by Lloyd Toone. Courtesy Peggy Dillard.

Page 46: Renauld White: Photograph by Charles Tracy. Courtesy Renauld White.

Page 47: Beverly Johnson: Photograph by Ted Dayton. Courtesy Fairchild Publications.

Page 48: Pat Cleveland with Thierry Mugler: Photograph by Marou. Courtesy Fairchild Publications.

Page 50: Iman: Phtotgraph by Michael Thompson. Courtesy Iman.

Page 52: I-Threes: Courtesy Island Records.

Page 56: Patrick Kelley: Photograph by Marou. Courtesy Fairchild Publications.

Page 57: Alvin Bell: Photograph by Jerri Crooks. Courtesy Alvin Bell.

Page 58: Jeffrey Banks: Photograph by Lynn Kohlman. Courtesy Jeffrey Banks.

Page 58: Gordon Henderson: Courtesy Fairchild Publications.

Page 59: LL Cool J: Photograph by Glen E. Friedman. Courtesy Rush Management.

Page 63: Karl Kani: Photograph by J. Letourneau. Courtesy Fairchild Publications.

Page 66: Spike Lee's Forty Acres and a Mule line: Photograph by Kyle Eriksen. Courtesy Fairchild Publications.

Page 71: Bethann Hardison and Tyson Beckford: Photograph by Karen Pugh.

Page 72: Patrick Robinson. Photograph by David Lawrence. Courtesy Patrick Robinson.

Page 74: Silk knit T-shirt designed by Patrick Robinson. ACI Advanced Copy.

Page 92, 95, 96, 97, 98, 99, 100: African Fabrics: Photographs by George Chinsee.

Page 102: African-inspired head wrap with business suit: Photograph by Marc Baptiste. Model: Margaret.

Page 114: Relaxed black style: Photographer unknown. African-print dresses by Therez Fleetwood. Models: Magic, Etta and Dione. Courtesy Therez Fleetwood.

Page 124: African-inspired evening wear: Masai-beaded gown by Ralph Lauren. Model: Naomi Campbell.

Page 129: Therez Fleetwood's design in Guinea Brocade: Photograph by Wayne Summerlin. Courtesy Therez Fleetwood.

Page 132: Plus size dressing: Photograph by Matthew Jordan Smith. Stylist Darlene Gillard Jones. Makeup: Cynde Watson for Bobbi Brown. Hair: Oscar James for Ken Barboza Associates. Model Audrey Smaltz. Suit: Anne Klein at Lord & Taylor. Cardigan coat: Joan Vass. Boots: Donna Karan. Necklace: OMO Misha.

Page 144: African gelee. Photograph by Gilles Bensimon. Model: Brandi.

Pages 148, 150, 151, 152, 153, 154, 163: African accessories. Photographs by George Chinsee.

Page 160: Black Cameo: Photograph by Corinne Simpson.

Page 164: Lingerie Style: Photograph by Daniela Stallinger. Stylist: Darlene Gillard Jones. Makeup: Tadree Coppedge. Hair: Phedra Pryce. Model: Audra. Lingerie: Inside Out, NY. Shoes: Manolo Blahnik.

Page 174: Wedding gown with cowrie shells by Therez Fleetwood: Photograph by Wayne Summerlin. Model: Nina Shay. Courtesy Therez Fleetwood.

Page 178: Nigerian-influenced bridal gown and groom suit by Gboyega Adewumi at Nigerian Fabrics and Fashions: Photograph by Eric Von Lochart.

Page 181: Bridal gown by Therez Fleetwood. Photograph by Wayne D. Summerlin. Model: Nina Shay.

Page 182: Photograph by Joe Grant. Makeup: Roxanna Floyd. Model: Phina. Courtesy Roxanna Floyd.

Page 189: Photograph by Joe Grant. Makeup: Lanier Long. Model: Roshumba.

Pages 192, 194: Oprah Winfrey. Photograph by Victor Skrebneski. Courtesy Oprah Winfrey/Harpo Productions.

Pages 192, 197: Toni Braxton. Courtesy Arista Records/LaFace Records.

Pages 192, 196: Diana Ross. Courtesy Ross Records/Motown.

Page 192, 198: Jessye Norman. Photograph © 1995 David Seidner. Makeup: Bridgitte Reiss-Andersen. Hair: Coleen Creighton. Opera Coat: Fernando Sanchez.

Pages 192, 199: Susan Taylor: Photograph by Matthew Jordon Smith. Courtesy Susan Taylor/Essence Communications.

Pages 192, 201: Tina Turner. Photograph by Gilles Bensimon.

Pages 192, 202: Naomi Campbell. Photograph by Albert Sanchez. Courtesy *Women's Wear Daily.*

Pages 192, 204: Patti LaBelle. Photograph by Albert Sanchez. Courtesy MCA.

Pages 192, 205: Whoopi Goldberg. Photograph by Ted Dayton. Courtesy *Women's Wear Daily.*

Page 207: Erykah Badu: Photograph by Marc Baptiste. Courtesy Marc Baptiste.

Page 208: African-style male headwrap. Photograph by Edward Wilkerson. Model: Donovan.

Selected Bibliography

Alder, Peter, and Nicholas Barnard. *African Majesty.* New York: Thames and Hudson, 1992.

Alexander, Lois K. *Blacks in the History of Fashion.* New York: Harlem Institute of Fashion, 1982.

Arnoldi, Mary J., and Christine M. Kreamer. *Crowning Achievements (African Arts of Dressing the Head).* University of California, Los Angeles, 1995.

Clarke, Christa. "Brooklyn Museum Knew How to Sell, Too." *New York Times,* February 21, 1997, p. 34.

Dunning, Jennifer. "Bernard Johnson, 60, Dancer, Choreographer and Designer." *New York Times,* February 1, 1997, p. 26.

Encyclopedia of African American History. Schomburg Center for Research in Black Culture.

Fisher, Angela. *Africa Adorned.* New York: Harry N. Abrams, 1984.

Hinds, Patricia M. *Essence: 25 Years Celebrating Black Women.* New York: Harry N. Abrams, 1995.

Hull, Richard W. *Munyakare: African Civilization before the Batuuree.* New York: John Wiley & Sons, 1972.

Kenyatta, Jomo. *Facing Mt. Kenya.* New York: Vintage Books, 1965.

Morris, Jean, and Eleanor Preston-Whyte. *Speaking with Beads.* New York: Thames and Hudson, 1994.

Picton, John. *The Art of African Textiles: Technology, Tradition and Lurex.* London: Lund Humphries, 1995.

Polhemus, Ted. *Street Style.* New York: Thames and Hudson, 1994.

Rodney, Walter. *How Europe Underdeveloped Africa.* Washington, D.C.: Howard University Press, 1974.

Segal, Ronald. *The Black Diaspora.* New York: Farrar, Straus and Giroux, 1995.

"The Soul of Seventh Avenue." Pamphlet accompanying show sponsored by Fairchild Publications, New York, N.Y., August 1989.

Southern, Eileen. *The Music of Black Americans.* New York: W.W. Norton, 1971.